EMILY SHORE

THE TEMPLE TWINS
Copyright ©2019 Emily Shore
All rights reserved.
Printed in the United States of America
First Edition: November 2019

www.CleanTeenPublishing.com

SUMMARY: Trapped by Force, Serenity is required to become Yang—the bearer of her father's dark Temple legacy. Her new persona requires using a whip on her shell of a twin sister, but Serenity has even bigger problems. Most chillingly, a series of corpses with swan symbols carved in their chests. More than ever, Serenity needs Sky… and he will be there to protect her. No matter what it takes.

ISBN: 978-1-63422-369-0 (paperback)
ISBN: 978-1-63422-370-6 (e-book)
Cover Design by: Marya Heidel
Typography by: Courtney Knight
Editing by: Cynthia Shepp

Young Adult Fiction / Dystopian
Young Adult Fiction /Social Themes / Sexual Abuse
Young Adult Fiction / Social Themes / Self-Esteem & Self-Reliance
Young Adult Fiction / Fantasy / Dark Fantasy

For more information about our content disclosure, please utilize the QR code above with your smart phone or visit us at www.CleanTeenPublishing.com

To all the ones like Bliss.
In the words of For King and Country:
God only knows what you've been through. God only knows the
real you.

PART
One

One

BrOtherly LoVe

LUC

I REACH THE PENTHOUSE IN THE same moment a fleet of guards embarks into Serenity's room at the end of the hall. Part of me wishes I'd remained where I was in the Hall of Angels—a brief journey for inspiration regarding Serenity's next exhibit.

Instead, I steel myself to investigate. Two medics carry out an unconscious guard, blood gushing from a broken nose. When I arrive in the suite, my suspicions are confirmed—Skylar. There is my brother thrashing with half-a-dozen security members, but he is well-pinned. Blood lines his cracked-open knuckles. The first thing I do is cross the room to the bed where Serenity is asleep, but as soon as I approach, I realize she's more than asleep; she's passed out. And Bliss is just rising from her knees.

"Good of you to join us, Aldaine. Perhaps you can help me solve this dilemma," Force welcomes me, fist perched on his chin. "I assume you have some familiarity with the *subject*. Friend of yours? I know he's not some lowly Aviary guard as Serenity led me to believe."

My brother grits his teeth, snarling again, muscles swelling, straining to free himself. I'm certain he had more than enough reason to reveal himself. Perhaps if I'd been here, this wouldn't have happened. Ignoring him, I shift Serenity until she's on her back and tuck her under the covers.

"If only it were that uncomplicated, Director," I say while straightening.

1

"Hmm..."

He observes the level of animosity between us. Not so difficult when it's thicker than a haystack around a needle. Even if one were to sift through every piece of straw, all they'd find is a sharp point between us.

"I think the pieces are coming together," Force announces, fingers curling, intrigue soaking his voice. "Two jealous boyfriends. Both equally motivated."

"I'm. Not. Her. Boyfriend," Skylar growls.

"So, he does speak." More interested than before, Force bends down to address my brother. "Lover, then?"

"No."

"Please, tell me," Force urges, manic smile deepening. "I'm quite curious."

"I'm sure you are."

"Did any of you maggots search him yet?" Force commands the guards holding Skylar.

One of them starts digging through his pockets, finding a few minuscule objects but one that proves to be incredibly significant.

"Give it back," Sky demands of Force, who holds the ring up to the light.

Force begins to pace, eyes still on the ring. "Now, this looks familiar. Why is this so familiar?" A look of recognition. "Ahh, yes, I remember. May I ask what you're doing with Serafina's wedding ring?"

"It was a gift." Skylar offers nothing else. Why I should be surprised Serafina granted her blessing to Skylar is beyond me. She certainly wasn't going to offer me any.

"I believe I'll hold onto it for now. After all, I'm her father, and I have certain stipulations for any man who wishes for Serenity's hand."

"You're not her father," Skylar denies. "You're just a pathetic sperm donor."

Force chortles, a host of demons spicing the laugh. "Gutsy, this one. Persistent, too. Like you, Aldaine, but with no respect. Intriguing."

"Not so intriguing, given the circumstances," I reply, keeping my hands firm at my sides.

"Oh, and what circumstances are those?"

There's not much point in concealing our familial connection now. Force will log Skylar's DNA into the Temple database, and it will flag with mine.

"The circumstances of our unfortunate but similar DNA."

Force shakes his head and laughs again, this time smacking his thigh. "Brothers, then?"

"Half," Skylar clarifies, thrusting his head back.

Force laughs harder before turning to look at his sleeping daughter. Bliss remains quiet in the corner of the room.

"I'll have to remember to thank her when she wakes. She's made my life so much more interesting. In the meantime, I'll deal with you." Force turns back to Skylar before barking out orders for an InstaTat delivery. Permanent barcode for Skylar, then. One with a tracker chip. It's the only time InstaTat devices are used.

I must give credit where it's due because Skylar manages to get his arm free from one of the men on his right, and he uses his newfound momentum to strike at the others. By tomorrow, they'll lose count of their own bruises. This is not my fight, and I don't intend on joining, but at least I don't stand by and watch in an amused fashion like Force. Unfortunately, Skylar's defiance will only prove to be a delay tactic. I can see even before a drone arrives with the InstaTat. While my brother is distracted with holding off the guards around him, Force presses something to the nape of his neck. A sleep patch, judging by how Skylar swipes the air behind him, but Force easily steps away to avoid the blow. It must have been a larger dose because my brother topples to the floor.

Force wipes down his shirt. "Well…now it is over, so we can commence with the blood sample and the barcode. Hmm…" he glances at Serenity before determining, "Perhaps a different room. Would you care to stay and watch?" he extends the offer.

"No." I shake my head. "I'll remain with her."

"Oh, good, then. I can dismiss Mara."

It's the third time I've caught myself staring at her. I've acknowledged her presence more than Serenity's. During this whole time, she's reminded me of a ghost—the type who knows her power lies in observing, not interfering.

Force extends a hand to his daughter. "I was going to ask her to stay through the night with Serenity. Or Serafina. But if you're volunteering—"

Bliss steps forward for the first time to interject, "I'll do it."

She blinks a few times when the guards haul Sky out. Whatever my brother did, it certainly had an effect. Whether she'll reveal that or not is difficult to say. Her eyes don't linger on Force; in no way is she concerned with her father's antics, considering how familiar she is with them.

"I'll let the two of you sort it out. Goodnight," Force says before closing the door behind us.

"Should we alert Serafina?" I inquire of Bliss, then pull up a chair next to Serenity's side.

Bliss sways to the bed to join her sister on the opposite side. "No. Let my mother rest. It's late, and I will tell her in the morning."

Weary from the day, I lean over and rub a hand down my face, only to realize that other than retrieving a chair to sit in, Bliss does not seem tired whatsoever. No ringed shadows under her eyes, no slumping posture. On the contrary, she remains astute as a swan's pinions before liftoff.

As if sensing my reflection, Bliss nods my way and explains, "It's not normal for me to sleep at night. I run off little rest."

"That is understandable."

"Night is not meant for sleeping. At least not in the traditional way," she hints, lashes descending halfway—seductive moth wings.

I bristle. "You don't always have to do that."

"Do what?"

"Your only method of interacting with a man is the art of seduction, isn't that true?"

Bliss just shrugs, eyes glancing at one of the volumetric swans swaying across the room. "We all have our talents. I could always opt for a different method. You prefer the chase?"

"I prefer what's *real*," I counter, straightening in my chair.

"Oh, please, Luc. We both know reality isn't in your vocabulary. After all, where were you during Serenity's hour of need earlier?"

I don't respond.

She goes on, ignoring my desire for explanation. "You were

gleaning inspiration from other levels, harvesting as much as you could. Just so you may turn her into another fantasy. It doesn't take much imagination to know what you do in your room, especially when the walls are so close to mine."

"Stop," I request, firmly at first, fingers nearly leaving prints on my pants.

"Sometimes, I can hear you reviewing her feeds," she strikes with the expertise of a cobra. "Watching her performance every time. Her transformation is your drug."

Bliss's words harpoon me. They are a million needles transcribing ink into my skin, labeling me with titles that identify me, ones she can recognize. But I have nothing of her. No words to debate. Nothing to counteract what she's said. Impossible to read a girl who wants nothing.

"And what of your fantasies, Bliss? Your desires? Your wants?"

"I am here to *fulfill* desires and wants." She opens her legs a little, a gesture to mimic her words. "Not the other way around."

"Everyone has wants. Otherwise, we are mere empty shells of existence."

She grins. "For once, you're catching on."

"You enjoy this, don't you?" I brace my fingers on the chair's armrests, trying to control myself. "You've deluded yourself so much into accepting this life."

"If reality and survival are delusions." She yawns.

I rise to confront her, weaving my way around the bed. "And what about living? Is there no such thing for you?"

"No." Her expression is un-provoked, putting me to shame. "Don't you know, Luc? Ghosts can't live. And I'm full of many ghosts." Her smile spreads like a drop of ink in oil. "But you only have one, don't you? One you'll never catch. Because someone's already caught her heart."

Infuriated, I turn around—back to her—trail both hands through my hair, tugging at strands. Bliss is too good at what she does because I didn't even hear her footsteps; she is right here, body printing against mine from behind. Her hands link together, framing my waist, fingers slow-dancing up to the skin at my collarbone.

"You'll never catch her, Luc, but perhaps *I* can help you come

5

close."

The scent of her is overwhelming. A potent perfume that is just my style—exotic and enticing. Her warmth sidles into my own, combining with it, flirting with it, daring it. For once, I imagine what it would feel like without any flimsy barriers. To have her naked body sealed against mine. My thoughts breeding new ones, each one more potent and dangerous than the last. And Bliss undoes one button and dips her hand below the fabric of my shirt. Thrusting my head back, I shove my rushed inhale down my throat from the touch of her soft hand on my skin.

"Bliss—"

"Shh," she murmurs, her feather-light words in my ear, nipping the lobe and stirring a wildfire inside me. She's too good at what she does.

After planting a light kiss on my neck, Bliss pivots around slowly, working her way to my front but keeping her arms around me. Then, she eases them up to my neck and stares into my eyes, shattering the glass windows there with ease. I dip my head toward her, meeting her as she tiptoes to greet me with a subtle kiss. Nothing passionate about it. Just a mere invitation. Too inviting. Those lips are soft, supple, and house more secrets than I could ever hope to imagine. She is the dark side of the moon wrapped in a black silk shroud. Her fingers coiling in the ends of my hair, tugging on them softly, makes it damn near hard to think, to focus. Her whole body is a tempting labyrinth I want to explore.

Leaning up toward me again, Bliss murmurs in my ear, "I could be your Swan."

I take her by her wrists, forcing her away. Nothing in her responds with any sort of fight. No battlefield to step on. No castle to storm. The only thing I can manage is to let go of her and walk away before I do something I regret.

Or not?

Two

My Sister

Bliss

"HE DID A NUMBER ON you, didn't he?" I mutter, thumbing the space just next to the raised flesh from the splicer.

I look around the room before locating a washcloth in the closet.

After running it under warm water, I dab it gently against my sister's temple, washing away the blood that stains the side of her head. To see her like this is almost eerie. Her cheekbones, carved replicas of mine, the bridge of her nose, the way her eyes have softened now in sleep, there is Serenity in every bit of her sleeping form. Only when we are awake do we show our true forms—of lightning and a ghost mountain.

Rinsing the washcloth, I wet it again and finish scrubbing off the dried blood. On her shoulder, bruises are starting to show. I try to deny the panic I felt when I saw her crash down the stairs. No, the panic came before—when I saw Force move. Predicted he would move because I am still more familiar with his patterns than Serenity. Considering my sister's recklessness, I form the conclusion. She should not have tried to attack him.

I should have warned her.

For the first time, I reach out, fold my hand into hers. Perhaps it's because she's sleeping—a shared ability between us. After all, we have no other common traits; even how we breathe is different. Despite all my talents, the one I've never managed, much less mastered, is water. Now, I understand why. It is Serenity's domain. I am more than willing to let her keep it. Water is too unpredictable.

7

While a man's heat may surround me, it will never trap or drown me. There is nothing familiar about water. It's always changing, always moving. Much like Serenity and her lightning emotions.

Curious, I glance down. Did her hand just squeeze mine? It happens again. Undeniable. Even in sleep, Serenity can't help but move. Smiling, I shake my head. My smile doesn't last because I understand how far I've come. Retrieving my hand, I touch my forehead and sigh. This wasn't supposed to happen. But I can't help it. How she acted with Sunshine, how she risked everything, what almost happened to her…why should any of it matter to me? But it does. One threadbare vein of her lightning has crept into me. Just a hairline fissure in my mountain of ghosts. Not in my heart but certainly hovering at its border.

I've stopped calling her just Serenity. And I realize why I care…I am her sister.

Three

InteRogation

Sky

UGH. Feels like someone shoved a bunch of rabid monkeys with drums in my head. Just beating away in there. I'm hunched over but somehow still standing. My arms feel cold. When I open my eyes, I see metal cuffs attached to my wrists that keep me in a forced sort of stand with my back against the frame of a metal wall. The rest of the room comes into focus like a lens sharpening. It's an interrogation room. Force even has a shiny little table full of sharp metal instruments and needles with chemical vacuum tubes. He stands before them.

I'm touched, really.

"Good, you're awake," he remarks.

If this is what awake feels like.

"We will start with something simple. Name."

Guess he broke his promise about dinner.

"Skylar Lace."

My name and background do not matter much. Pandora's Box already opened. Not like he can hurt me. There's only one person I care about. Well, three. Still haven't quite figured out the fourth, considering his more recent actions.

Force begins to pace all the while eying the table. "That was surprisingly effortless. If you'd lied, the cuffs would have registered it and stunned you. Let's try another, shall we?"

"Fire away when ready."

"How long have you known my daughter?"

"All her life."

9

"Fascinating, please enlighten me." Force presses his fingertips together, curiosity practically oozing from them. "Serafina hasn't been very forthcoming about filling in the blanks."

Huffing, I manage to hoist myself up a little. "Are the cuffs really necessary?"

"Oh, I should think so."

"I know about the heart implant. I'm not going to kill you."

"No, but I wouldn't put it past you to render me bodily harm." Smirking, he wanders toward the instrument table to finger a surgical scalpel. "And I quite like my body unharmed."

I shrug. "Guess I can't argue with that."

Sighing, I figure it's better to cooperate. The faster I get this done and over with, the faster I can get back to Serenity. It's not like him knowing about our past makes much of a difference now.

"I met Serenity when I was four years old. Since Serafina knew you'd hunt her all her life, she believed a protector for her daughter was in order. Kerrick became my mentor and trained me, Serafina became...an adoptive godmother of sorts."

"And what was Serenity?"

I narrow my brows, harden my jaw. "I'll thank you not to insult her honor or mine in any way with your presumptions."

Force chortles, tapping an unfamiliar device against his palm. "I don't need presumptions. I know my daughter's virginity is intact. But I am so very curious as to your relationship and how you've managed all these years." He examines me, surprise arching his brows. "That sort of fortitude contrasts with mine on the extreme end."

I grit my teeth. "I'd rather not discuss it."

"Well, unfortunately for you, I'm her father. So, I make it my business."

I don't bother repeating my last statement. Not like he's gonna listen to arguments involving Serenity's freedom and independence and right to choose who she loves, etc.—those will just go in one ear and out the other.

"Humor me, Skylar," he pressures, eyes lowering to my cuffs, which emit a low volt of electricity into my system. Only enough to make me wince.

I huff again. "You just don't quit, do you?"

"Consider you my pet project."

He means *other* than Serenity.

Groaning, I roll my eyes before finally giving up the truth. "Hasn't been easy. But she makes it worth it."

"That doesn't give me the reason why. You're both of one mind in this, I assume." He starts to pace back and forth, examining the floor as if my confessions are etched there and he's trying to piece them together.

"To put it mildly."

One mind, one heart, one soul. Just not one flesh. Not yet.

"So, why deny yourselves? You've had more than enough opportunity," he points out, approaching to stand in front of me.

I make the argument. "Serenity is still very young."

"Legal age by far."

"Call me a nonconformist."

He studies me, eyes probing. "But you want to."

"Someday," I reply, working hard to rid myself of any indecent thoughts. Picturing her eyes helps. "When the time is right."

"How do you judge when the time is right?"

"Ring gives you a clue."

Force withdraws the aforementioned item from his pocket. Fiddles with it. "Fascinating. Holding to such traditional ideals in this day and age."

"Plenty of people still get married."

"But white is such an antiquated and ironic color for brides today, wouldn't you say? After all, so few come untainted." Force pockets the ring again. As if any girl is truly *tainted*.

"I'm no better than anyone else if that's what you're trying to imply." *Her eyes, her eyes, her eyes.*

"I imply nothing. I merely observe and weigh what I see." He plants a finger on his chin.

Sure, you do.

"One look at you, it's obvious you certainly don't have anything to prove to anyone. Perhaps you're in denial over something?"

I roll my eyes. Force's petty implied insult over my masculinity bounces off me as easily as a blown-up balloon. Just a method of baiting me, goading me. I'll have to remind Serenity she differs from her father in this way. No mind games. What people see is what they get.

"Nice try." I only chuckle.

"Come now, Skylar. There's no use for such things like chivalry anymore. Our society has come too far." He paces again, hand open as he tries to convince me. "Girls themselves willingly take on Temple work and enjoy it. Ones who don't learn their place. Eventually, everything is consensual."

I ball my hands into fists. "Whatever helps you sleep at night, Force."

Force twists his whole body toward mine. "My goal is to determine what will help *you* sleep at night. After all, I'm not entirely convinced of your purity act. Rest assured, I will put it to the test." Force holds up a cleaver to the light. The metal catches it right before he shoves it toward my right eye.

"Do your worst," I dare, thrusting my jaw out.

"Not *my* worst, my boy."

Force turns around and walks the few steps to the door, which he opens. He steps to the side to allow access to a young woman. I'd wager no more than seventeen—wearing little more than lacy lingerie with a pair of white feathered wings bouncing in the air on each side of her body.

You've got to be kidding me!

"Halo." Force's smile is silky and sinister—a satin-dressed serpent. "I trust you will take care of my friend here."

"You're a real piece of work, Force," I spit the words.

"So I'm told. Consider this dessert instead of dinner. Bon appetit, Skylar. "

Don't hold your breath, you sick bastard.

Unlike Force's, Halo's smile is as bright as her name. One I imagine she's practiced. Even her body emits a sort of glow with tiny beams of light radiating from her fingertips. Digital luminescence implanted under her skin.

Her scent is sickeningly sweet. When she grinds her body up against mine, I concentrate on that scent as much as I can. Damned if it feels like I've just been dunked in a vat of vanilla cream, which keeps my attention somewhat off her movements.

"What's wrong, handsome?" she asks while sliding her hands up my chest. "You been a bad boy?"

"No, as a matter of fact." I keep my eyes on the ceiling. Not much to look at up there, but I manage to make out a blurred reflection of sorts. It helps. A little.

"That's too bad. I was hoping to redeem you." Pausing at the buttons on my shirt, she fingers the skin just beneath them.

"I'd rather you didn't."

"Something wrong?" She tries to beckon me, head darting back and forth as she searches for my avoiding eyes. "I'm fairly good at improv. Just tell me what you want, and I'll do it."

"Think you can get me out of these cuffs?"

She glances toward the door. "I'm not sure. I was just told to follow Temple procedure and give you whatever you wanted."

"Cuffs, if you don't mind."

Halo bends, giving me a fleeting glance of her ample rump, too exposed by her pittance of panties. Reminding myself of my ingrained lessons from Kerrick to be better than the average man, I yank my eyes upward. Back to Halo's face. At least she finds the release button, but the sudden inertia sends me to the floor.

"Oh, no! Here. Let me help."

Halo looks all too concerned, plump lips parted with corners curled down, the heads of her brows curving in a distressed manner. She's good. Her hand dips into my shirt while the other fiddles with the buttons of my shirt.

"These look like they haven't been washed in weeks."

"Pretty close." I shrug. Not like Serenity could explain to the staff why she needed men's clothing washed. And Luc's clothes wouldn't fit me. At least I managed to get showers, so that counts for something. Shaking my hands out, I make my way to a stand and crack my neck to the side just as she approaches. Halo arches her neck and squares her shoulders to thrust out her bosom, but I pick a spot on the wall behind her when she volunteers, "I could wash them for you, while you're still wearing them."

"Thanks for the offer but no thanks."

"Something else you want?" She seems so hopeful. Whether that's genuine, I can't tell.

"Yes, just stay right here." I press one finger to the floor before I stand and walk to the furthest corner of the room, then turn and face the wall. Ooh, goodie. Camera there. I give Force my most obliging "fuck off" glare as I flip him the bird.

"Is this some new fantasy trend?" Halo asks from behind me. One momentary glance and I can see she hasn't moved.

"Nope."

"Did I say or do something that—"

"Please, just stop," I interrupt, raising my hand. "Don't ever let anyone tell you you're not good enough, Halo."

"Just not good enough for you?"

I push both my hands against the wall, flattening them, restraining myself. I'm seriously screwing this up. I stick to the truth. "Let's just say I'm spoken for already."

"She doesn't share?"

"Neither of us do." I keep my statements simple, to the point.

"That's too bad."

"Not really."

"Isn't there anything I can do?" she presses, her words trying to find a home somewhere on my back, but they just meet with more body armor.

"No, you're fine there."

"But this isn't following Temple procedure," she protests, her breath coming out harder.

I decide to glean her for information instead. "What's Temple procedure?"

"The Temple prides itself on adhering to a wide variety of clients. We're trained in the art of seduction because exhibit introductions are included in each level's flat rate, but an interaction costs more."

Doesn't surprise me. Just another way to take advantage of the chain of supply and demand. Free enterprise at its grandest. Hell if men care whether the merchandise happens to be human souls.

I jerk my head when Halo presses herself against my back.

"I could lose my job here if I don't follow protocol." I don't blame her for leaving her spot and trying harder.

I give the camera another glare. Of course she will.

"I could take off the wings if it'd make you feel more comfortable," she suggests. Probably because she can't manage to slide under my outstretched arms with them on.

"Why do you beat yourself up like that?"

"Excuse me?" Her brows sink. Good. At least that's real emotion and not just this cheap performance.

"I'm giving you every opportunity here." I tilt my head toward her, eyes scrunching down. "You don't have to try with me. You can be yourself, you know?"

"Screw you," she says, raising her voice. "I'm lucky to be where I am. I'm on a higher level, they give me decent food, I have a soft bed to sleep in, and, most of all, I'm here so my little sister doesn't have to be."

I lower my head. Seriously. Screwed. This. Up. Apologizing seems moot, but I do it anyway. "Sorry about that." I pause, then look into her eyes. "They threaten you?"

"They don't need threats. They own me!" She presses her hands to her chest. "They own a lot of us. You're born into Family houses, and you die in them. Simple as that. Started with my grandmother. My mum had us girls in a Family foster home. I could be in the Glass Districts, but Force's underlings sent me here. It's better money than anywhere. And every penny goes back to pay off my sister's debt."

"And you?" I decide to turn around, leaning against the wall this time.

"What about me?"

"You hurting? You tired?" I wonder.

She braces herself, pressing her small lips together. "I can't afford to get tired. At least they screen and treat us for viruses here. Not like in the Districts."

A growl builds in my throat at the mention of that, but I shove it away because the last thing she needs to be reminded of is how neither the Districts nor the Temple bother to screen the clients for anything.

"If you could get out?"

"There's no out. It's the life we're born into."

"If I could get you both out?"

"You an activist or something?"

I smile, pivoting my head a little. "Or something."

"No thanks. Don't trust activists any more than I trust clients. Least here they got security if clients get too out of hand."

Except in Bliss's case.

"And if security gets out of hand?" I tighten the muscles in my shoulders when I consider the reality.

"As long as we give them what they want, they look out for us. Besides, I know what to expect here. It's what I can't see coming that scares me."

"You feel safe here? How'd you get that bruise on your neck?" I motion to the chokehold marks, subtle beneath the makeup that tries to conceal them. My guess is her manager gave it to her. Force might be director of the whole Temple, but the floor managers still run each level.

She pauses before answering. Her wings look heavy. Too heavy for someone her age to carry. Wonder what it must be like to cart around that weight every day. I have a feeling Bliss knows.

"I feel safer in here than out there," Halo finally tells me. "Men make promises all the time. Not like they can carry them out. Or they go back on their word."

I don't tell her that's not the case with me. She's not in the frame of mind to listen.

Then, she brushes her fingers on my bare arm. "Is that what it's all about, handsome? Because you know I need to be rescued? I'm a lost angel. You want to save me."

Throwing her arms around my waist, she presses her face into my chest. Lord, give me strength! Halo's going back to the only thing she knows. When I don't answer, she takes a moment to follow procedure again. This time, she removes the belt at my waist, but I take her by the wrists before she can do more.

Halo tilts her neck, swinging her strawberry-tinted hair to the side. Before I can thwart her more, Force opens the door and extends a hand to her.

"Good girl, Halo. That will be enough for today."

I release her wrists.

"Maybe I'll see you around," she says, leaning up to kiss my cheek.

I don't lie to her. "I doubt it."

"Later, handsome."

Once she's shimmied her way past the door, Force taps his closed mouth but does not embark farther into the room. "Rest assured—" he informs me, brows narrowed, threatening, "—I'll find another flavor to whet your appetite."

"Keep telling yourself that."

"You'll stay in this room until I do."

"What about Serenity?"

His mouth curls into a knowing grin. "You can't honestly expect I'll allow you near *my* daughter, can you?"

I barrel toward him but only end up smashing into the door after he proved too quick for me. Fast as an eagle swooping in to seize its prey, Force prods the nape of my neck with a stunner. At a high enough level to incapacitate me.

He leans over, lava breath on my skin. "You behave yourself, and I'll see you transferred to better accommodations. Until then, food and water will be brought for you. Pleasure to make your acquaintance, Skylar."

I pound my fists at the door, but it does no good. Even throwing my whole body to smash against it doesn't make it shake. Force strategically engineered this room for the purpose of no possible escape. Looks like I'll be here for a while.

Four

AnGel

SERENITY

"WHERE IS HE?" It's my first question, my first demand, when my father finally meets me for dinner. Over the past couple of days, I've gone stir crazy, searching every room possible, but my limited access is preventing me from finding Sky. Bliss knows nothing. Luc is good for nothing. And my father has given me nothing.

"Nice to see you, too, Serenity," he comments while removing the lid from a tray, which steams in response. A hearty cut of red meat greets him.

I don't sit at the dinner table yet. "Where is he?"

"And which *he* would that be? Seems like you have countless of men who are interested in you."

I circle the table until I arrive in front of him. Then, I proceed to grab his plate and slam it on the floor with enough force it breaks. "You tell me where he is right now!"

My father stares at his ruined meal, more pity for the meat than the thousands of girls in the Temple.

"Honestly…" He dabs at the splattered sauce on his vest, which is printed with swirling yin-yang symbols. "There's no reason we can't have a civilized meal together."

"Since when have *you* ever been civilized?" I challenge.

Quicker than ripping open a wound, Force seizes my jaw, forcing me to my knees before holding me there with a pressure point to my collarbone. My eye is in exact line with a twirling yin-yang. As if he is purposely reminding me of his greater plan.

18

Amidst my struggling and protests, he leans to murmur in my ear. "Make no mistake, Serenity, you may wear the Temple Face, but I am its body and heart. I control what goes on here." When I raise a hand to attack, he only increases the pressure. I recoil, whimpering from the pain. "I have been incredibly patient with you, and you will show me respect. Or at the very least, you will *pretend* to show me that respect."

On that point, we can agree because I will never respect him. Not in this lifetime or any other. Pretending is the most I could ever do. Even that concept feels like a million spiders devouring my butterflies, discarding the wings. Even pretending feels like swallowing a smoldering yin-yang symbol, branding my insides.

"Now…" He shoves me back so I hit the ground. "If you can manage to sit through a meal with me, I will give you some insight into what will happen over the next couple of weeks."

Glaring at him, I get to my feet and return to my chair on the opposite side of the table.

"Good girl," my father commends when I sit just before ordering another filet mignon. It would seem ironic he could have things much quicker by using the transporter tubes with delivery bots or 3D food printer, but my father enjoys having personal staff. It gives him a sense of power and dominance by using servants rather than servant technology.

"Unofficially," he says while waiting for his food, "remarkable assertiveness. Provided you learn to channel that animosity and veil it under a thin layer of respect, you will go far. That's why I've been training you to endure my Temple's pressures, to understand its atmosphere and way of life."

"And whipping my own sister?" I turn my eyes into sharp green diamonds.

"Training and a coping mechanism, obviously." Raising his champagne glass, he swirls the silvery liquid.

"Not where I'm concerned," I deny, then pick up a hunk of bread and shove it in my mouth.

"To use the old vernacular, 'could have fooled me'."

After I get done chewing the roll, which tastes more like a cooked pillow with my wrecked appetite, I dig my fingers through my hair and plead, "Please, please, please just tell me where he is."

"Very unlike you to beg, daughter." He wags a finger, and I notice a new accessory. A jeweled yin-yang symbol embedded into the very skin at the base of his finger. "I can see you care about this one a great deal. My only question is how he cares for you because his little demonstration in the bedroom is not enough for me. All your suitors must be tested."

"Except the ones you choose." I wrinkle my nose.

"Oh, I vet them, but I understand them. Like Director Aldaine, who requires no such fruitless tests. Your method of testing is simply outright refusal. But trust me, this paramour of yours requires much more testing."

"I want to see him."

"I'm afraid I cannot allow that at the present. But soon."

"My word should be enough," I insist, fiddling with a silver spoon to give my hands something to do.

"Perhaps if you weren't so biased."

"Biased!" I drop the spoon and plant my hands on the table, trying to control myself.

"Yes," my father confirms just as the staff arrives with another filet mignon.

He enjoys the process of slicing it into plump chunks. Gazing at the cheese and fruit platter I ordered, I decide to indulge in the imported Brie. At least the creaminess stems the lightning in my throat for the moment.

"Biased, daughter." He dabs at his mouth, then sips at his champagne again. "From what I've heard, this young virile is the only man you've ever spent your time with other than Aldaine and the late Kerrick."

"And Neil," I interrupt.

"Ahh, we both know Neil is a boy and always will be. So, tell me, how can you make a full assessment if you haven't encountered others?"

"I don't need to." I grit my teeth, hiring back lightning, chewing bolts. "He's the only one who matters."

"All I ask is the opportunity to have you make a fair assessment."

"Because life is so fair," I drawl, spreading the cheese onto a cracker and topping it with a heaping glob of preserves.

"Be that as it may, I am still not convinced of this young man's faithfulness to you. Especially given his more recent actions."

"He was only protecting me like he always has."

"Protecting you…or Mara?" He refers to the other night.

Both, I don't bother to respond, remembering Sky's words, which extend to my sister—*your promises are my promises.* Sky would never allow Bliss to be hurt on his behalf.

My father sighs. "Once you choose a suitable suitor, then we can put this matter to rest."

More resolved than I've ever been in my life, I hammer my hand into a fist and promise my father, "I won't choose anyone but Sky."

"And Luc?"

I groan. "Stop bringing him up."

"Luc has proved his dedication with the surrendering of his Museum. Something you seem to deny," my father scolds.

I lift my chin. "I don't deny it. It doesn't hold me hostage anymore. Not after he assaulted me."

Force rolls his eyes. "Come now, Serenity. Please don't pretend you don't want that man."

"I want Sky." More than want. Need him. It's him. It's us. Always us.

"Just as you may want others. Drake's son has inherited his enterprise, another personal friend of yours." The way he uses the term "friend" so loosely gives me a sense of foreboding. I wait for him to reveal the answer. "You might remember Tristan's eager mouth before his name."

Revulsion for the memory alone multiples inside me. I press my lips into a thin line.

"After he sees to his business affairs, he will join us for dinner along with his cousin. Until then, your other suitor will undergo more testing until I am certain. I am curious to see how long he holds out."

"Holds out?" I grip my butter knife. "What are you doing to him?"

"At ease, Serenity. He is quite unharmed, I assure you. Just the opposite in fact." My father chuckles, far too amused for his own good. "In return for your cooperation to meet more suitors since your judgment is also clouded, I will give you a sustained amount of time in which your training will not include whipping your sister."

I perk up. "How long?"

Leaning back in his seat, he thumbs the edge of his glass. "Three months."

"A year," I press.

"Six months," he negotiates.

"Nine months."

"Done."

He smiles before speaking an order. "To celebrate, I've ordered a signature dish for you this evening.

A staff member arrives with a gold-trimmed plate bearing a decadent arrangement of gold-plated vessels—one in the shape of a swan boat that houses an ornate arrangement of strawberries dipped in edible gold. My father gives me a proud rundown of the other delicacies.

"The world's most expensive cake, gold infused, wrapped in an edible gold sheet, imported vanilla beans from Uganda, and Italian ganache for your strawberries because the quickest way to my daughter's smile is through her sweet tooth."

He watches as my fingertips light on the chocolate shavings decorating the cake before I raise it to my mouth to help my salivating tongue. Then, I go for a strawberry and practically drown it in the ganache. "Is it ever exhausting?"

"Come again?"

"Dressing your evil up all the time? Playing these silly little games?"

My father stretches out his arms in an exaggerated fashion. "Every day. I take pride in my abilities, but I do enjoy a good round of self-pity every now and then. After all, it's exceedingly difficult to shoulder the responsibilities as the most powerful man in the world."

"I'm sure," I drawl, sarcasm decorating my tone.

"But the greatest gift is watching you bloom to carry on my legacy."

Don't hold your breath. That's when I catch the stray thought. Why didn't I voice that out loud? And I realize the yin-yang symbols on his shirt seem to have grown claws and weigh on me heavier than the entire Temple.

I PROGRESS DOWN THE HALLWAY, headed for the elevator, wishing I could visit Sharky, but I don't have access to the lower levels at this time of day. Far too crowded in the evenings. Maybe after my exhibit. So, I make my way to the roof to swim in the infinity pool.

As I pass the hallway to Bliss's room, I notice Luc standing just outside her door. Curious, I linger there and watch them speak. Unfortunately, I can't hear what they're saying since their voices are too low. Luc is too stiff. Spine rigid, fingers curled like they want to tighten into fists. My sister closes the door and he turns around, brows lifting at my presence. I walk away.

"Serenity," he calls, but I do my best to ignore him.

He catches up to me in the elevator. I move to the side, remembering our one encounter in here.

"I only wish to speak to you regarding your next display," he states.

Luc confounds me. Never before has he had a grander opportunity. With Sky out of the way, this would be prime time for him to pull one of his stunts, but I'm grateful for the lack of attention. And the discussion of my next display is more than welcome.

"Any hints?" I quip a little, pressing the button for the roof.

"Your father has forbidden hints, but I imagine Neil will enjoy this display the most."

That is a hint in and of itself. An offering of sorts. When Luc touches my hand, just the tips of his fingers, but then retreats, I gaze at him, shocked.

"What?" He notices my parted mouth.

I shake my head, stare forward to the opening doors. "Nothing."

That's when he pursues me by snatching hold of my arm. "You were expectant."

"No, surprised," I correct. I try to step out, but he tugs on me, just enough so I'm back in the elevator with him. I brace my fists, steeling myself, but nothing comes except for the tilt of his head, his eyes an otherworldly blue when they meet mine.

Speaking my name in a whisper, he then cups my face, his hand not as insistent as it has been in the past. "What do you want?"

"Swimming would be at the top of the list right now."

"Tell me," he urges again.

"Luc..." I sigh and lick my lips, remembering. "You did nothing. You just stood there. You let him take him away."

"Would it have made a difference?"

I drop my eyes to the floor, defeated. "Probably not."

"Does it make any difference now?"

"Why are you doing this?" I challenge. "Is this just more manipulation? You hound me, you force yourself on me, and now... is this some kind of trick?"

"Perhaps I'd settle for penance." He circles his thumb on my cheek.

"You don't need my forgiveness."

"Yes, I do."

I can't feel my breath anymore because all my butterflies have stolen it, keeping it from me. This is a side of Luc I've never seen. No self-pity or self-loathing—no trace in the creased lines in his forehead. His brows have their own dialect, but for once, they're still and silent. This is a straightforward apology. More than telling, he's *showing* with his hand stationed on my cheek, gaze soft on mine, but not once does he try to kiss me. Through this eerily submissive display, I recognize he is trying harder than ever. More than the night he killed the graphickers, more than the night he beat Gull's abuser, more than giving up his Aviary or taking me to the Garden or the night he tried to seduce me, Luc's humility is an open door to his heart. To do this must mean one of two things—desperation or love.

Maybe both.

"Luc, I need you to let me go."

He searches my eyes. "In what way?"

I glance behind me. "Right now, I'll settle for swimming, but you know what ways."

"Don't be long. Your exhibit opens in just a few hours."

I nod before turning around, then rush out into the glass hall that opens onto the rooftop. Even before I hear the sound of laughter, I see them there. Guess he must've just come back from overseas. It's not the first time I've seen him swim, but at least his lower half is clothed this time. It's the girl with him who catches me by surprise.

Naamah.

"Care to join us?" Neil offers. Judging by the way his body sways to the side, I can see he's had a few drinks. "Wine on the table behind you," he says, confirming my suspicions by pointing to one of the pool tables.

It seems odd, considering how unusual this is. Neil must have used a Temple pass for Naamah. Perhaps because Force offered him a complimentary interaction. All Naamah does is remain on the side of the pool, legs dipped in the water, the rest of her dark horse body clothed only in a white-feathered bikini. She's so still... as if this is more of an exhibit and not an interaction.

Something about her...not right for Neil.

He wades through the water, arriving at the shallow end to greet me.

"Do I get a welcome-home kiss?"

I lean toward my brother with a beguiling smirk, right up until the point where I smack the water with both hands, splashing him in the face. Then, I dive under, slipping past him with ease because I can match anyone underwater. When I surface closer to the deep end, Neil is shaking his fist at me from the other side.

Naamah hasn't moved once.

When Neil approaches, she gives him a half smile. One full of the same mystery as the fallen angel she portrays. The black raiment of her hair is long enough to brush the tiles behind her. Even as he plants his hands on either side of her, Naamah's eyes follow mine. Even if the angel lens doesn't distort them to black orbs with blue veins ebbing along her skin, the way she tracks me is unsettling.

Suddenly, I'm not feeling much like a swim, so I tell Neil I've changed my mind.

"Wait!" Naamah's voice, deep-set and smoky, follows me.

I spin around, more surprised at her boldness of leaving the water and pursuing me. Fortunately, my brother doesn't seem too disturbed by the faux pas.

"Swan…"

I resist the urge to grind my teeth when she calls me by my exhibit name. It's how so much of the world has labeled me anyway.

"Please, I must speak with you." Her eyes uncork mine, full of intent and urgency. They remind me of *Arabian Nights*—full of dark nights spent by fires, embers eavesdropping on romance and secrets.

"About Neil?" As soon as I say the words, I know they are a mistake. Especially given the way she glances back at him, brows tapering.

"Neil…" Her voice lowers almost to a whisper as she shakes her head. "No. He's been more than generous."

"Generous?" I steal another glimpse at my brother, who waves and then stretches his arms above his head.

"Yes, with the vaccine," Naamah declares, but at registering my confusion, her mouth parts, eyes falling toward the ground. "Oh, more generous than I realized since he kept it private, even from his own sister." She joins her hands together. "After high-profile exhibits, we are always blood-typed for viruses. The system red flagged me, but Mr. Bodelo arranged for me to have access to the early form of the vaccine."

At once, I feel guilty for assuming the worst of my brother, for assuming he just caved into my father's lusty suggestion. More than a tight hug is warranted this time. In any case, what else could she possibly have to talk about?

Shifting her weight, Naamah offers a hint. "A situation has been unfolding down-Temple. I feel as though you're the only trustworthy one."

"Does this have something to do with the murders?"

Naamah blinks once, but the way her eyes waver to the side reveals it does.

"I don't want to put him in danger." Her eyes flick to the side, indicating Neil.

And she has no doubt assumed one of two things—either I am already in danger and therefore she can trust me with something potentially more dangerous…or I am exempt from the danger because of the swan carvings.

"I have an exhibit tonight," I state, but then propose. "I can see if I can host you for a meal after. Or in the morning."

"Thank you."

"He's in love with you," I tell her before she has the chance to walk away.

Nodding, she licks her lips. "Many men are."

"He's different."

She smiles, but it's not as soft as it should be. No doubt the Temple has chiseled that smile into what it expects.

"He is different," she agrees. "That is not the question, however. The real question is for how long can he afford to be different?"

And just like that, Naamah dethrones me.

Five

WhAt ShE NeEds

LUC

*A*s I PREPARE MYSELF TO check on Serenity's progress, I reflect on her response to me earlier. All the while, I know I'm just fooling myself by fooling her. An act born out of desperation, one I resort to, not one I trust. My father's voice resounds in my ear.

Never submit yourself to a woman. It's her role to submit to you.

I wonder how my brother manages the balance—the art of mastering respect but not submission because I've never caught him overthrowing his masculinity before her. At least my actions gave her pause, but will that pause linger? Doubtful. But I'm not ready to give her up yet.

Glancing behind me to ensure Queran is still following, I continue forward. Tonight, two preparers unite. He's outdone himself with the wings, the way he's interlaid them one over the other, shaping them in a delicate fashion. Each one is designed to withstand this onetime exhibit. After tonight, they will be auctioned off as a collectible. Feathers would have proved too reminiscent of the Swan. Tonight, Serenity will be the Angel.

And what an angel she is with every strand of her silver-pearl hair straightened to a degree it swings past her bare waist, a few strands brushing her soft, even stomach. My Aviary brand on her shoulder is a nice addition to the rest of her from the silver cuff on each arm where a sheath of transparent fabric drips to the diamond and tulle. Embellishing the center is a brooch of floral-inlaid crystals and a diamond dangling three inches down.

By the way she brushes her hands down her bare stomach and to the silver latticework that extends from her hips to cover her sex, I can tell she's uncomfortable with this costume. And she must know there will be no water this time. Neither air nor land is her domain, and her anxiety is showing through her trembling fingers.

I'll need to get her through this just as I did for her first Aviary exhibits. Self-serving and punishing myself at the same time.

Queran attaches the wings to the back of the costume. That's when I notice the preparer place an object in her hand. She holds it up to the light and smiles at the origami angel, then kisses his cheek before placing the folded paper on the dressing table.

"Sweet girl." Queran touches her cheek. If I didn't know any better regarding his sterile status in more ways than one, I'd have an issue with his affection.

"Give me a moment," I tell the other two preparers. "Serenity, you're shaking," I say once they've left.

She holds her arms now, bending. "I know."

I cup her shoulder, brushing my fingers across her tattoo. "I doubt you'll ever get used to it."

She shakes her head.

The fabric curling down the sides of her hips and between her thighs flirts with her naked legs, and the sight is driving me damn near insane. I know I'll regret this, but I capture her face with my hands and drive my mouth to hers, opening it. At first, she resists, then crumbles, resists, and crumbles again. Her hands don't know what to do. Mine are all too certain of what they want, but I only drift my fingers to her neck, permit myself that and no more as I ease into her mouth from another angle. Tastes as sweet as honey and chocolate, sweet sin and wine, mouth just as soft and warm as ever. Her getting winded was my goal, and I've achieved the result when I step away and leave her gasping, cheeks reddening, mouth swollen. I'm not ready to stop. The ache is an indelible chain connecting me to her, but for once, I recognize it's held together by a link that is in danger of fracturing.

Serenity is familiar with the dynamic, so she doesn't speak any lethal words. All she does is lick her lips, folding them over each other, then touches her forehead. She's making it difficult to concentrate, and my gaze drifts over every patch of open skin,

29

forming thoughts about how I could create more. Of taking her into my arms, into my bed, and into my heart to make her my Swan, my mermaid, my angel, and everything else that is beautiful in the world. Forever. And how beautiful we would be together. But the fantasy deteriorates with every second, and she shatters it to smithereens with her next words.

"Please, not again."

At least I've given her something else to think about, which was the goal. She performs better when she doesn't plan or think beforehand.

I don't tell her there will be no need for quite some time after tonight. These three are the triumvirate displays. From now on, votes will be taken for other options, but that process will last a good month. Until then, Serenity's exhibits will be off the market.

Her body leans away from mine as I escort her, but I can tell she's trying to force it. Good. Better for her to dwell on me than her exhibit. If she was prepared as a mermaid, it would be different, but Serenity won't be able to lose herself like she always managed in the Aviary.

Security has been increased on Force's orders. Through the curtain, I notice one standing sentry before the center of the exhibit. More are on each side of the display, but I am the only one with access to this backstage area. After I lead Serenity to the winding staircase on the opposite side, I offer her my hand. Swathes of white fabric lick the steps as she follows. The sounds of an impatient audience crowd the air.

"Where are we going?"

"Catwalk. You'll be dropped from the middle."

While I prep the cables to attach to her wings, I survey her expressions. She doesn't appear too surprised. Not much of a revelation that Force wants his little angel to fly. If only I could tell her to fly for me, but words have never helped her. Serenity responds more to action, so I grip her jaw, keep the quiver there steady, and force her eyes to meet my own.

I whisper her name. Follow it with, "Shh…they're waiting for you."

I let her go, then signal Force through the earbud that operates on our own frequency. The show commences.

BLISS

EVERY MURMUR AND WHISPER ARE rendered silent as soon as the exhibit dims. Serenity's figure, illuminated by the spotlight glow, appears. She has some power over them because all eyes are trained on her. I wonder what it must feel like. To fly like that. Or rather... to float through air.

I'd be happy just walking through the absence, but she takes advantage of her cables by spinning, pirouetting, twirling, and dancing in midair. It's not in her nature to remain still. Perhaps she's imagining water instead because her body moves through the air similar to when she's immersed.

Father outdid himself on the exhibit. The moving clouds in the background appear to be real, the lights playing on them changing color according to the notes of the song. Soft and light hues to mimic the high, fluttery melody, dark gray shadows for the thunder and bass that follows. The sudden sprite lights sparking on one side and then the other, seemingly at random, don't deter Serenity. In fact, she bonds with them, responding to each crackle, playing along with them like they are her instruments. My sister, the Lightning Angel.

The cables do most of the work, but she follows along well enough. I would need to practice for days before such a thing, weeks even. Not been content until I'd mastered the art. My sister works well on the fly, pun intended.

"Beautiful, isn't she?" Luc remarks, and I find it intriguing he managed to find my solitary nook just next to the lighting booth. I conclude his only reason for monitoring this area is for security.

"Her ferocious grace is capturing."

"Ferocious." He ponders the word, then gives his commentary. "I was going to say passionate." He stands against the wall, back almost as stiff as mine.

"Much more than passion." I recognize the wrath in her expression. I've seen it every day of my existence. Wrath I could never erase. Wrath I could only suck into myself, but my father always had more to spare.

Luc studies her for a moment. "Yes, there is a fine line between fear and anger. I only needed to send her over the edge."

"Oh?" I can predict where this is going. "Did she attack you for it?"

At first, he seems hurt by my interest, but it seems Luc is learning to follow along with my little games. Or perhaps he's surrendering. "Resisted, but she understands the pattern. It's what she needed. What do you need, Bliss?"

I stare blankly, making my eyes cold. "I don't need anything."

He opens his mouth, but the telltale thud echoing all over the exhibit, followed by the sudden screams, sucks away his words. We both flick our eyes to the exhibit. There, on the ground just before Serenity's feet, is the soaked body of another angel. All her sharp angles and her dark river of hair are familiar. The Angel of the Year. Naamah.

Luc is gone, and I catch the sight of him running down one of the exhibit staircases. He isn't going for Serenity, but why would he? She doesn't seem frightened in the least. On the contrary, she's furious. I imagine her expression must echo Father's. I hear it in his voice even as he tries to quell the fleeing crowd, assuring them it was an accident as a result of a suicidal girl. So much chaos, no one notices me hurrying down the stairs to get closer to the exhibit where I understand this was no suicide.

By now, Serenity has been lowered to the ground and is standing over the body of Naamah, staring down at her chest, bare between the silk fabric of her angel gown. From this angle, I can make out the image carved on Naamah's chest. A swan.

"*Serenity*," I call even as people push past me and guards haul her away.

She drags her feet for a moment before obliging them.

Out of the corner of my eye, I see a security detail ushering my father out a side door. Instead, I follow the crowd, managing to slip behind the curtain at the last second, evading another guard. Finally backstage, I see two guards standing around Serenity, who sits on a chair, her face full of rage from her compressed lips to a jaw tenser than a tightrope. Father must have ordered them to keep her here. Behind her, a door opens. Luc appears. Serenity tries to stand again, but one of the guards pushes her back down.

"Cut that out!" She smacks his hand away, annoyance smearing into her fury. "Luc, tell these gorillas to back off."

I approach her from the front while Luc approaches from behind.

"You should be receiving orders to turn her over to my care now," Luc stipulates before the guards confirm and exit the stage area.

"Did you find anything?" I ask, referring to the door he'd just come from.

He shakes his head. "No one permitted through that exit but the preparers and me. And Lindy and Queran both have alibis."

"Neither would do it," Serenity denies, and I agree with a nod.

We all turn at the savage yell coming from the exhibit. Our brother stands behind the glass, fingers clawing for Naamah's corpse. I'd always known she was special in his eyes. Up until now, I didn't understand how much.

Serenity tries to run toward him, but Luc grabs her arm, preventing her. "It's a crime scene, Serenity," he warns. "You can't get near the body, and neither can he."

Tearing her arm away, Serenity lashes out, but I hear her voice cracking, "Why doesn't he come for me?"

We both know she's not talking about Neil.

"He's escalating," Luc returns. "He's left this one right at your feet as some gift in his demented mind. I don't believe it's his intention to kill or harm you."

I listen to Luc, deciphering every word, but Serenity scans around her, unable to concentrate.

Luc tries to summon her by tapping her jaw. "This obsession reeks of idolization. It's nothing like the Aviary occurrences, but I have seen it in other cases."

"So, why doesn't he come for me?" she repeats, her eyes tightening at the seams.

No tears squeeze through. My sister's fists still haven't loosened, and the skin on the back of her hands is too white. Blood will have to return at some point.

"We will protect you."

I notice Luc doesn't say "I", and I wonder what 'we' he could be referring to because the way he says it leaves me to believe Father is not the only participant.

"WHY ARE YOU HERE?" I ask my mother when I arrive at my door.

"I'm here for some answers," she says in a straightforward tone without betraying confidences. It's one of the reasons Serafina and I relate to each other.

"Why don't you ask your other daughter?"

"I saw you both come in with Luc. The last thing she needs is someone asking her questions. Serenity's not in that frame of mind. And it wouldn't be in mine or Luc's best interest to ask him questions at this time." My mother rubs one hand up her arm. Goose bumps have already grown there, but I notice how her flesh is fuller on her arms. As if all the recent events have only strengthened her. Motherhood comes with such a high price. It's unfathomable to me. How can she handle that her two greatest weaknesses belong to Father?

Sighing, I use my barcode to unlock the door. I find Queran inside preparing for tonight's interaction because life never pauses in the Temple. Father is having Serenity and me perform our Yin and Yang display as always.

Serafina closes the door behind her before confronting me. "Are you concerned?"

"For Serenity?"

She shakes her head. "For yourself."

I glance over at Queran. Whether he shows it, I realize he's listening to every word. This conversation would be better served in private, so I ask Queran to give us a few minutes.

"Why would I be?" I ask my mother once he's returned to his adjoined room.

"Your life could be at stake in this, given what I know of the victims." She reaches out to touch me, fingers settling lightly on my shoulder, a cloud overlapping the moon.

"They've been targeted due to their high status," I try to reassure her. "I'm out of the public eye."

"Even though you and Serenity have been separated all these years, I've already seen how ultimate the competition can be between two sisters, particularly identical twins."

I take a seat in the vanity chair and touch a curl, one of the few things Serenity and I have in common. "You should be more worried about her. Not me," I say.

"I am concerned for you both."

"I'm a lost cause, Mother."

She approaches me, eyes reflecting in the mirror. They hold empathy, fathoms deep as cemeteries, yet just as full of regret and longing. "Any daughter who calls me Mother is never a lost cause."

Had I said Mother? I don't recall having called her that before, never truly acknowledged it until now.

She places her hand on the back of my head while the other reaches for the brush on the table. "Perhaps when or if you have children of your own, you will understand."

While she eases the brush through my strands, I shake my head. "There will be no *if* or *when*. Father has seen to it."

"What?" She pauses.

"Father has...*seen* to it."

In the mirror's reflection, I notice her fingers tighten on the handle, memories almost forming a whirlwind in her eyes. "You and your sister were the only decent parts of my life that came from the Temple. The only light in the darkness. Never forget that, Bliss. Please. The choice should always belong to you."

"No choices belong to me inside the Temple. Only my reactions to them."

She continues brushing. Resolutely nods. "I understand."

"I know you do. It's your other daughter who doesn't."

We both chuckle at the thought. "Yes," Serafina reflects. "Serenity has never hidden a reaction in her entire life. Even as a baby, she was quite colicky. A high-strung child. Spirited and active teenager."

"How did you manage to keep her secret all those years?"

"We couldn't have done it alone."

"Yes, the infamous Skylar." Exhaling, I relax my shoulders. "I've had the pleasure but not the background."

"It's difficult at times to remind myself he's not my son." Her eyes become lost in my curls as if she can summon memories from them. "After all, he doesn't take after anyone, but he embraced our family, our values, our wisdom and knowledge—all with open arms."

"He must have remembered something. Serenity tells me he was four years old. Why didn't he ever want to return to his real family?"

"Blood does not make a family, Bliss." My mother is very firm on this since her eyes wander back to mine. "Blood may have a role in dictating your genetics, but it does not make a family. He was, *is*, family to us. Just in a different way. He's become a touchstone we can always rely on. I never had any qualms leaving Serenity under his care when we left to search for you."

"Why?"

"Because his eyes never lost that spark from when he saw her for the first time. Because he's always loved her." A smile tempts her features. Some otherworldly glow that permits her to spread the corners of her mouth. Had motherhood given her that glow? Love? Freedom? Any one of those concepts seems so foreign to me. Especially love. Lust and shadows—breath and bruises—on my skin are more familiar.

I stare at my hands, noting, "And she loves him."

"I suppose she only realized it this year, but it has only deepened their bond. Their roots couldn't be stronger."

"Indeed."

Serafina works at a knot, however few I may have. Serenity has no patience to untangle the strands, unlike our mother.

"Do you know where Force may be keeping him?" Her hand begins to slow. My curls resemble more sea foam with how much she's brushed them.

I shake my head. "He has a holding center in the Temple, but I don't know where." I've only left the Penthouse a handful of times. I couldn't begin to guess where Father is keeping him.

Our time is drawing to a close. Soon, Queran will return to prepare me, so I give her what information I can. "I can't tell you much about the murders. Luc simply says they are escalating. Due to media attention, Father has been tending to the backlash, offering complimentary return visits and special offers. Since the incidents have coincided with Serenity's exhibits, he plans to close them for a time. But you could learn more from Luc. Why don't you ask him?"

My mother puts the brush down, its sound mimicking the

firm shake of her head. "Luc is more interested in pursuing his fruitless desires. I've spoken to him already, and that will suffice for the time being."

"You speak like him sometimes," I comment, almost wishing I hadn't. She knows who I'm referring to.

Serafina doesn't need another explanation judging by the way she pauses, eyes on her feet before responding. "Yes, well…I spent a great deal of time with him. As you know, he's quite fond of his own voice."

"Did you ever love him?"

"Yes." She gathers my curls into a knot at the back of my head. "Or at least I convinced myself I did, that his hurting me was what he needed, what made me valuable. But your sense of worth should never be dictated by someone else. It is intrinsic." She cups my chin, coaxing my face to the side so she may peer into my eyes. Hers are so similar. Blue echoes, my genetic footprint contained there. "You are a human being with a heart and soul. That is what makes you valuable. Most importantly, you are my daughter. You will always be priceless to me."

No one has ever called me priceless before. I don't know what to make of it. Her conviction is so certain. Does she say these things to Serenity? No, Serenity doesn't strike me as someone who needs to hear it. I wish I could discount my mother's words, tell her she doesn't understand, doesn't understand what it's like to have ones soul crushed and reshaped into something black and wrapped in ice, capable of holding a mountain of ghosts, but she understands all too well. Her mountain is simply one giant ghost while mine is comprised of thousands.

Six

LoYalty

SKY

*I*ORCE DROPS OFF ANOTHER GIRL before he declares he must be "someplace". Convenient. I've learned my lesson with Halo. Turning my back isn't the answer. She's still a girl. A human being who deserves to be treated as such. I just keep training myself to keep my eyes higher where they belong.

I wasn't the only one who learned a lesson. The last time he opened the door, I nearly made it out. Force's taser—or hurts-like-a-dick stick as I prefer to label it—didn't let me get too far. Now, he keeps a thin collar around my neck like I'm some sort of dog. Little zap if I get too close to the door. My invisible fence, as it were.

Before he closes it this time, I ask him to send in some food. Other than the collar and keeping me shut up in here, he's been accommodating, asking me if I need anything, telling me nothing is off limits. Apart from Serenity. In his twisted mind, maybe he thinks it will make me more likely to pursue an interaction.

"What would you like?" I ask the entering girl.

By the way Force's lips thin, it's obvious I've struck a nerve, but one side of his mouth curls as if intrigued. All a game to him. Curious as to anything I might try or want.

The girl looks dumbfounded—as if no one has ever asked her what she might want to eat. She must be a lower girl, judging by the simple lingerie and chamois over her dark skin.

"Um…" Scraping her nails together, she shifts her weight. "Peanut butter and banana sandwiches. And lollipops."

I put in the order to Force. "Peanut butter and banana sandwiches and lollipops it is, then. Throw in some milk with that, along with a couple of beef jerky sticks if you don't mind."

Force nods, but the revulsion on his face is hard to miss. I smirk. The food is too crude for his hoity-toity palette.

Kicking my foot up behind me, I flatten it on the wall, lean back, and ask her, "So, why do you like peanut butter and banana sandwiches?"

She paces the room, rubbing her hands along her naked arms. "It reminds me of my past."

"Are you cold?" I point to her arms.

"I'm fine."

Rolling my eyes, I remove my jacket. Another gift from Force was a change of clothes. Strange, considering I figured he'd be eager to get rid of mine, but it's just another manipulation to make me feel more comfortable.

Without approaching, I toss the jacket to her. She has to be cold in that getup. More reminiscent of what Serenity would wear—sleeveless white dress but much thinner and more transparent. At first, she fingers my offering, then peers up at me from beneath her lashes.

"Don't you want me to take it off?" She motions to her dress.

I shake my head. "Not really. More interested in those sandwiches."

"Why?"

I shrug. "Call it a hobby."

At first, she purses her lips as if debating. Does it cost her more to surrender this information, I suddenly wonder? "You don't have to—" I start, but she opens her mouth.

"My father used to make them all the time. Before he got sick."

"I'm sorry." I lean against the wall. "Is he better?"

She glances at the floor, shakes her head.

"I'm sorry." It's all I can think to say. When she puts her arms through the gaping jacket holes that swallow them up, I add, "You must've loved him a lot."

She nods. "Was always just him and me. Mama ran off after I was born."

"How'd you end up here?"

"Centre bills are expensive."

She doesn't need to say anything else. Wouldn't be surprised if that's how a lot of girls end up here, working to pay off their endless debts since Force's system is to take out a fair chunk for housing, food, medical check-up expenses, costuming, makeup, and anything else he can use to rack up the debt.

Our food arrives a minute later, and she goes for a lollipop first. I sense she doesn't get the opportunity to try too many sweets in her position. My surprise comes when she doesn't eat it. Instead, she throws it on the floor and crushes it under her shoe.

"Huh," I speculate. Nope, coming up empty. I have no idea what that's about. "What did that sucker ever do to you?" When she doesn't answer, I wave a hand. "Nah, never mind. I'm too nosy. Just forget it. What's your name?"

"Rosie."

After a few minutes of eating our sandwiches in silence, Rosie finally pauses to tell me, "He gave me a lollipop on my first day here."

"Force?" I assume around a chunk of jerky.

Rosie nods. "Told me I had potential, and it'd be the fastest way to work off the bills. I could either go the Temple or he'd let the Syndicate deal with me. They make you pay only one way."

Blood. Truth be told, it's the most effective. Dastardly, cowardly, but effective.

"Anything about this place you like?"

At first, she debates, chewing one side of her mouth before answering, "I like Christmastime. They decorate all the levels in twinkle lights, and we get to wear fur coats."

"I know someone else who likes twinkle lights." I think of Serenity. "Can't say she's into fur coats, though."

"It makes me think of that one girl who walked through the wardrobe into another world."

I smile, remembering the old children's story. "Now, wouldn't that be something?"

"Are you finished?" She points to my empty hands. Guess I wolfed down that sandwich. "Should we get started?"

"I thought we already were."

"I was sent to—"

I hold up a hand. "I know. But we could just talk instead," I suggest. I lower to the floor, back against the wall.

40

"Talk?" Her face screws up in confusion.

"Yeah." I gesture, circling a hand around the small room. "We just sit here and have ourselves a friendly conversation like we're friends."

"Friends?"

I raise my brows, chuckle. "Am I not speaking clearly? Should I talk slower?"

That seems to make her giggle, so I take advantage and go for the gold. "Let's see, what else could I try? Sign language." I hold up my hands, flash her a defeated expression. "But I only know two or three words, and those would be *boy*, *cow*—don't ask why I know *cow*—and *baby*." She laughs, and I scan the room, continuing, "Um, smoke signals! Ugh, guess that won't work. No fire. Ooh! Shadow puppets! Check it out. I can do a mean crocodile."

When she holds her stomach, I know I'm succeeding.

"Course…I could always just beat my chest and stomp my foot like one of those ancient warriors. That'd be something."

She breaks from her giggles to tell me, "I could see that."

"But I left my war drums in my other suit." I snap my fingers before dropping my hand to my side like a chess king tipping over. "The effect would never work without them."

"Maybe next time."

"Maybe." I bow my head to her, hand on my chest. "Was nice to meet you, Rosie."

Our time is short. Force is relentless. He sends in a new girl every hour. Sometimes, I have to work harder because they're wearing next to nothing. Offer my jacket every time, and it always takes them a bit of time to get used to the idea. No such thing as 'no strings attached' in the Temple. I keep things light for them, finding it also does the trick for me. That and food. Who knew the quickest way to a girl's heart was through her stomach? However long Force decides to keep this up, I'm going to show him it's not about overcoming him. It's about showing them a kindness or two they never get inside these walls. And it's about waiting for *her*. I don't care how many girls he puts in my path, she's the only one for me. I don't need to prove it to myself. I don't need to prove it to him either.

I'll spend the rest of my life proving it to *her* every day.

Seven

Grief

SERENITY

Y SENSES KEEP FIRING ON all cylinders. The sprite light sunbeams radiating from my costume match my inner landscape. Unlike me, Bliss manages to synchronize hers. Even after our third interaction together, she reminds me of a stag in winter. She's built a thick hide and strong limbs to survive in the cold. All this time, she's done this with our father's suckers lodged in her like fangs. They stick to my skin, too. Each sucker bears the names of people I love. And now he has Sky's name. At least I still fight. Just a matter of time before I take a battle axe to every last one to sever myself and everyone I love from him.

Queran washes my back to erase the paint from our earlier Yin and Yang interaction. This time, our interaction style was more reminiscent of wedding dresses reflecting the sun and moon. Bliss's was black with sheaths of fabric infused with digital sprite lights that displayed constellations and galaxies. The high-tech crystals that scintillated in her hair are now turned off, sitting lackluster on the table. She is just Bliss again. Queran removes the remainder of my costume from the sinuous waterfall of gold lace and silk with its sprite light sun technology.

Now that Force has halted my exhibits, he is adamant about maintaining our interactions. I no longer have access to other floors. Only the Penthouse. Can't even visit Sharky. If it wasn't for my mother, the rooftop pool, and the tanks with miniature dolphins and whales, I'd drive myself insane. How Bliss has managed to stay cooped up here for this long—I stop myself, remembering all the hotels I grew up in. At least I got to see the outside world, even if I couldn't exactly be a part of it. Why should I complain when Bliss has never gone anywhere? Does she even want to?

"Haven't you ever been curious about the outside world?" I ask her.

Bliss shakes her head, donning her customary silk robe while Queran finishes tends to the back of my legs. "I get pieces of the outside world every night. And I can see the view fine from the windows."

"Not once?"

"Not once."

"And you've never wanted to become an exhibit?" I throw a different question her way.

"I enjoy my solace."

Queran pauses now because it's part of the routine. After he wipes away the hard-to-reach spots, I take a shower to deal with the rest. I don't stay too long under the spout. Just a quick hot shower enough to scald my body, warm my insides, and let the air cool my skin. I wipe the fogged-up mirror to stare at myself. My reflection seems warped like some carnival mirror—body long and languid because Force has stretched me out, pulled harder at my too-thin seams. He'd rather bend me since he knows I'll never break. Just bend me enough, knowing I'll bow and stretch as long as he's holding my family prisoner. Let him pull harder. Quitting isn't a word I recognize. No rest for the wicked.

I can still bleed, shiver, and fracture. All this time, Serenity has never let go. Even with the monster taunting her, even with the ghosts of the Swan, Skeleton Flower, Undine, and Angel, she's the one who keeps the lightning stoked. Despite how physically frail I am, my father can't break the spirit inside me.

But Bliss—she's broken pieces all fused back together. I can still see the cracks even if she doesn't want to show them. And she's somehow stronger for them. She won't let herself be weak. Or vulnerable. Somehow, I must believe there's still a little girl somewhere inside her.

After shrugging into a simple white dress that falls to my ankles, I walk out of the bathroom to see Queran applying white feathers to Bliss's cheeks.

"What's going on?" I ask, gesturing to the eerily familiar costume.

Bliss raises her chin as Queran pastes feathers along her throat. "A special client has reserved me tonight, and he's requested a Swan costume."

I dig my nails through my soggy curls before walking away, slamming the door behind me. Let Bliss think whatever she wants. After all, we don't walk on eggshells. I'm not mad at her. Just my father.

"There she is!" I hear the familiar voice as I round the corner of the hallway leading to my room.

I look up to see Neil standing by my closed door. Or rather... he's wobbling with Lindy grabbing him by the arm to stabilize him.

"There's my corpse flower!" He tips a bottle of vodka back and then drops his arm, but the action causes his body to shift to the side.

"Skeleton Flower," I correct him with a roll of my eyes as I approach them.

"Found this drunken fool wandering around the Angel exhibit after hours," she explains, blowing out aggravation through her nostrils. "He would've ruined all my work if I didn't do something."

"You...and your magic hands," Neil slurs while dragging out the last vowel.

I let him drink, but I take his other arm and prop it up over my shoulder before directing Lindy, "Thanks, Lindy. Help me get him inside. What's he doing here? His room is on the other side of the Penthouse."

Groaning, Lindy kicks open the door after I scan my barcode. "He wouldn't go. Said he had to take a picture of the only angel left before it was too late."

"He's a little late. I'm not an angel anymore," I remark, hearing Neil belch. As soon as I get a whiff of his breath, I cringe and fan a hand in front of my face.

We decide to opt for the couch instead of dragging him up the staircase. After we manage to wrangle him into lying down, he reaches for the bottle again. This time, I retrieve it and dump out the remaining contents in the bathroom sink.

"Aw, Serenity," Neil whines from the other room.

"You've had enough." I wipe my hand on my dress, marveling at how well the jinx is working. "It's my own fault. I wanted a distraction from Bliss."

"I could get naked. That'd be a real distraction," he offers. Lindy and I both shoot him down, but she's more sympathetic than I am since she covers him with a blanket.

"Neil." I put a hand on his arm as he raises his wrist to summon the voxel camera attached there. "*Neil*," I try again. "I'm not an angel anymore."

Shaking his head, he points to me. "Always be an angel to me."

I turn around, denying him the privilege. "Not tonight."

I peer over my shoulder, noticing how he drops his arm, dejected. It can't be helped. The last thing I want is for someone to take my sprite light.

Sighing, Lindy smoothes a lock of his hair from his forehead. Then, she picks up his hand holding the camera and points it toward herself. "Go on, Neil."

"What?" Doing a double take, he nudges her. "You never let me—"

"Take the damn picture already, Neil."

He widens his eyes, brows almost dumbstruck as the irises. After another moment, he raises his wrist and taps on the cuff there, the telltale hum and laser technology capturing Lindy. She doesn't strike any poses. Lindy just sits there next to him, staring and playing with his curls.

"You're not an angel." He taps her nose, which wrinkles from the statement. But then, he follows through, "You're a goddess."

I smile when his head drops to the side, and he starts snoring. Only Neil.

"I'll stay with him if you don't mind," Lindy says.

I don't mind at all.

Eight

WhAt She WaNts

Luc

AYS PASS. I PREOCCUPY MYSELF with investigating the circumstances of the last murder—reviewing footage, exploring the exhibit, and searching for unknown angles. Skylar is better at this. I am so well practiced in the art of killing I can't see the big picture; I focus on the endless details instead.

The body is the same as the others, killed in the same manner and style. Whatever this individual's frame of mind, I know he or she—still leaning toward he—is intelligent and knows the grid layout of the Temple. Only one possible escape route: the rafters. They were scanned for fingerprints, but I doubt the system will discover any.

At least nothing sexual was forced on them. Not that it's much consolation in the Temple. There's simply a personal angle I haven't quite ascertained yet. It's almost like he's dumped this new body right in her display as a gift. As if he's trying to prove something to her. If he knew who she truly was, then he'd recognize Serenity is less than thrilled.

On my way back to the Penthouse, I stop the elevator, go down the security staircase, and then scan my barcode at the door to grant me access to this level. Down this hall is where the security magic takes place from a station comprised of the latest in technology with an interface and database to monitor the top half of the Temple to a training and fitness room including a jogging track, pool, and virtual rooms simulating various environments. I've already explored the security station in the interest of finding

46

a weakness for Force's implant but have been unsuccessful thus far.

That's not why I'm here tonight.

After I scan my barcode once again, I open the door to the holding center, bidding the girl to leave.

"Looks like our time is cut short," Skylar tells her, then gestures farewell. "Nice to meet you, Winter."

If Force is not present himself, he reviews all the footage at the end of the day. I wonder how he'll react to Skylar using the staff call button for flowers, dolls, and teddy bears since the floor is near covered with them.

Skylar picks up a stuffed bear. "Have you ever tried hugging one of these things? It's quite therapeutic." He tosses it at me, but when it bounces off my chest, he rolls his eyes. "What's wrong? Not secure enough in your manhood to squeeze a child's toy?"

"Cheap shot."

Shrugging, Skylar stuffs his hands in his pockets. "Discovered the girls love them. That's where you really see they're just little girls deep down inside."

"How many?"

"One each hour. Must be on some sort of synchronized schedule." He starts to pace, eyeing me from the side. "So, speak of the devil, what are you doing here? Since you're obviously not here for the teddy bears or interested in my social life, I take it you want to discuss some other things? Need to give me an update on something perhaps?"

I almost anticipate my brother will clench his fist, but he does nothing of the sort. He doesn't even approach me.

"What sort of update are you expecting, Skylar?" I ask.

"How is she?"

"You mean in general or do you mean in regard to the latest murder victim, which was dropped right in front of her during her exhibit?" When he doesn't respond, no doubt sorting through his own thoughts on the situation, I respond with, "She's asked for you."

"Course she has." He blows through his nostrils as if it's the most obvious thing in the world.

"Apparently, Force has entered into a negotiation with her. In return for her cooperation in indulging more suitors while he tests you, he's agreed to a ceasefire from her whipping Bliss."

Sighing, Skylar lowers his shoulders. "Guess I can't fault her for that. Oh well, my latest escape idea wouldn't have panned out anyway."

"And what was that?"

He levels with me. "You as a hostage. I'd prefer a Christmas tree ornament, but you work with what you got."

"I haven't done anything," I inform him, referring to Serenity. "She's been spending her time with her family—breakfast with her mother and sister, lunches with Neil, dinners with Force."

"Oh, I'm certain you've tried. Couldn't pass up the opportunity with me out of the picture, could you?" Now, he tenses, but I'm still surprised at his control, given he hasn't raised a fist to me yet.

"You don't seem too concerned by the fact."

"That's cause she and I have a little thing called *trust*." He winks and sifts one hand through his hair, tightening his pony. "You should try it sometime."

"Trust only goes so far."

"Not in our case. Even with you and me, I know there's only one way you could make her yours. And we both know you won't."

"How's that?"

Sky sniggers, leaning up against the wall, brows tapering down, muscles flexing. "Because you can *trust* I'd rearrange your whole body if you so much as tried to force yourself on her again. You can also trust she'd tell me. Steal a kiss here and there—I'll make you pay for those later. But anything more, Luc...I'll kill you."

Even though my brother is no killer, I believe him. At the very least, permanent damage would ensue. Serenity is slipping from my grip the more I try to hold onto her. She's becoming an illusion while another has taken her place.

I DROP BY SERENITY'S ROOM since I agreed to give her an update. At least, that is the excuse I give myself. She is just closing the door behind her, escaping into the hallway when I arrive.

"Queran?" She raises her brows, staring at the figure behind me.

Considering I'm a former assassin, it does not bode well that a preparer has managed to stroll up behind me with no forewarning. Then again, Queran is no ordinary preparer. He has Temple blood inside him. He knows the routes of the Penthouse better than even I do. Letting him pass, I observe him approach Serenity with cupped hands, which he then opens to present her with an origami angel. I recognize the object from earlier.

"I forgot it after…everything." She accepts the token. "Thank you, Queran." She leans over to peck his cheek.

Queran points to her and then to the angel. Sighing, she stares at the paper, trailing her fingers across the thin edges of the wings.

"I don't feel like one. More like a monster."

Queran's brows crease. I'm keenly aware of every move he makes when he withdraws a piece of paper from his jacket and starts to reorder it. His expert fingers craft a monster-like figure within mere moments. After holding it up to her face, he reaches for the angel and makes a growling sound with his throat before he uses the angel to strike the monster. It falls to the ground. Serenity smiles. I haven't seen that sort of treasured smile since she looked at Fawn or Finch.

"Goodnight, Queran," she tells him, and he leans over to whisper something in her ear before departing. He doesn't meet my gaze once.

Again, if I didn't know any better…

"Luc," she says while scooping up the fallen paper monster. "If I am an angel, I definitely have monster parts stuck in me."

"We both know even monsters can take beautiful disguises." I want to cup her cheek, but I restrain myself.

"What are you doing here?" she asks.

"I could ask you the same question."

"Neil got drunk and Lindy's with him, but his snoring is so loud I'll never be able to sleep. And no, I won't sleep in your room. I'm going to my mother's."

"I wasn't planning to ask."

She avoids my gaze. "What do you want to ask?"

"Serenity," I say, trying to summon her, but she doesn't want to look up at me. So, I tread lightly, urge her ever so little by coaxing my chin upward. "I'm asking this time. Will you let me?" I lean toward her, rubbing her bottom lip with my thumb. Feasting on the sight of that mouth, I realize it's still tempting, but not in the same way. The way she uses it is...wrong.

She shakes her head. "No."

"Because of my brother?"

"Because I love him." She steps back, and I drop my hand as she finishes, "And because *we're* right, and you and I are *wrong*."

"Wrong for each other," I confirm, feeling the last pieces of her crumble and blow away like diamond dust.

"I'm not sorry, Luc."

Surprisingly, neither am I.

WHEN I KNOCK ON *HER* door, it's Queran who opens it. Of course it is. Her interaction is over. It's no surprise he's here to help her return to Bliss. I try to convince myself his presence here will help me avoid any manner of temptation. It's a flimsy excuse, but I hold onto it.

Until I see her.

Deja vu strikes a chord inside me when I survey the white feathers sealed so tightly to her throat, the birdcage veil, the thigh-high white stockings—wrinkled—the bits of lace around her sensual regions, some already ripped from too-anxious fingers.

I would savor her longer. She is far too overwhelming to be taken in one gulp.

"Enjoying the view?" she asks while Queran sets to work with the remover, easing a tiny brush underneath each feather. I'm certain NAILS could remove this much faster, but it seems Bliss enjoys the gradual process.

"Here," I volunteer, putting enough authority in my voice for Queran to register I don't mean this as a request. "Let me."

He still eyes her for confirmation. She waves a hand, and like the little lapdog he is, he retreats to his bedroom. Picking up where he left off, I dip the peeler in remover and nudge it underneath the feathers.

"This must be a switch for you. Removing the Swan instead of creating her." Nothing about her voice is coy or flirty. She's fallen into the similar pattern of goading me.

I challenge her. "But I get the sense I could never remove enough of any guise to see what's truly beneath the surface."

She doesn't respond, which is confirmation in and of itself. Neither of us speaks while I finish removing the feather collar strangling her neck. Beneath it, her skin is soft and fair as swan's down. The tattered lace on her shoulder tempts my eyes lower to her cleavage line. Tonight, I welcome the thoughts. I let them breed.

My wandering eyes do not escape her notice.

"You'd enjoy seeing more. Admit it."

"I'm more interested in what you want, Bliss. Who you are behind that beguiling smile?" I brush my index finger along her upper lip.

She stands, retreating from my touch. Tempting me and pulling away in that expert way she does.

"So, my smile is beguiling, is it?" Bliss spreads her lips, one side crooking. She's toying with me.

I'm not having it tonight.

"Damn it, Bliss." Grabbing her by the shoulders, I shove her up against the wall, nostrils flaring from the effort. "Just tell me what you want!"

Bliss's lips part, but nothing comes out. Her eyes zero in on me, but I can tell she's stunned by the question. What is so difficult about it? Does she even know? Does she even feel anything? Does she even know who she is? She glances at the bedroom for a moment, then back at me before biting down on her lower lip.

"I want whatever *you* want, Luc."

Hell, I won't stop this time. When I drive my mouth onto hers, I'm digging my own grave. When I raise her into my arms, feeling her legs respond to climb my body and anchor themselves around my waist so I can carry her to bed, I'm digging my own path to hell. And so be it. I don't move fast. Instead, I peel her stockings off, leaving my fingerprints along every inch of skin as possible. I move agonizingly slowly—preserve this, kissing every inch of her glorious body. My lips seek hers, then voyage down her throat, across her collarbone, before descending lower.

I feel her shiver once I'm inside her.

"Am I hurting you?" I murmur.

"Shh..." she whispers, then opens her swollen mouth below mine, inviting me inside even more.

She unearths me only to bury me. This time, I've found a way inside her, but the instant I pull away from her mouth and peer into her vacant eyes, I recognize one truth—Bliss's heart will be my grave. But I'll have to work much harder, crawling through layer after layer until I reach it. Because she's given me nothing but her body.

And that will never be enough for me.

Nine

LuC's GhOst

BLISS

WHAT DO I WANT? How can he ask me that? The first twelve years of my life were spent training in virtually every art. The first twelve years of my life, my eyes were already closed, mind asleep before my head could hit the pillow because the days were filled with muscles wailing from how they were contorted into every imaginable dance pose, toes bleeding from shaping them into ballerina points…and for what? They've always been more interested in ripping the tutu before I've finished the dance. Their mouths salivating too much to wait for me to complete the song. Their hands itching to land on me before my very last dance move.

They're all just open shells. They close their jaws over me, thinking I'll fill them, but I never do. I slip inside but drift easily through their cracks as if I were a ghost. But they leave pieces of me inside them. A finger here, a crumb of a beard there, half a crooked smiling lip, a starved iris. They all become a second skin—one sown into me. Destined while I was in the womb. My fate sealed because I was not the chosen twin. No one has ever chosen me. Because I'm not worth it. And I never will be. To him or anyone else.

So, I can't fathom why Luc pretends to care. All he wants is to fit me into his preconceived notion I could have a dream similar to his. That we could share something together. But nothing is ever shared. Nothing is ever given. It's just taken.

Why else would he do this on the night I'm dressed like the

Swan?

So, I add more to my last answer. One that is practiced. One I've rehearsed for years. "I want whatever *you* want, Luc."

He may be different, but he's still the same. He goes slower than the others, more interested in what pleases me. At first, I think it will make a difference. Many men walk me through their precise flavor, show me sprite lights of what they are searching for. Luc does none of that. He takes his time. Kisses every speck of my skin, mouth slow and lingering.

Every now and then, he pauses to ask me questions. None are about him. *How are you feeling? Am I hurting you?* It's quaint really. His sweetness.

Clearly, he knows how the game is played, considering how *practiced* he is. He knows where to touch to send electrical currents through me, but he doesn't realize how many years I've spent turning them off until they're nothing but dying light bulbs. I adopt a routine I haven't needed to practice in years. Surely, he must understand. He's a former director. Tapping his jaw, I whisper honey words in his ear, brush my fingertips in all the right places, and even giggle at the right times. I keep everything soft fluff. So much, I almost think we're making love on a bed of clouds.

I've never had one linger after. Wanting to cuddle. It's unexpected, but I squeeze into the new mold because it's what I do. Pleasing men is an art form, and I am Picasso, Van Gogh, Degas, and Da Vinci. Harnessing a man's fantasy and fulfilling it is a symphony, and I am Mozart, Beethoven, and Bach.

I even fulfill his fantasy twice because it's such a change from the norm. Tomorrow, I'll probably end up with another one who takes me from behind, riding rather than folding me into his body like Luc does. Might as well enjoy it while we have tonight. I'd hoped something would change. But the ghost of every man in the Temple still covers my eyes, and Luc has just added his to the mix.

Ten

The TrUth

SKY

I'LL LOVE HER UNTIL I stop breathing. Until my heart stops beating. Even if I was in a coma and on life support, she'd be there inside me. With me.

She makes it hard. I have to work harder for her. Feels damn near like picking a scab open every day, but on the days we fit—oh, those days! Like cell regeneration. Instant healing. Not even a memory of scars. But this damned Temple is one giant scissor, wanting to cut us in half. And the hours I spend boxed in this room stretch on endlessly like child's play goo.

At least I have something to occupy my time with all the visiting girls.

I start telling them stories.

"Sometimes, I'd risk dropping into her bedroom during the day just so I could smell her. Just so I could touch her pillow, knowing it's where her hair was," I say, relating the events of those first weeks to the latest girl.

Star plays with the ribbon on a teddy bear's neck as she listens.

"Sometimes..." I lean in as if we're sharing a secret. "I'd even walk out onto the balcony and gaze out at the city because it's what she enjoys doing every night. Just like in the hotels where we grew up."

"It's a beautiful story."

Leaning my head back against the wall, I look to the side because of how Star is dressed to mimic her namesake in nothing but body glitter, but at least the teddy bear she's holding is a decent size to cover her chest.

"It's real," I tell her.

"A lot of men are in love with the Swan. They make up stories."

I shake my head. "I don't lie."

"All men lie."

I could list off a myriad of facts from Serenity's birthmark to her blood type, but Star wouldn't believe me. Guess I can't really blame her, considering what she's experienced from the majority of my miserable gender. What's important is I know the truth.

What does she always say? Paper flowers in the attic? We should've known the wind would've blown us away eventually. And now, we've landed smack dab in the Temple Penthouse right where her seed was first planted. Harder than ever to escape. Can't kill Force without flatlining Serafina.

Serenity can't lose another parent.

Neither can I.

Just need to bide my time. Somehow, I'll get Serenity, her mother, and her sister the hell out of here. And this time, we won't stop running.

Eleven

HeArt MurMur

SERENITY

I PREPARE TO KNOCK ON MY mother's door. More than any-one else, I want to see *her*. Whoever this killer is, he clearly has an obsession, and no one knows about obsession more than my mother.

But when the door opens before my knock lands, I flinch, leaping back.

Right now, I must have a heart murmur. Too much blood forcing itself there, beating too fast. My valves are overworked. Butterflies suffocating. Someone has plucked at their wings. They commiserate together at the bottom of my stomach. I can't so much as summon lightning because this is too much.

"No."

It comes out more as a whimper. I sink to the floor, drawing my knees up to my chest to protect my taxed heart. I rock myself back and forth, trying to deny the sight of my father buttoning his shirt, his hair tousled, cheeks flushed, and body more relaxed than ever.

"Come now, Serenity," he croons, reaching to touch my hair.

I flinch even more, shrinking away.

"You didn't think I agreed to a generous nine months on your actions alone?"

"Go away," I whisper, recoiling. "Go, go, go."

I want to go.

I want to fly…into the sky. I want—no, *need*—Sky.

My mother appears in the doorway, wrapped in a silk robe

57

like Bliss wears. When I see him lean toward her, I spin my head around, but I make the mistake of forgetting my ears. I still hear the sound of their kiss. Still hear him address her.

"Thank you for a lovely evening, Serafina. Until tomorrow night."

"How could you?" I whisper once he's gone, slowly rising.

My mother folds her arms across her chest, striking a defensive pose. "You wouldn't understand. You wouldn't understand any of it."

"But *she* would."

"Yes, Bliss would."

"Does she know?"

"No. It's no one's business but mine."

I flatten my hand against the wall behind me just before I smack it. "Like hell!" Unearthing my lightning, I confront my mother. "I've agreed to be his toy, his Yang, his prodigy. I've whipped my own sister…and all for *you!*"

"I never asked you to." My mother and I are the same height, but right now, her shadow engulfs me. "I never wanted you to. And we both know it's never just been for me."

"What?" I keep my nails on the wall, keep myself stitched together any way I can.

"You've satisfied your own desires even in the midst of the sacrifice. You've loved every moment of every exhibit. And you love the power of the whip."

I open my mouth to protest, but my mother raises a finger, halting me. "Don't say another word, Serenity. You're looking at someone who can smell it from a mile away. Even now, you can't understand anything past your own anger and how this affects *you*. I'm not trying to hurt you because not everything is about you."

As soon as she speaks the words, I close my mouth, shake my head, and turn my back. She doesn't pursue me or try to urge me back. She just lets me walk away. Had my mother ever truly escaped? I feel like a storm-tossed boat, trying to stay afloat until another wave careens into me.

It comes when I open the door to her suite. Tiptoe toward the door left ajar into her inner room. When I see *them* in bed together.

58

I scream, alerting them both. Bliss doesn't move. Luc just stares. He doesn't try to come after me. He stays with her. Desperate and knowing I can't return to my own room, I make a beeline for the closest one, so thankful it's open. Regardless of whether Luc will try to follow or not, I slam it behind me and turn the lock.

Hundreds of origami shapes fill the room, some dangling on strings from the ceiling, others perched on the bookshelf and nightstand—more on the floor. His room is smaller because he's getting up from the bed a few feet away. Without his shirt, Queran is lean and wiry. Soft, subtle muscles as soft as his voice.

When I break down right in front of him, he approaches and gathers me up in his arms as I cry into his shoulder.

"Shh…sweet girl." He pats the back of my head.

When I'm finally all sobbed out, he raises a finger and motions to his right. To the dresser. He opens a drawer to withdraw a shirt before pulling it over his head. Then, he takes my hand and stands me in front of the dresser before producing Bliss's object—her tetra-star shape. After he holds it up, he takes another object out of his pocket—an owl. He acts out the scene of an owl diving through Bliss's star, but he rips right through one of the star's layers in doing so. I lick my lips and nod. Why is it I can understand Queran with his silly, silent shapes, but I can never understand my mother even if she were to speak a million words? Or wrote in her journal?

Queran signals for me to wait before he retrieves an origami heart from one of his desk drawers along with another paper swan. Side by side, he holds up my swan and Bliss's tetra-star before raising the heart so it invades the center between them.

"Beat, beat," he whispers, and I manage a smile, however weak it feels.

I scan the door, grateful there is no knock. Then, I catch the time on the holographic clock. With how late—or rather, how *early* it is—sleeping seems almost pointless even if it's what I want more than anything. So much has happened in one night. Rest is a temptation, a luxury, and a necessity all wrapped up into one. Part of me considers going up to the roof to swim, but I know my father does early morning laps, and the last thing I want is to see him.

Instead, Queran makes the decision for me.

He gestures a hand to his bed, then unfolds the sheets for me. Sleeping in his bed isn't such an alien notion when he's seen every inch of me. Prepares me every week. For Bliss, it's control. For me, it's trust.

"Sleep, sweet girl," he whispers, tucking the blankets around my frame. He grabs a blanket from the end of the bed before he heads to the couch.

I study him. "Queran?" He pauses, and I chew on my lower lip for a moment before asking, "Would you mind staying close? Just for tonight, please?" I point to the floor right below the bed.

When he returns with a smile, I relax a little and lay my head down. His pillow smells like sandalwood and spices with a hint of lavender. Not what I would've pegged for him, but I don't mind it. It's nothing like my father's blend of rich vanilla, nutmeg, amber, and an underlining of rum. Or Luc's watery linen scent. Above all, I miss Sky's earthy musk. I miss our lake house with the noisy pipes. Miss skinny dipping in the lake. I miss the lightning playing with the thunder, illuminating the rain over the surface of the water.

What I'd give to go back.

After sinking deeper into the pillow, I hear the sound of crinkling paper. Sliding my hand underneath the pillow, I latch onto an origami shape. Another swan. I crook one side of my mouth into a sheepish smile. It would almost be disturbing, but Queran keeping me under his pillow is a compliment. I glance at the desk where Luc's owl and Bliss's star sit. Maybe Bliss isn't so much like that star as she is a puzzle box game. Just needs someone to line up the right squares to form the right pattern.

Maybe Luc is the one.

Twelve

DeAd

Luc

*I*T'S LATE.

I assume it's rare for men to spend the entire night with her. So, I'm not surprised when she tries to leave the covers, but when I tug on her arm, she obliges me, leaning into me. Her body meshes well with mine. For once, I'm dissecting it, but not comparing or contrasting. For once, I'm not formulating endless sketches in my mind or tracing imaginary anatomical lines. Bliss's body is an island—a world all unto itself. The bed is a conglomerate of our aromas. I can still smell ylang-ylang extract on her neck as well as exotic citrus.

She kisses me back, but I sense an undercurrent of pressure. She's trying too hard.

"I'd say you got your money's worth." She taps my jaw, her words confirming her previous actions.

I harden my jaw. "I don't remember seeing a bill."

"You don't think Father will let you off the hook so easily?"

I thrust her away from me to swing my legs off the side of the bed, planting my feet on the floor. Unfortunately, I feel her behind me a moment later, and I have to grit my teeth when her soft breasts rub my back.

"You should know by now, Director Aldaine, there are no secrets in the Temple."

I sigh, defeat cloaking my heart. "Did it mean anything to you, Bliss?" I examine her over my shoulder.

"Everything has a cost. Everyone has a price. Even love is for

61

sale."

I grunt. "And what would you know about love?"

"I wager I know as much as you," she counters expertly.

I rub my hands down my face. "All just part of the game then? You give me everything I want but nothing of yourself. Nothing that means a damn thing."

"Whatever it means to you."

"Stop that!" I snap, but Bliss doesn't flinch—as if she's expected it.

"Director Aldaine, I was your Swan last night."

I grab both her wrists. Force her against the pillows. "I want *you*, Bliss! Not the Swan."

Astonished, she raises her brows before studying me, staring back with those ghostly eyes of hers. "Bliss doesn't exist."

I let her go, but I have no intention of believing her.

What I haven't worked out is how far I'm willing to go.

I need answers.

THIS SEEMS LIKE THE ONLY logical place to get them at the present.

He was right—Force is relentless.

My brother looks haggard, all dark shadows and bags under his eyes as if he's spent the night tending to girls. Force is good at getting what he wants, and I have the feeling he intends to do it by wearing Skylar down to the breaking point. I dismiss yet another girl so I can speak to him alone.

At first, we say nothing, but I can tell he's taking stock of my un-tucked shirt, the traces of lipstick on my collar, the lack of shower, the scent of lingering perfume, my unkempt hair. He doesn't brace his fist, but he does tense.

"Who?"

"Bliss."

A pause.

"Shit." Another pause. "Real piece of work, you know that?"

"I wish that were the whole of it, but she saw us."

Skylar curses again but thankfully refrains from using his fist on me, even if he does start pacing, foot kicking up a few teddies along the way. More stuffed items than before. Plush dolls, too.

"You go back to her, you hear?"

"Which one?"

"Both. Understand?" He points a finger, brandishing it like a katana. "You made your bed, now lie in it."

"She's nothing like her sister," I tell him, kneading my brow. "It was all nothing to her. She gave me everything I wanted but nothing that lasts. Her eyes were on me the whole time, but she never even saw me. They're not watching anything. Just dead."

"We are the choices we make, Luc." Sky's right hand forms a fist. "Life might deal us a bad hand. In Bliss's case, the devil—Force himself—got his claws into her when she was little. Only thing we can control is how we react. How we live with the sin and the grit. Who we trust along the way. Gonna be really hard for you to get Bliss's trust, especially with what you've gone and done. But if there's one thing I know about you, it's you don't back down from a challenge."

Every word is a razor tooth cutting into me.

"So, tell me, brother, what is your challenge with Serenity?"

Pausing, Skylar straightens. "Each man's gotta follow his own course. For me, that girl is stronger than the call of nature. First moment I looked into her baby eyes and heard her gurgle, she hooked my four-year-old heart and she didn't just wrap it around her finger." He chuckles and finishes, "She damn well ate my heart right up. Knew I'd downright be her slave if she asked me."

I brace my chin against my fist, contemplating, questioning. "How do you work with a girl whose known nothing but slavery? How do you teach a girl who's been a slave since birth about freedom?"

Sky blows frustrated breath through his flaring nostrils. "She's never seen sex as love. Nothing more than physical to her. No emotions, no bonding, no good old-fashioned commitment, no romance, no spirituality. No intimacy. None of that. And like most people, it's gonna take a lot more than just words. Words whisper. Actions scream with a bullhorn."

"How on earth can I show her all that? Tell me, Skylar. You've had a lifetime to show Serenity. How much time could I possibly have with Bliss?"

"One day at a time, Luc. One day at a time."

I KNOCK ON QUERAN'S DOOR.

He answers.

Beyond him, Serenity sleeps in his bed, but the blanket on the floor below her does not escape my notice. He doesn't move aside.

Despite my desire not to, I decide to try for courtesy this morning. "Please, I'll keep it brief. And I won't even wake her."

"Too late."

We turn at the sound of her voice. It doesn't surprise me. She's always been a light sleeper. At least she waves a hand, motioning me forward, but neither does she dismiss Queran. His shadow follows me. Plants itself near the wall just behind us.

I lower into a chair across from her, lean over, and fold my hands, waiting for her to begin the conversation. So certain she will react with her lightning at any second, I prepare for her outburst, her nails, her shoving hands, her screaming words launched in my face.

"Why her?"

Her soft question stuns me.

I can only consider one response. "Could it have been anyone else?"

"It doesn't make it right."

"I never said it did. I knew what I was doing." I stare into her beautiful eyes—a frosted fantasy forest. The one thing their DNA has separated…

Bliss's eyes are an early winter morning—all frost and fog. "There are no excuses."

She holds onto the sheets tighter. "What are you going to do now?"

"Haven't quite figured it out yet."

Now, she strikes with more force than ever. So much so she barrels right into me, knocking me back to the floor, but she recovers and puts one foot on my chest. Another first for me—I don't try to thwart her. Remaining where I am, I let her eyes burn lightning holes clear through mine. She deserves her say.

"You don't get to do that!" She presses her foot down harder, almost sinking it into my throat. "Not to her, do you understand? If my respect—if my *trust* in you—is worth anything, Luc, then you damn well *better* figure it out! If you leave her now, you're just like the rest of them, and I refuse to believe that!"

I deserve all her words. Each one is an acid chip dissolving in my throat. There are no arguments, no debate, and no defense. If she insulted my honor by calling me a coward, I would be fully prepared to agree with her. But this time, I can't shove it into a deep pit somewhere inside me like every other one-night stand I've experienced. Last night will fester under my skin like a plague. Bliss is a sweet poison I've ingested. She will never go away.

"You go back to her. Right now," Serenity orders with her fist raised, and I hold up my hands and agree.

At a loss for words, I merely stand, leave the chair on the floor, and turn around to follow her bidding. She opens the adjoining door, and Bliss is sitting at the table in the middle of the room, sampling on breakfast and reading a screen. Betraying no emotion, Bliss eyes us just before Serenity gives me a shove.

"I'll be in my room if you need me."

Serenity slams the door behind me.

I prepare to meet Bliss.

Thirteen

ExpecTatIons

BLISS

EVEN AFTER HE'S GONE, I try not to remember Luc's arms around my body this morning. How his body heat just nudged inside ever so little and thawed my veins, but his words became needles dipped in frost probing me. Why couldn't he leave it alone? Let our bodies do what came naturally and left the rest. No matter that he wanted to stay. No matter how tender he was with me all through the night. *It's all an illusion*, I remind myself. Aviary manipulation.

Like I told him, there will always be a cost—strings attached and ulterior motives. No man is above them. No man loves forever. They all grow bored. They leave or they abuse. Never satisfied. The only way to keep a heart from being broken is to pretend love is an illusion. Like touching a sprite light. People can interact with it, manipulate it, but it's all an illusion. Artificial. Because a girl like me can have no heart. Or if a heart is there, it's been numb since the day I was born.

I don't want to lose myself in a man. That's what happened to Serafina, and she became the Unicorn. I wear what I need to—all just masks, but no emotion in any of it because I can never let down my guard. I feel nothing. He must understand that, but he doesn't.

A brief time later, I receive a client appointment that appears on my schedule feed. *Luc*. So soon, then. By now, I've showered for the day, put on my normal lingerie and robe, but beyond that, there is no time to prepare for anything else. If Luc cares for anything else, he'll have to pay extra to watch my preparation.

When he enters the bedroom, his eyes are like wrought-iron stakes ready to spear. I remain where I am at the breakfast table, drinking my morning coffee. I must convince him this is a waste of time. I'll provide him with a warm bed, but anything else is out of the question.

"What do you want, Director Aldaine? I don't normally get repeat clients," I mock him with a grin, my eyes hard as flint.

"I'm not here as a client."

"Then, what on earth did you pay my father for?"

"Let him think whatever he wants."

He takes one step in my direction before swinging his body to the side and striding toward the window. What else could he possibly want? Perhaps I'll help him along.

Just as I get close, he thrusts his head up, breath growing; he's smelling me. Good. I string my arms around him. Press my body against his back. He tenses. He's fighting it. Resisting. Why? Perhaps because of how different Serenity is. Perhaps he needs that. Something familiar. I weave my way around to his front, noting the desire plaguing his irises. So, why doesn't he touch me? Just slip the robe off my shoulders and repeat last night? His eyes dive to my cleavage, across my stomach, to my lower regions. Telepathy may as well be a talent in my repertoire because I know exactly what he's thinking—lust is inscribed all over him. It wouldn't take much. With one hand, I curve my fingers into his hair, my other hand dipping to grip his—

"Stop, damn it," Luc pleads, fingers kneading his eyes, body shuddering just a little.

Creasing my brows together, I don't move but question him, "You want something more, Director Aldaine?"

Luc takes my wrists in his grip, painstakingly wrenching them from his waist in order to paste them to my sides. This is...new for me. And he's far too observant because his eyes wander across my fluttering fingers. He smiles, which unsettles me because he must know I'm having trouble keeping them still. Far too used to using them.

"I can give you more," I offer, then stand on my tiptoes to whisper in his ear. "Much more."

With a rushed inhale, he jerks his head back, mouths some obscenity, then states firmly. "I want you to call me Luc."

Hmm…he wants more intimacy. I can do that.

"I can be whoever you want me to be, Luc."

"I am not here as a client." he repeats again, firmer this time.

"Then, what?" I am genuinely confused. "Are you here to complain about my services?"

"In a manner of speaking."

"Customer is always right. Let me make it up to you." I sneak my fingers across his neck.

"Damn, you're relentless," he curses but follows with, "No, Bliss."

Frustrated but adopting a calm, very Yin-like pose, I remember my lessons. Grabbing the sides of my silk robe, I fold my arms across my chest. "You're here to talk about Serenity, aren't you?"

"What?" Now he's the one who's taken by surprise. Good.

"I'm not an idiot, Director. I've seen the way you look at my sister. Were you hoping for my blessing or something? It's not like you need it. It's not like it's my business."

He steps back. "I slept with you last night, and it's none of your business?"

"Exactly. One night, Director." I raise a finger. "I gave you what you wanted, and that's the end of it."

Turning around, I hear Luc groan and then mutter under his breath. "I'd take a bullheaded Serenity any day over this stony nightmare." Perhaps he didn't mean for me to hear.

"I can explain it to her if you prefer. What happens in the Penthouse…"

"Bliss, I'm not in love with Serenity."

I smirk, seeing right through his facade. "As one who is a keen expert in love-related matters, Director, I must take the unfortunate necessity to relay what a piece of horse shit that really is."

"You want to know the truth?" he levels with me, chin lowering.

I give him nothing. "Not particularly. It has nothing to do with me."

"I *loved* your sister. Past tense. I am choosing a different road now."

I commend him. "Good for you." And turn around, heading in the direction of my vanity. If he's not here for an interaction, it's not my business.

Still, he pursues me, seizing hold of my arm to swing me around. "That road is you, Bliss."

My other methods haven't worked, so it's time to try something else. What Luc needs now is some cold, hard truth. "Ahh... so that's it. It's not just a different road you've chosen. She *won't* choose you. And this is your fantasy instead." I draw a line down my chest, towing his eyes to my hearty bosom. "You can't have her, but you can have the next best thing. She rejects you, so you fall into my arms and pretend. Fill my eyes with her eyes and kiss my lips, but taste her instead. But once isn't enough." I push, picking up on the strain in his eyes. "Especially not when you're so close to her all the time. It's not just about what you want, it's what you *need*. But I'm not rejecting you, Director. I'll even dress up as your pretty swan if you want me to. Let's get it done with. Over and over again until you crush her face once and for all."

I place my hands on him, but he grits his teeth, hardens every muscle in his jaw. His anger is almost tangible, but I keep my emotions in check as I've always done. Though I'm certain Luc is capable of violence, I doubt he'd raise his hand to me, but I'm more than equipped to take a blow.

Instead, he lets me go, so I walk the few steps to the vanity, take a sip of my coffee, and finally decide to ask, "What did you expect, Luc?" Perhaps I'll get a straight answer if I call him by his first name.

"I don't want my own pleasure at your expense."

"Too little too late." It's all men ever want.

I pick up my reader screen, thin as a magazine page, to browse the morning gossip circulating around the Temple. A few moments later, Luc's shadow overlaps my body, and he gently pushes the reader down before urging my chin upward.

"Would you give me the chance to convince you otherwise?"

I give him a blank expression because I can't so much as acknowledge the notion.

"I'll pay whatever fee your father wants. But I won't sleep with you again until you ask."

I pause from the reader screen. "And how do you propose we spend that time?"

"You let me handle that."

"Don't keep me in suspense," I flirt, arching my neck toward him.

He shakes his head, tightening his brows. "Not going to work this time, Bliss."

It's not the first time a man has withdrawn from my advances for one reason or another. I simply have to adjust my tactics. According to Force, if one behavior doesn't work, another surely will. I just have to learn to be creative, flexible, and innovative.

"Perhaps if I change into something more comfortable," I opt as I begin to untie the sashes on my robe.

Luc seizes both my hands in one of his, preventing them from completing the picture. I groan a little in protest. "What do you want from me, Luc?"

"Much," he says.

"I can give you anything you want. You know that."

"In your sister's words 'it's not about what we want, it's about what's right that counts.'"

NOT LONG AFTER LUC DEPARTS, Father comes to greet me.

"Good morning, Bliss." He takes a seat on the opposite side of the table, then helps himself to a croissant. "I must commend you on your work with Aldaine." He makes a show of quiet applause, tapping his palms together. "I was beginning to get concerned he would never fold, and his obsession would drive him to the brink of madness. Well done."

"He's already mad."

"Oh?"

Flaked croissant bits tumble onto the table before him, but none land on his clothes. As if even they have an aversion toward him. I'm the only one who's ever managed to tolerate Force in large doses.

"He's making plans for some sort of encounter that doesn't involve me sleeping with him," I relay, ever the loyal daughter.

"Play along but remember what you're paid for."

I'm paid in lodging, food, clothes, costumes, preparer labor, and the endless lessons I've taken throughout the years—a fee which I'll never be able to repay. My credit was maxed out long ago. Serenity's credit will always be new.

"I'm certain you of all people can change his mind. Charge his account for a base interaction. When he's ready for the full encounter, the full amount will reflect on his account."

Sitting across from me, Father appears different. Not the stiff shoulders I'm used to. No, he is far more relaxed. Even his gait upon walking in didn't betray an ounce of its usual hyperactivity. No chaos. No twitching of the muscles in his jaw. I've never seen him so relaxed. It can mean only one thing.

"You spent the night with her."

My father pours himself a mug of coffee, steady hand never spilling one drop. "A portion of the night," he confirms.

I don't rationalize it because the syndrome is common in the Temple. We both knew she could never escape him. That's why it's best not to form attachments because I'm certain he will break her. Unlike me, Serafina has just come back to this world. It will be like an overdose instead of building up immunity as I've done. Force will keep erasing the parts of her that are alive, fill them with Temple porcelain, chrome, glass, and tech until she is more Unicorn than woman. I've seen him do it with others. Others who have fought just as much as Serenity. Perhaps she will buck and prance and cater to his every whim. But perhaps she will also adopt new coping mechanisms, survival strategies like me. Not that I don't have faith in her; I just have more in the formidable foe who is my father.

Now, I understand his bargain with Serenity and why he's agreed not to whip me for the next several months. He has a new subject.

"How is your other project coming along?" I wonder, referring to Serenity's lovesick young man.

"Not successful in any sense of the word, but I'm confident he will break in time. His brother did. Hmm..."

I look up to see Force stroking his chin. "What?"

"I have an idea."

I can see where this is going. If I can give my sister one kind-

71

ness, it will be this. Based on the little I know of him, Skylar strikes me as the type who would never embark where his brother did, but I suppose I could prove that wrong. Either way, it's a win/win. If this works the way Father wants, then he will finally release Skylar and give him a lifelong pass to all the Temple's levels except the Penthouse, and Serenity will know the truth. If Skylar refuses, then perhaps Father will give up this petty battle because I'm the ace up his sleeve.

If this doesn't work, what else will he have to fall back on?

Fourteen

LaSt REsoRt

SKY

I ASSURE FORCE THIS TIME WILL be no different than others when he bids the last girl away, preparing to send in the next. With all due respect to Serenity's pet, Force has the anatomy of a shark. Never stops swimming. Or hunting. When he closes the door, I take up my position against the wall and keep my eyes fixated on the chrome striations nearby. And then, she enters dressed in full Swan garb.

"Oh, come on!" Groaning, I roll my eyes when Force starts to close the door.

"Enjoy your time, Skylar." Force flutters his hand in an 'adieu' gesture.

I curse, then decide it's time to turn around again and face the wall. Anything to keep my eyes off her familiar body, her long shapely legs housed in tight stockings, the white feathers clinging to her—*no*! Focus. Say something. Anything!

"Didn't think he could manage a new low. Your father's ruthless," I tell her, gritting my teeth as she approaches me because I can smell her.

"He's testing you," Bliss echoes.

"You don't say."

She moves closer. I can hear the soft whisper of her bare footsteps. Feel her scent wafting all around me. Too exotic of a scent, too much spice and fruit. Overstated. Good. Serenity has always smelled like water—always at her best just after a swim with her hair soaked and sticking to her skin. I imagine her in Bliss's place,

73

but I still jerk my head back, arching my neck and groaning in response when her sister slides her arms around my waist.

I grind my teeth together. "Damn it, Bliss!"

"Cameras," she states simply as her hands curl downward. "All girls must perform. It's part of Father's special package for any client. They pay a flat price, and the girls must perform in order to entice clients to pay the extended price for an *encounter*."

"I know."

All the other girls have tried the same, but at least they back off when I resist. Bliss doesn't.

"I'm not a paying customer," I counter.

"The rules apply."

Her hands roam to my rear.

"Do you have to be so *thorough*?"

I can hear the smile in her voice when she grabs me there. "It's my style. Think of it as a secret we can both share. A little performance for Father."

"Snake in a business suit," I define him better.

"Serenity prefers parasite."

"That'll do, too."

She leans in to me, nearly naked body pressing its warmth into my back. I snarl but then her words offer a reminder, and I look up at one of the many laser cams and give it my best righteous glare.

"Serenity talks about you."

"Oh?" I feign surprise. "What does she say?"

"That she loves you. And something about paper flowers and lightning and thunder. I didn't know what it—"

"*I* know," I interrupt. "How is she?"

"Wearing thin but holding her own."

"How are you?"

She pauses in her pursuit. "It doesn't matter how I am."

"The hell it doesn't. You're the sister of the girl I'm going to marry, and she cares about you, so it matters to me."

Bliss dips her hands below my shirt. "Obviously since you exposed yourself on my behalf. But I've been in this world since birth. You should be more concerned about Serenity."

"Trust me. I am." I rip her hand away, twist the wrist downward. "But my concern isn't limited. I care about her mother just as I cared about Kerrick, and so I care about you." I survey her eyes, but can't turn around yet.

"What about Luc?"

I bristle. "Luc can take care of himself."

"Hmm…" She picks up on my tension. "You have a history."

"Not as long as my history with Serenity."

"Yes, that's clear, but you two are very similar in some ways."

"No, we aren't," I deny her words just as her body winds her way to my front. "Ack, Bliss!" I shut my eyes, screwing them down tighter and harder than a war drum, wishing I could expel the image of her in the feather-clad lingerie.

"Your denial speaks volumes." She places her hands on my chest. "It's not so surprising you both became rivals for her heart. There isn't a man alive who doesn't want her."

"All I know is no other man alive is good enough for her."

"Except you, right?"

"Wrong." I lift my head. "But I'm still the only one for her. Only one who matters. Only one right for her."

"You're incredibly determined. What is the harm in tasting a little of what you two could share together?" Bliss tries harder when she takes my hand in her grip, inches it toward her waist.

I retract it, leaning one hand against the glass instead. "Cause I love her. And I won't disrespect her. In public or in private."

"Even if she never knows?"

I shake my head. "Serenity's worth far too much to me. You are, too."

"Excuse me?"

I groan, launching my head back and trying to explain. "Shouldn't be like this, Bliss. Last I checked, it's your body."

"You can do whatever you want to it." She shrugs, hands sweeping down, inviting.

"Exactly…" I point out the hypocrisy of it all, meeting her eyes and nothing else. "It's always what the *client* wants. They set the rules. Force sets the rules. But you're worth more than that. Human beings should never be commodities."

Bliss falls silent. I maintain my defense, knowing Bliss isn't offended. Her expression is unreadable, but I do wonder what's going on in that head. Whatever the case, I hope this will be the last straw. After this, Force will have two choices—shoot me and be done with it or leave me the hell alone. Hoping for the latter.

I've never been so grateful for my height or the stark difference between mine and Serenity's because Bliss stands on her tiptoes, plump lips inching toward my face. Raising it, I tighten every muscle in my neck and jaw, but she presses her mouth to the base of my throat instead, leaving lipstick prints there as she wanders farther down my chest. I sense she's trying harder.

"Force isn't the only one testing me," I note, my tone sharper than frost-covered claws.

"She *is* my sister."

"Glad to hear you say it. But you can stop now."

I prevent her hands from wandering underneath my shirt, and I don't stay where I am. Instead, I begin pacing because it gives me something to do. And a way to avoid her.

"What will he do now?" I ask.

"He may try harder. Send more than one girl in at a time. Or he may leave you alone, but I would wager on the former."

"I'd wager you're right."

Terrific.

PART Two

Fifteen

FatHer's PlAns

SERENITY

WEEKS PASS, OVERLAPPING ONE AFTER the other like folding cards. Wintry weather strikes early even though it's barely autumn. Swimming three times a day helps to keep my mind off things. Since I no longer have exhibits, I have more time on my hands. Until my father discovers the perpetrator, he's ordered no more exhibits, and thus far, they've stopped. Even the Yin-Yang interactions have been scaled down, but he can control those more easily. Every time, it's a different set of foreign diplomats, which I prefer. They always speak in their foreign tongue, and ignorance is bliss in my case, though I can't speak for my sister.

My father is a creature of habit as he keeps arranging suitors for me to meet every night. After a week, they all start to look the same, and I measure them against Sky. His chin is wider than this one, more chiseled than that one, eyes richer of a brown, muscles far larger, etc.

Neil and Lindy help fill the daytime hours. With the Penthouse costume room, which includes BODY and NAILS, we have a ball dressing in different outfits and helping ourselves to Neil's complimentary services as a graphicker. Provided the sprite lights are private. There are millions of activities in the Temple.

I don't see Bliss or Luc too much.

Whatever they do is their own business. I don't visit her during the evening. We haven't spoken more than a few words to each other since that night. I knew exactly what to say to Luc, but every time I think of bringing the subject up to her, my veins seem

78

bloated, blood running free, so it rushes up to my head and makes me dizzy. All I want to do is forget the sight of them together. I want to forget the sight of my mother and father even more.

"You can't keep pretending it doesn't exist," Mom finally combats me at the dinner table one evening. For once, Force hasn't joined us, and I'm not about to look a gift horse in the mouth. Like Bliss and I, she and I haven't discussed *that* night.

I stuff another bite of salmon in my mouth, then another and another, but my mother sees through the pointless action.

"You're not getting out of this, Serenity. Finish chewing and then talk."

The fish in my mouth seems thicker than rubber, hard to swallow, but I drive it back somehow, coming up with the best non-lethal response I can manage. "I just don't understand."

"You don't have to. You just need to trust I know what I'm doing. This is my choice."

I don't believe her, but it's not up to me. I've come to understand that. Swimming helps me cope. Visiting Sharky helps me cope. Talking doesn't. Right now, it feels like an earthquake is shifting the tectonic rib plates in my chest, causing the bones to collapse. I can't do anything. For once, I can't embark into this territory because it's not just forbidden—it's alien. It would be easier to puff myself up with helium and float to Venus than try to figure out what my mother is doing or why Luc goes back to Bliss every night but leaves the room just as frustrated. I hold onto swimming. I hold onto sanity. I hold onto Sky.

For weeks, I've asked Force every night for Sky, but he still says he's in the "testing" stage. How long can this possibly last?

I pick up a glass of water. Down it in a series of back-to-back gulps. It's unusual for Mom to eat so much, but she's cleaned her plate.

I don't get a chance to ask her about it due to the knock on the door.

"Lindy," I say, a little surprised when I open it.

"I'm here to prepare you for tonight."

Confused, I narrow my brows. "What are you talking about? There's no exhibit tonight."

"It's not a public exhibit as far as I know. I was just ordered to prepare you. You'll have to talk to Director Force afterward."

"I want to talk to him now."

"I was ordered to take you straight to the preparation room."

I roll my eyes. "And you always do as you're told."

"Trust me, honey, Neil can attest I don't." She blinks a few times, one side of her mouth curving. "But I don't want to lose this job either. My fingers would never forgive me. And they've been itching to get themselves on you ever since I got the order. Wait…" She pauses. "That didn't come out right."

I almost grin because Lindy's just managed to take a foreboding experience and turn it into something I can stomach. For her sake only, I follow her to the preparation chamber, fully prepared to have words with my father later.

First, Lindy pins up portions of my curls with decorative pearl combs. All the rest are left to dangle down my naked back. Next, she reveals a costume eerily reminiscent of what I wear every day. A long skirt and blouse, but the blouse is loose enough to dangle below my shoulders, neckline plunged low enough to show much of my cleavage. Material on both parts so thin, it's transparent in certain areas and reminds me of the first Skeleton Flower dress. This ensemble doesn't seem ostentatious enough for my father or creative enough for Luc for that matter; I can't imagine what he has planned.

Speak of the devil.

Force comes up behind me and dismisses Lindy.

"Not what I would select, but it's not for me, now is it?" he admits, smirking, gesturing to the see-through clothing.

For a moment, bone-crunching panic sets in. Is my father taking me to an interaction?

"I think you will enjoy this night," Force eludes right before cupping my shoulders.

I crane my head to each of his hands. They remind me of Luc's but not as young, and my father has more calloused killer hands than calloused artist hands. Considering how his nails dig into my skin there, they could be vulture claws for all I know.

"First, I have something to show you."

Force summons a sprite light screen on one of the walls so it projects footage into the center of the room. There is Sky. He looks so real. I can reach out and touch the sprite light, my fingers straining to touch his, hand longing to sink into his until our lines overlap. But then, I see the angel girl…Halo. Clothed in nothing but feathers as she gyrates her body up and down against him. I narrow my brows to a menacing point. Not because of her—she was following orders. Not because of Sky—his back is to the wall, every muscle in his body is tense, and his eyes are pinched and strained in concentration to resist her. No, my eyes turn sinister. Directed at my father.

He reaches over my shoulder to swipe the screen so a new sprite scene commences, this time showing half-a-dozen girls issue into the room. Dressed in harem-reminiscent clothes of rich-colored silks, bangles and baubles, and bejeweled bustiers, they besiege Sky like he's some sort of present to unwrap. But I smile when he keeps himself tighter and more resolute than a war drum, rejecting them one by one. Still, he acknowledges them, interacts, and greets them. A giggle ping-pongs in my throat at the sight of him placing his hand on his chest and bowing his head, all gentleman-like. If he had a fedora, I could imagine him tipping it or removing it before them. My smile must brighten because I feel the butterflies in me glowing at the sight of all the teddy bears and flowers on the floor.

Only Sky.

Force shows me footage after footage. Every time, the room gains more teddy bears and other varieties of stuffed animals. Sometimes, Sky will pick up one or two, tap their noses, tug at their ears, or hand them to the girls who enter. At some point or another, each girl ends up picking up a stuffed animal and clutching it to her chest. One of the last videos shows a clump of girls huddled in a semi-circle around Sky. I can't hear what he's saying, but they're leaning toward him, eager for his words. Sky always was a good storyteller. He had to be to keep me entertained through the years. I grit my teeth. All these weeks, and he's seen dozens upon dozens of girls. Not me. I try not to feed my inner jealousy they've had pieces of him instead of me.

One last scene to show me.

He swipes.

I feel sick.

The sight of my sister coiling her arms around his waist cuts through me as easily as a cookie cutter plowing into dough. She grabs him. Twice. Sky holds his own, jerking his head back every now and then, thwarting her advances and even gripping her hands at one point. Bliss is good. Much better than any of the other Temple girls who came before and after since the footage is time stamped. Force must have added more girls after Bliss's failed attempt. Despite Sky's victory, I'm angry at Bliss. I shouldn't be, but I'm angry she put her hands on my Sky. Every part of him belongs to me, and I'll be damned if any girl gets to touch him, especially my own sister.

Most of all, I'm angry because she never told me. She knew where he was, she knew what Force was doing, and she never told me.

Would it have made a difference? a voice in my head challenges.

I could've sneaked in to see him, I argue. Even if it was just once before Force would've caught us.

Finally, he shuts the screen down. "One must admire his fortitude despite how misplaced it is."

"So, what now? Are you finished *testing* him?"

"Not quite, but I'm confident he will break tonight." Force's grin is wider than Sharky's mouth. "I'm sending someone very special to him just as I'm sending someone very special to you."

"You're wasting your time. And I thought our agreement was only for dinner."

"Call it an after-dinner snack."

"In my suite?"

My father shakes his head, beguiling grin teasing the corners of his mouth.

Not five minutes later, he escorts me into the pool area, keeping a hand on the small of my back. Light as a spider's legs settling after floating down from a cobweb string.

"What do you think?"

He's enhanced the pool area. Twinkle lights string every tree while hundreds of holographic candles of all shapes and sizes project everywhere on surfaces and on the floor—faux ones float in the pool itself. Each one casts the scent of vanilla and spice into the air. Along with them are dozens of Skeleton Flowers scattered about in no order. Curling from the corners of the room is a sultry fog, hovering like shifting bedsheets on the tiled floor. All the blinds tethered to reveal the city lights glittering like a treasure horde. They give the stars some fair competition, but the full moon always gets the last laugh.

I shiver when my father traces a finger along my bare arm just before whispering, "Enjoy your swim, Serenity."

And he departs.

No one is here. I don't stop looking around the room, almost afraid someone will catch me by surprise, but no one does. I get the sense my father will do nothing until I'm in the water. Instead, I draw it out, remaining defiant for a time by walking around the tiled floor, my long skirt wisping along the holograms, candles flickering out of focus because they aren't as reliable as sprite lights.

After several minutes, I grow impatient. The pool is too inviting, but everything about the circumstances seems too convenient. Force is giving me the perfect atmosphere—one I can appreciate, one I could wish for.

It's still my choice.

I hold onto that as I slide into the water and dive, surfacing after a few minutes. Wiping my hair down, I tip my head back and exhale a long sigh. That's when I notice the figure out of the corner of my eye. Immediately, I tense, but the tenseness abates after one mere second of recognition. Sky is standing in the doorway.

No wonder Force created this grandiose display. *I'm* his final test.

SKY

EVERYTHING IS QUIET AT FIRST, then she rises out of the water like a siren. All her sultry curves and lines showing straight through the thin fabric clinging to her soaked frame. I turn my head, avoiding the temptation to stare, wanting nothing more than to take in every speck of her. Instead, I zero in on her eyes, notice the recognition there. Her first instinct is to rush forward before I raise my hand in warning. She pauses, bites her lip, catching herself, and hunches lower so the water conceals her more. She's conflicted. I share her pain. Our first reunion after weeks apart shouldn't be like this. Force has dished out another form of testing torture but worse than anything before. What I want most is to hold her, but if she comes out of the water, it's more than a man can stand. All sorts of impurities slither around in my mind like serpents. I take a battle axe to each one and chop off their heads, but they still wriggle around, fangs bared.

The first thing I do is look around for a towel, but *no*...that'd be too easy. Nothing in here we can use except for what's on my back. I start undoing the buttons on my shirt and shrug it off, dropping it on the tiles at my feet before I turn around and face the door. Droplets colliding with the floor betray her ascent from the water. Every nerve ending in me fires with the desire to turn around, to steal one glance, but I tighten my hands into fists to prevent myself. It doesn't matter she belongs to me or the feeling is mutual. This is neither the time nor the place, however the circumstances may suggest. I won't take the girl I love in one night of passion. There's so much more I want to share with her.

Our terms. Not his.

But I pause to wonder how he'll react. If he'll separate us both forever if we last the night. I don't use it as a justification or as an excuse because that would mean I'm no stronger than my damn dick. Or Force.

"Sky," she whispers.

Wagering it's safe, I turn around to see her standing a couple of feet away from me. My shirt swims on her, falls to her thighs, and clings in some places since she's still wet, but it'll do. I do up the last button, securing it around the base of her neck. My hand lingers there just as my eyes meet hers. With the candles lending their glow all around us, her eyes have turned to a silver green. I could easily mistake the spark there due to the firelight catching them, but I know better than that. That half smile cooking the corner of one side of her mouth and the way she tilts her head just a little to the floor betrays how happy she is to see me.

I'm not that subtle. I scoop up her whole body, rewarded with the way her legs wind around my waist while her hands dig through my hair. I don't kiss her. I just enjoy the closeness, the skin-to-skin contact of our heads touching. How her wet curls brush up against my cheek. How her breath and the scent of her overshadows each vanilla-scented candle.

We don't say much. Words don't have much of a point right now. At first, I try to lower her back to the ground, but she tightens her grip, legs and arms squeezing. I can take a hint. With her still wrapped around me like a leech, I carry her to one of the lounge chairs, sink down into it, and take one long, deep breath and relax for the first time in weeks. Dead tired from lack of sleep thanks to all of Force's *gifts* every hour, I know it won't take me long to pass out. Of course, her lips on my cheek and then on my nose, on my forehead, and traveling down my neck might hinder that. She pauses there. Inhales. I don't know why. Can't possibly be smelling anything good, given I haven't had a shower in a while, but she doesn't stop in any case. A chuckle rises in me, but I keep it at bay, not wanting to wreck the moment. One of her feet rubs up and down my calf, but her hands don't roam anywhere. They just nestle into my chest right before she sinks her cheek into my collarbone region, nose rubbing my throat, not caring about the metal cuff around my neck. Force's failsafe.

Holding her like this, falling asleep with her, was worth it all.

Sixteen

PlaYing AlOng

BLISS

LUC REMINDS ME OF A spyglass. Polished and pleasing to look at on the outside, but inside is another world bright in detail. Up until this point, I've simply been playing along with his new antics while cunningly trying to steer him in another direction. The last thing I want to do is get anywhere near that lens. No amount of adjustment will change my perception of him.

He is still just a man.

"Are you certain you don't want to change into anything more comfortable?" he asks while setting the table for dinner, adopting the similar pattern he has for weeks.

"I am comfortable." I glance down at my ensemble. It's abnormal for me to wear much more than this robe and lingerie. Clothes seem more burdensome where others might count them as a necessity or luxury.

Bodies speak much more than any words. And I've mastered their language. Luc has held his own, resisting every one of my efforts. For several nights, I haven't given up on tempting him from this fruitless cause, but I've also read the resolve in his eyes and body. More in his eyes. It's when he turns from artist to bordering on killer within a split second. I don't have the slightest amount of fear. All my life, I've dealt with wrath and abuse, so I can recognize it and steel myself before the blow comes. However, I must admit Luc's control is praiseworthy. He deflects every last one of my taunts. Every shrewd, seductive play he avoids.

During these times, I find myself admiring his own language

whether the strength in his stride, the way he focuses on these seemingly menial tasks: spreading the cloth over the table, smoothing out the wrinkles, setting up the candlesticks, laser-lighting both wicks, straightening the silverware. Etched in his hands is a careful care, a steadiness in his facial expressions, stability in his shoulders.

I try another tactic, one I've neglected up until now because it's a sharper, more obvious way, but he simply isn't taking any of my other hints.

Leaning over just as he places the silverware, I murmur in his ear, "How many times did you do this with Serenity?"

Other than a calculated pressing of his lips, none of Luc's features betray frustration, and he responds, "In her last days at the Aviary, we took our breakfasts together. Dinners were most often spent with the other Birds."

He keeps everything straightforward without revealing details.

"Why didn't you ever try harder then? Why didn't you ever just take her? Not man enough to take a little fight?" It's a well-known attack but an effective one.

I'd hoped my attack would produce something else. A knowing smirk is not what I anticipated or wanted.

"I did try once. It was a mistake. It was no better than assault."

Now, I'm intrigued. Possibilities term in my brain. "What happened?"

"Why do you want to know?"

"Is that what you want, Luc? More fight?" I lean in closer, placing my hands on the table, curving my fingers. "Do you need the challenge? To feel like you've *dominated* something? I can give you that."

He shakes his head, smirk growing. "Trust me, Bliss, you fight much harder than she ever has. You have multiple levels. You're challenging enough."

"Have you had your fill of wining and dining me yet? You finally ready to get down to business?"

"Not until you trust me.

"I'm not Serenity. I will never be her."

"That is the most truthful thing you've admitted to me. And I couldn't be happier for it."

LUC

"How far are you going to take this?" Bliss challenges me.

"As far as it goes." My answer may be vague, but it's the truth. "I want you to trust me."

"And what reasons have you given me for that?"

"Not much."

"Good to see we agree on something."

She turns around, directing herself toward the door. I don't pursue her or try to bring her back. Sometimes, one must choose their battles. My father would tell me this is ridiculous. Backing down from any sort of confrontation is a sign of weakness. Weakness in my profession would have earned me nothing more than a coffin. For me, my efforts with Bliss are proving to yield more than mere weakness. Vulnerability. A territory unfamiliar to me, and I have no guide.

Control was my greatest advantage as Aviary director. It's more than difficult to shed that skin, which is why it has taken weeks for Bliss and me to connect in any sense. I'm used to giving the orders, in having them followed to the letter. Bliss would do even more than a letter. She'd give me the whole book. No, the whole library. She would give me anything and everything except herself. Only her mask. And I'd be nothing more than a cheap John only interested in my own empty pleasure at her expense. Now, I've begun to see that loving Bliss will be like sailing the ocean in a paddle boat. I've just pushed off from the shore.

My patience is wearing thin but not so much I'm ready to give up. So, after a few minutes, I follow her, wondering how long she's going to continue pushing me away and shutting me out, how long she's going to keep herself away playing these endless games. Tonight is new because she went for a stabbing technique by bringing up her sister, showing she still doubts my intentions—I'm only here because I could not have Serenity, though I want nothing more in the world than to know Bliss. She's testing me. Good.

I find her in the VirtuRoom. She's selected an outdoor scene—a quiet city street with a steady falling rain. Real enough to feel the droplets soaking our skin. As if she's trying to rinse away the Temple, though this is all artificial. Standing in the rain with her eyes closed, she reminds me of a classic film still. Timeless beauty.

Her body is the mirage—an illusion over what she's truly made of, which is stone. No battering ram or forcing can break that stone; it will only strengthen it. All these nights, I've been contemplating different methods on how to see through that wall or how to scale it, but there are no shortcuts. It must be chipped away slowly and methodically. So far, I've managed to distract myself, resisting her advances, countering every mocking word and scoffing glance. I haven't so much as touched her.

Perhaps that's the problem.

I pause to stare at her. Raindrops continue to skitter down on us, and I notice the gooseflesh erupting on her skin, the ashen cheeks, the telltale shiver she tries to conceal, the way she keeps her arms at her sides lest she betray herself by folding her arms to warm herself. Shaking my head, I realize what a fool I've been. Bliss is human. As human as any girl. I can't keep avoiding her this way. Resistance will only go so far. And no number of candles, flowers, or dinners will aid me because they cannot muster a connection, cannot replace what I've declined to try up to this point. It's going to be more difficult. More control will be needed to keep myself in line, but I can't continue pretending her body is nothing more than a mirage.

So, I remove my jacket and wrap it around her shoulders, stepping closer to secure her frame inside it. Surprise registers in her lifted brows. Good. That's something. I do up the buttons, taking my time with each one, pausing only when I reach the collar before touching her cheek, fingers sucking up the rain droplets there.

Cautious, I search her eyes while I slide the rest of my hand along that cheek, my fingers pressed into her damp curls. "You asked why I care what you feel. Because I'm in love with you. I care about what you think and feel. I care about what's inside your soul. I want you to share that soul with me."

She avoids my gaze.

"Look at me, Bliss," I say to her, more urging, less a command.

"Stop."

"No."

She shifts her weight, eyes like a critter before the predator. She has multiple defense mechanisms. Which one will she use now?

"It's impossible, Luc."

Lies.

I close my arms around her body, feeling her resistance building with the need to escape this and return to what is familiar, what she can understand. She can't understand love. I can't tell her. I can't use gimmicks. I have to show her. Lowering my head, I brush my nose on the side of hers, my mouth a millisecond from hers, but I don't settle them just yet.

"Stop running from me, Bliss," I whisper, then say her real name three times.

She pulls away again. "I'm not Bliss. I'm Mara."

So, that is how she truly sees herself. Through her father's eyes. I shouldn't be surprised. Somewhere inside, she still must be that little girl.

I wish I could prove it to her. "You think I can't swallow it? Anything you deal to me. I'm just as twisted, Bliss. The world doesn't owe us any favors," I try to convince her.

"This world hasn't given me a damn thing!" She struggles against me, but I deny her the benefit because she's finally reacting with something other than a cold indifference, something other than her pleasure party, something other than a mask.

I grip her by the neck just enough to keep her close, keep my other hand stationed around the base of her waist.

"No, it hasn't. But you don't have to be alone anymore. I'm here. I'm not going anywhere. What are you feeling, Bliss?"

"Cold."

"Cold inside?"

She sighs, closes her eyes, hand stationed on my chest, fingers curled as if debating on whether to resist more. "You don't make sense. Why won't you take anything when you want everything from me? You want too much. You'll never get it."

"I don't intend to."

I kiss her, combing my fingers through her hair. Breaking my rule, I kiss her. For the first time, I feel her resist, so I know I'm gaining some ground, but she relaxes against me. I spend six seconds breathing the scent of her Temple-glass skin and tasting her, but that is all. It doesn't take her long to sink back into her familiar pattern. She angles her mouth, unfolding her lips, permitting me to go deeper and luring me with her body. No.

"You're going through the motions," I rebuke while pulling away, shaking my head fiercely. "I'm not going to let you go back to that. I can determine what's fake and what's real," I tell her, cupping her chin. I've spent years differentiating, memorizing the difference between a real smile and a fake touch. For once, Bliss and I are equally matched in this, but what little standing I have is overshadowed by the night I took her to bed.

All that time spent wanting Serenity's soul, I'd peered inside it just like I'd looked in her heart—even held it for a few precious moments. But I'd never once belonged to it. She'd swallowed Sky up long ago. And for the first time, I realize I'm not jealous of my brother. Serenity is uncaged. I've let the Swan fly away. All I feel is relief and pride because a better man is flying with her. I'm not so arrogant as to believe I'm better than my brother. On the contrary, he bests me in many ways. I might be a stone-cold killer and older than him, but Skylar outranks me. He is the right man for Serenity. They've been soaring high together for years now. Like a fool, I believed I could pull her from the sky and wind her around my heart. But she's flying with her soul mate.

If only I could grow wings for Bliss. I wish it were as simple as creating them like I've done for so many of my Birds. But she must grow them herself. Some days, it seems impossible.

Seventeen

SkY's ChaNce

SERENITY

"**I**'VE HAD JUST ABOUT ENOUGH of this."

I wake first when my father's voice intrudes upon Sky and me. He's the deeper sleeper, and a good night's rest has been long overdue thanks to my fathers forced extracurricular activities. Make that *failed* extracurricular activities.

Force grabs my wrist, hands clamping down with the power of wolf jaws, wrenching me to my feet. That's when Sky is roused, but he doesn't groggily stir. No, he shoots to his feet, blinking and taking in the sight of my father's hand chained around my wrist. I could've told Force it was a mistake, but I enjoy watching Sky show it instead when he applies pressure to Force's arm until his hand breaks its hold. No part of me is concerned, not even when my father raises his taser. The electric current crackles, but Sky's far too accustomed to a different sort of lightning.

Catching Force's other arm, Sky manages to knock the taser to the ground. I pick it up as it rolls. It's still vibrating in my hand, and I sense how with just one click from the button, it will pulse to life again. A moment later, I hear my father's frustrated growl as he pinches his eyes closed. Sky has him pinned to the ground, but it doesn't last. Instead, Sky tumbles back, body seizing. That's when I see the metal cuff around his neck. A built-in electric-shock.

My father rises. Now's my only chance. I'm doing this. Every last one of my butterflies dons their body armor. While my father is distracted, I bring the taser down on the nape of his neck. Once is plenty enough, and the sight of him tasting his own medicine, body shaking and twitching like a petrified chihuahua, is well worth the assault of the guards who surround us moments later. Whatever electricity pulsed through Sky's body is gone, but I still tense, brandishing the weapon and sticking close to Sky's side.

Force makes his way to his feet. I smirk, admiring the telltale burn mark on the nape of his neck. He turns to face me. His expressions compete. First with the faintest curl of his mouth, but no rising chuckle. Soon, his eyes pinch together, brows besieging the lids below them as he addresses me.

"Give me the taser, Serenity," he orders with a hand stretched out.

I tighten my grip, lean against Sky, and reply, "No."

My father takes one step forward. "*Now.* I won't be using it on you or your little beau."

Sky summons my gaze with the turn of his head. "Did he just call me little?"

"Touché, Mr. Lace. I'll have to hone my precision of language. The taser if you please, Serenity. If you try to use it again, the next pulse into your paramour will be a lethal one."

Acknowledging my father's trump card, I surrender the weapon. Part of me knows it could be easily taken, though a few guards would go down in the process. As my father smirks, I hand over the weapon. One second passes before he turns it on his head of security. Only Force doesn't stop with one or two. He keeps the taser crackling against the security guard's neck until the man stops crying out in pain, stops twitching…stops moving altogether.

"Let that be a lesson to the rest of you ingrates about what will happen if you don't do your job correctly. I don't know why I don't replace you all with drone bots. Pick him up and dispose of him," he orders to the other guards before directing his attention back to us.

He spends a few moments pacing, gaze flicking every now and then to us. Sky keeps one arm banded around my waist, securing us together. Closer than the moon's glow that's just a silvery reflection of the sun.

Finally, Force shakes his head and addresses Skylar, "Congratulations, Mr. Lace. Seems a position has opened, and you are a candidate."

"Come again?"

"Tonight, you will compete along with several other candidates to fill the slot of my head of security for the Penthouse. Should you win, your duties will include overseeing my security staff, monitoring security feeds, and escorting the Face of the Temple to every interaction and encounter she may have."

Sky's eyes widen. I bite my lower lip, brows lifted in anticipation. Of course Sky will win. There's no one better than him. Like he's said in the past, no one in the world could protect me as well as he does.

"I hope you're happy, Serenity," Force spits out the words.

"I'd be happier if you were in a shallow grave, but yes, I'm happy."

"Pair of star-crossed lovers." He rolls his eyes.

Smiling, Sky squeezes my shoulders. "I've always thought of us as storm-tossed, wouldn't you say?" His mouth brushes the side of my head.

I grin, silently agreeing with him.

Even though Sky and I are forbidden to see each other for the rest of the day, I'm not complaining about it. And I welcome Neil when he comes for lunch.

"Where's Lindy?" I wonder as I close the door behind him. "Did she finally come to her senses and drop you like last week's news?"

He raises an arrogant eyebrow. "Please, sis. I'll always be on the front page. Right up there with you," he adds with a wink. "Actually, I came to get your advice instead."

"On what?"

"This."

Neil fishes in his pocket before he brings an object up to the light. My jaw hunkers down low when I examine the ring. Just the idea of it would be a surprise, but Neil has managed to shock me even more by the understated style. I figured he'd pull out all the stops with a rock the size of a knuckle or at least digital glowing gemstones or singing pearls or something. Instead, the ring before me is a classic gold band with a simple round-cut diamond in the center. Nothing more.

"Are you serious, Neil?"

"I bought the ring, didn't I?"

"But it's only been a few weeks," I point out.

"I don't want to wait years. I don't even want to wait one year. I've traveled all around the world, I've photographed thousands of girls, no two of them alike, but she is—" Neil pauses, running a hand through his hair. "Serenity, name me one other girl who would stay with me all night after I got drunk over someone else, then clean up my puke to boot?"

I give him a blank stare. "Coming up empty on that one."

"I knew as soon as I got her sprite light." He chuckles. "You know what I did? I printed it and then burned it. No picture can do the original justice."

I lean over to kiss his cheek. "I like her Neil. I like her a lot."

"Good to know." He puts the ring back in his pocket. "I'll ask her to elope, so don't be surprised if you don't get a wedding invite."

I laugh. "If I had a wedding, you'd be my bridesmaid." I pinch his cheek.

Neil rolls with it. "Hey, I'd look adorable in a big ol' bow." Then, he winds one arm around me, squeezes tight, and announces, "I'd better get going. Would love to hang up here with you with a bucket of popcorn and watch the show, but it turns out Lindy got us tickets for the performance. Sounds like she goes all loco, screaming from the stands and everything."

"Actually, Force is going to escort me," I say, referring to the security competition. "He's got some sort of private box lined up where he can oversee the whole thing and make me watch. What do you know about it?"

"Set up like a giant obstacle course, but it's one big free-for-all. Anything goes. Centre sees to quite a few concussions on fight nights. The remaining participant goes head-to-head with a final challenger at the end. But don't worry, I put all my money on your lover boy."

"He'll win." I shrug.

"I know." Neil grins at me, posture prouder than a peacock's. "Looking forward to it. I'll get a nice little honeymoon egg out of it. I'd ask you to wish me luck, but—"

"You won't need it," I finish.

Eighteen

ObStaCles

SKY

IT'S THE SECOND TIME I'VE had a visit from my brother. Suspicious as to how he'd know I'd be here, I keep working on my exercises but pause to ask, "Force let you know?"

"Neil told me about the fight," Luc confesses. He starts to pace without saying anything, so I know this is going to be rich.

Groaning, I jerk up on the bar until it moves higher and higher, hauling my body upward. One of many exercises in my typical training with Kerrick. Even when I was in the Aviary, it didn't stop. And the Garden put my body through hell, but made it stronger. But over the course of the past few weeks, my muscles have taken a beating, so to speak. Sure, I could practice my sit-ups, do what I could with the walls in the holding center, but it was more of a *psychological* strain. Emotional, too. I chuckle, thinking of how much more emotional it is with Serenity. All the girls Force sent me…less emotional hassle than my girl. And I wouldn't have it any other way. But with my brother…oh screw it!

I swing down. "What do you want, Luc? Just spit it out."

Luc strokes his jaw, back and forth like a sideways swing. When I tense, he must take the hint because he drops his hand to his side. "What if it's too late?" I lower my brows as he continues, "What if Force and thousands of others have ruined her? What if she can't ever accept my love?"

I cross my arms over my chest. "Ready to give up so easily, pretty boy?"

Luc glares. "I've been working my ass off, Skylar. Don't cheap-en this. For once in your life, just be straight with me."

"What if, what if, what if…" Sighing, I run my fingers through my hair, then yank it up into its usual bun. "You're still just as dense as ever. Stop wondering what if. One question, Luc—is she worth it?"

I hear him pause before he questions, "What?"

"Fuck, Luc," I curse. "You've been with a woman. Now try *staying* with one. Love her. Don't lust for her. Love her through the lust. Through the pain. Through the deadness. Don't treat her as some fucking conquest. She's not a mountain to scale. This isn't a battle. And she's not a prize for first place. Just…*love* her! No conditions."

"What if I can't prove it to her?" Luc challenges, eyes averted.

I bite down, try to remember my brother's background, to remember how our father must have groomed him. "Love wears many different hats. Looks different depending on the situation. Sometimes, it's leading. Sometimes, it's fighting. Sometimes, it's protecting. And other times, it's healing. If I had my guess, I'd say you've been leading and fighting. Maybe it's time to try something else."

I've worn a lot of hats when it comes to loving Serenity. But now, it's time to fight for her. More than I ever have in my life.

Nineteen

PrOtecTing

Luc

ON MY WAY BACK TO the Penthouse, I stop by the security center to ensure everything is in order for the fight. Spectacles like this attract a great crowd. Plus, it will be televised. Naturally, Force has a stadium in the center of the Temple. Takes up three levels, holds hundreds of people. Drones are stationed in their correct places, ready to monitor, scan, and intervene for any security breaches. Only armed with electric shock but enough to dismantle a weapon and prevent any attempt of an attack. I don't expect anything. The murders have only occurred during Serenity's exhibits, which is why Force stopped them for a time.

An hour until the fight.

Enough time for me to speak to Bliss.

But when I arrive at her room, the door is locked. I summon my interface and try to contact her, but she doesn't respond. Then, I get a message from Force and refrain from rolling my eyes at the sight of his face projected above my arm.

"You won't find her there, Luc. Mara is in the middle of an interaction. If you wish, I could relay a message…"

I shut down my interface, closing off the signal. All this time, she'd had no clients thanks to my due diligence. I've checked her records. None have ranked higher than my requests, my price. How could this happen?

There are only three interaction rooms within the Penthouse. One is the conference room, but I know she won't be there. My search turns up nothing. I don't pause whatsoever before I use my barcode to open the last door.

I swallow back bile.

The holographic walls are pink with white dandelion fluff clouds swishing this way and that. A little girl's bed in the center of the room decorated in lush bedspreads gushing like a bird's pink plumage. And there is Bliss on the floor beside the bed. Dressed in a pink tutu and white stockings, the silver waterfall of her hair parted into pigtails with pink ribbons like serpent tongues dangling from them.

Unaware of my presence, the client stands behind her, belt in his hand. "Bend over, beautiful. That's a good girl. It's time for your spanking, my sweet."

Over *his* dead body.

It's what I deliver. Turning the belt on him over and over again until he's bruised and bloodied. The blood must clash with the pink ruffles of the carpet, but I don't notice—all I see is red. And I realize how different this kill feels. The only one that came close was taking down the Annex pedophile ring. Not even the night with Gull's abuser. That was a mere conceited, selfish desire to impress Serenity and maintain control over my Aviary. Now, another instinct rises inside me. More than anger. More than hatred. Something else propels me from beneath those vain emotions. Stronger than anything else. As my brother so neatly coined—love wears different faces.

This must be protection.

Bliss's reaction is far different than Serenity's when I'm finished. When the body of her client stops twitching once he's dead, she sheds no tears, but her eyes seem like they hold millions of them. Millions she's kept caged—a innate habit, as if she doesn't know how to anymore. But her lip quivers.

I kneel beside her. I don't know much of healing, but I try.

Keeping my hands slow, I remove one pigtail and then another, so her hair returns to its owner, covers her cleavage. Never once do my eyes depart from hers; I read every blink, every flick, every downward glance as I sweep my fingers to her stockings and slowly roll them down as if I'm opening a precious scroll. She doesn't deserve this. No girl could *ever* deserve this. Could ever want it. Once I've finished with her stockings, she closes her eyes and I stop. I stop everything.

"Please," she murmurs, voice softer than a wisp. "Don't stop. Get. It. Off." Her breaths rush between each word.

I don't question her. Simply reach my arms behind her waist, unravel the strings of the pink corset, peel back the guise covering her, along with the tutu, until all that's left is simply Bliss. She doesn't hide. But for the first time, she doesn't try to flaunt herself, doesn't try to lure me, doesn't try to seduce me. She just inhales deeply, then exhales the same. I hold this memory. The beautiful sight of her. More beautiful than ever because I see Bliss—no, a piece of Bliss—for the first time.

Finally, she whispers, "M-my first client. F-father designed…"

I cup her cheeks in my hands, my eyes summoning hers.

"Now, you've seen," she tells me. "Thousands of hands other than yours have touched me. Have stained me. He took my virginity when I was eight. Do you see now, Luc? There is nothing left of Bliss. There's just Mara and a mountain of ghosts. There will always be another and another."

I firmly shake my head. "I am the last."

I kiss her. Draw her in. And she accepts.

Twenty

PrOtecTed

BLISS

IT'S ALL TOO MUCH. THINGS were easier when I could just adopt who I needed to be. But all these weeks without clients and then, when my father informed me of an emergency client but refused to tell me who it was, I knew. As soon as Queran prepared me, I knew. The last time I saw him, I was ten.

Luc's eyes don't leave mine, don't drift. They are an anchor. Something I can hold onto because he sees me, and he's still... here.

"I have a hundred kills on my hands," Luc shares, pressing his palm to mine. "But the blood on my hands, despite how it will never wash off, is not the worst of my crimes. Every time I finished a kill, I returned to the Aviary. To the Birds I'd grown up studying, drawing. Father said it was a reward. Offering me a choice of any Bird as a prize after I'd killed. But it was just a healing attempt. A balm. I learned self-pity. Got incredibly good at it."

I almost smile. He's still good at self-pity, but I don't reflect on that. He's showing me something. Something personal. Something behind the director guise he's worn all these weeks.

"It helped nothing. Just made me feel emptier. You can never steal without feeling empty. I remember every single Bird. I remember the way their eyes looked. Even if they bowed to my every demand, I still remember their eyes. Some broken, some vacant, some melancholic, some hardened. None of them real."

"Until Serenity. How did she make you feel?"

"Alive." He doesn't lie. His hand swings from my cheek into

my hair, scooping up the curls.

"And how do I make you feel?" So tempted to arch my back and part my lips, to return to what I know, what is familiar.

"Like Luc." His words fracture my mountain, inject the cracks with their truth.

I purse my lips, try to deny. "You don't understand. You can't understand," I protest lowering my head onto his shoulder. "My past follows me wherever I go. Every man who's ever touched me is a loose noose around my neck. It doesn't tighten, but I still must drag them all around. And I'll never fly because I could never lift myself with all of them weighing me down."

"I understand perfectly, Bliss." I feel his lips on the back of my head. "Because I do the same in other ways. In my case, it's their eyes that follow me, their ghosts."

"Ghosts." I close my eyes and turn my face to the side, nestling my cheek into his shoulder. "We both have ghosts."

"But you never had a choice," he reminds me, a sharp edge in his voice. "Conscripted into you at birth by that man who's no better than a snake—who doesn't deserve to be called a father."

"Oh, come now, Luc." The deep voice invades the room. "Is that any way to treat your host who has been so accommodating?" Force quips as he wanders toward us, hands behind his back.

I lower my head into the customary designation my father prefers. Especially when I'm like...this. It's sweet of Luc, really. To remove his shirt and drape it around my frame, to do up the buttons. Doesn't he realize my father has screened my client interactions? That he reviews every one of my medical tests? That he has more intimate knowledge of my body than any client?

"All this time, I have been so consumed over Serenity and her new prospect that I regret to say I've neglected you, my dear boy," my father says to Luc while circling us. An action he enjoys far too much. "I knew you were paying for her, but it was my assumption Mara had become your Swan fantasy. Shame on me for not paying closer attention." Force gestures to the dead client. A name I will never forget.

"And what of it?" Luc combats him, standing with half his body overlapping mine. Is this what it feels like to be protected?

"Well, if it's my eldest daughter you wish to possess, Luc, perhaps we can come to an arrangement." Father touches two finger-tips to his mouth, continuing to move his body back and forth. Never stopping. "You know how much I love a challenge." I start to decipher the hidden meaning.

"What do you want, Force?" Luc asks, arm firm, muscle tense. I can feel it through his shirt.

"I want to see which man will come out on top. Serenity's or Mara's. Prepare to fight your brother tonight, Luc. Whoever wins will get his girl."

Twenty-one

ThE FigHt

SERENITY

As promised, Force comes for me. More than satisfied by my dress of choice, he takes a moment to observe me before ordering me to the elevator since he has no intention of showing up late. I pause in the elevator, noting my reflection. Tonight, I am lightning. For Sky's thunder. Thanks to my time with Neil and Lindy, I've become well-versed with NAILS as well as the body scanners. If there is one benefit of the Penthouse, it's this—no limitations. The silvery concoction I wear is one long lightning bolt with a train extending behind me like thousands of sun-sparkled pearls. Real gold lace designs fused with laser-technology swirl animated all over the dress.

"Someone's a bit pretentious…" Force plays with a few curls cascading from the messy bun.

"Not at all." I combat him with a worthy grin. It's no contest.

My father leans over, sultry voice beckoning, "You look like a phoenix!"

I don't bother refuting him. This ensemble isn't for him. "Is Bliss coming?"

Force straightens, pulling on the ends of his suit, which I know costs in the tens of thousands range. "Mara rarely ever leaves the Penthouse. Sometimes, a client will book an event experience followed by an interaction, but no client has claimed her in weeks." Again, there is a telltale smile bordering the edges of his mouth. Something is going on.

Weeks? That means Luc has…all this time. Oh! I guess I un-

104

derestimated him. No doubt, my father gives him a good salary, but with this information, I know he's been spending even more to keep clients away from Bliss. Is that why she's been free during the day—because her nights haven't been tied up? Why hasn't she bothered to mention it? I guess I haven't asked either. None of her client interactions propel my curiosity. I can't fault her when I've kept her at a distance ever since I saw her and Luc together.

After we descend in the elevator to the correct floor, Force escorts me down a long hallway and to a black door at the end. Even from behind walls, I can hear hundreds of figures cheering and an announcer bellowing through a microphone. When Force opens the door and motions a hand for me to enter the box, I swallow any tightness in my throat. My butterflies try to reassure me with soft tickles from their antennae.

I have nothing to worry about.

I want to laugh in my father's face. Somehow, I manage to contain myself, and my butterflies are content to merely dance a little jig as I survey below us and take in the obstacle course that laughs in the face of physics. A mixture of virtual reality and physical obstacles. Shifting platforms and obstacles. Chains to ropes to cargo nets to beam-walking to laser ladders to scaling cliffhanger gaps to unstable bridges, everything is designed to test a challenger's willpower and athleticism. Except this also tests reflexes by arming each challenger with a laser weapon they must use against virtual assailants.

Despite all those years knowing about similar, though not as exaggerated, courses where Kerrick and Sky would train, seeing one up close gives me perspective. I wonder if Sky is practicing meditative breathing—something he said always helped him break the course down in his head and offered him focus. That was always Kerrick's rule. Mental strength is just as important as physical. All lessons from Kerrick. Resisting the urge to allow memories of my real father invade my thoughts, I focus on Sky. And my biological father's words.

"There are five stages," Force explains. "As you can see, we have advanced the final stage to include the scaling of a makeshift mountain. It is climate-controlled, so he will be exposed to the natural *elements* as it were. I am very curious to ascertain your lover's stamina. As you can tell, upper-body strength, grip strength, and the ability to climb are all significant factors."

I don't respond. Sky will prove him wrong soon, and anything I say will just goad my father on.

"By the way, I've invited a friend to join us tonight." My father uses the interface in his head to summon the new guest. "You may come in now."

I suppose I shouldn't be surprised to see Tristan enter the box and take his seat right next to me. Whether it's my father's final attempt at suitor-hood in the likely event Sky wins or an attempt to unhinge Sky himself, I don't know. All I do is jerk my chin out without even acknowledging the young man. Instead, I focus on Sky. Not once does he lift his head to the boxes. Not once can our eyes meet, but maybe that's better. Maybe he needs to forget about me right now. If keeping me at a distance is what will help him win, then I hope his consciousness can erect a block so big, it will put Mount Kilimanjaro to shame.

SKY

HER HEAD IS TURNED WHEN I peek at the center box, strategically positioned to view all angles of the course. I stifle the rising chuckle, but I beam at the sight of my girl. Lightning incarnate. Time for me to be her thunder.

I remember Kerrick's lessons. Tonight, I fully intend to honor my days with him.

Adaptation is the most important. Every day, it was a new challenge even if it meant leaving in the middle of the night and having me scale an abandoned building or unfinished construction courses in one of the many urban sprawls where we grew up. In the Temple, I never know what to expect. The temptation to take this far too seriously rears its head. More is at stake, but Kerrick taught me one other crucial factor—over-focusing makes people sloppy. Relaxation is just as important when it comes to competition.

So, when one of the hired Temple girls from the front rows crowded with people whistles when I remove my shirt, I try not take it personally. Instead, I smile and wink at the audience. I recognize some of the Temple girls. Could name each one. Some of them point and others fan themselves as I roll my shoulders and prepare to take on the Temple course—seemingly impossible for any human to conquer. I banish every image, every memory, every speck of Serenity as much as possible. To get through this, I can't consider her whatsoever. I need to go another place. They say I won't need my weapon until stage two. I've chosen a laser blade in the design of a Chinese war sword—a cleaver. Kerrick would have gone with the cutlass or the Sabre. But this is my bastard blade. Wish it was the real thing. That'd be a thing of beauty, but no real weapons are allowed in the course. Or the Temple for that matter.

The first stage is more balance-oriented. I'll need speed to make it across the icy water. Other candidates for the security position go before me, and I welcome the extra time to breathe and harness my mind, forbidding any Serenity-shaped distraction but remembering to maintain relaxation.

Finally, the announcer says my name, and spotlights envelop me. I flex my muscles and pose at the moving volu-cam, winking, keeping things as light as I dare just before I leap onto the platform and swing my body up to grip onto the rocky handhold. Sharp slaps of wind gut into my back. The rocks are cold, but it helps me focus. I test each notch and groove, cautious but also steady. We only get one chance to begin again if we fall. And the course is timed.

Once I reach stage two, I'll remove the noise blockers from my ears. There's always a subtle hum and a vibration before each virtual assailant. I'll need all my senses to focus. Just like now.

My shoe slips, but I quickly regain my footing, remind myself why I'm doing this without summoning her image. Repeat my family's names once, twice, and then start climbing again. Toughest part is having to go upside down. Especially with my heavy body wanting to follow gravity. But I muscle through it, gritting my teeth hard against the mouth guard until I reach the other side and land on the platform. I'm only one of four to get here.

Stage Two.

SERENITY

TRISTAN LEANS OVER TO WHISPER in my ear. "Enjoying the performance?"

He motions to my hand, and I realize I've been digging my nails into the armrest, fingers clenched around the wood like it's a life preserver. Tristan's breath is warm in my ear, and he lingers there, reeking of far too much cologne. His fifty thousand-dollar suit is no doubt an attempt to impress my father. I should tell him not to bother since nothing much impresses my father.

Turning to Tristan, I spit out the sarcastic words, "Immensely, why do you ask?"

"I think we have our eye on the same candidate." He gestures to Sky, who is preparing to enter the second stage, which will pit him against a zip line and having to swing from a curtain onto a small platform in the middle of hypothermia-inducing water.

This course only appeals to trained professionals. Perhaps Force could tell Sky was one. Perhaps he assumed Kerrick's hand in the matter. Whatever the case, my father's plan—test—is a good indicator as well as complement of Sky's skill.

Gripping onto the armrest tighter, I hold my breath when Sky begins to swing from the zip line. I punch the armrest when he nails the jump to the unsteady platform, which starts to shift. I suddenly gasp when a laser creature slithers out of the water. Some sort of water serpent. But Sky whips out his cleaver within moments, then slices a clean cut so the serpent disintegrates into pixels. Sky falls once into the water, but he starts again from his last point. His body is shaking now from the cold, but the way he clenches his mouth and fists, it's obvious he's maintaining his control.

"The spider wall is my favorite." Tristan leans over, supporting himself on his elbow as he motions to the course. "All that upper-body strength on display. Muscles attract you, Swan? They sure aren't harming his cause."

Hundreds of Temple girls clamor at Sky from the stands. Some paparazzi. Somehow managing to swallow back my jealousy, I grit my teeth as he prepares to conquer the swinging chains challenge leading up to the spider wall. I stomp my foot, relieved when he swings from one chain to the next, not pausing between each one because they shift at body motion. Each time he gets to a new chain, the former one shifts up. But he nails each one. As soon as he reaches the last, there is another virtual challenge. Jungle-themed, several laser monkeys appear. Razor-sharp teeth designed to literally sear the skin. Maintaining his balance with one strong hand gripping the chain, Sky uses his other to grip his blade and cleave whichever monkeys he can. Still, he doesn't come away clean. When he makes it onto the next platform, a pause before the spider wall, he has a few singes on his neck and arms.

Only one other candidate has managed to keep up with Sky. Not as muscled, but that doesn't always give one the advantage. It's all about having muscles in the right places and the training to back them up. Sky has the willpower, too. That's his best asset.

Force stands, then adjusts his tie. "There will be a brief break before the final stage. You two enjoy yourselves. I'll return shortly."

He closes the door to the box behind him. Immediately, I rise to my feet and point a warning finger at Tristan. "Don't even think about it!"

Instead of coming onto me as I expect he will, given our last encounter, Tristan surprises me by remaining in his chair and waving a hand.

"Don't get your knickers in a twist, Swan. You're not a bad kisser, but you're not my type."

Unconvinced, I narrow my brows as Tristan takes a drink of his bourbon and motions to the stage. "Muscle man there, now *he's* more my type."

Placing my hands on my hips, I march toward him. "What the hell?"

He puts his glass down. "My father always had certain expectations of me—as well as doubts. Don't take it personally. Whatever happened during the interaction was a power play between him and me." He shrugs and finishes, "An act."

I slump down in my chair. "Glad to help you maintain your cover."

"Fortunately, I don't have to worry about that anymore, seeing as I'm the boss."

"Oh?"

"Let's just say *my* power play won out in the end."

I don't bother to ask what that really means.

"As long as you're being forthcoming," I incline my head toward Tristan, "I want the sprite light footage of my sister and me back."

Tristan looks to the side as if trying to recollect. "Oh, that. Yes, caught my father watching it in his office from time to time. I can arrange that. You realize *your* footage is splashed all over the web?" Tristan downs the last of his drink, then exhales. "Some of the popular graphickers have been quite *creative* in their alterations of your exhibits. And, of course, the Pleasyour app wasted no time in contracting your Temple footage for interactive programs."

Not just a fantasy in their heads anymore. My laser double pleasures their bodies.

Lightning quivers deep inside me. But even deeper is something else. More than any exhibit, the knowledge of this violation stamps a brand upon my heart. And it...*hurts*.

The stadium lights flash twice.

"Looks like the next round is starting soon.," Tristan comments, and I immediately scan the platform for Sky.

"By the way, back off," I warn Tristan, feeling lethal as I hold onto Sky's image. "He belongs to me."

"Ahh, fascinating," Tristan declares, measuring my eyes. "And do you belong to him?"

I take one look at Sky and grin, retorting, "Oh, hell yes."

"Good to see you're getting along," Force comments then, stepping toward me just before resuming his seat.

I straighten out my dress, prepared to watch Sky in the third stage.

So far, they seem themed around the elements with the mountain and the ice lake. Now it must be air-themed as Sky works his way through a large tube that slants at nearly a ninety-degree angle. He must chimney climb it. Nothing is ever easy since volts of air charge the tube, whipping away his bun so his waves fly all around him like dark wings in a storm. This one is the quickest challenge. Sky reaches the tube's end, jumps from it to the rope waiting for him, slides down, then lands on the platform in spite of the razing wind. More screams. More cheers from the crowd. No other candidates have progressed to the final stage; I knew Sky would be the only one standing in the end.

Stage Four. Fire-themed. Even if it's faux fire, concocted of laser projections, they still have the capacity to burn, especially given the hundred-foot drop. Each bar shifts. Sky keeps his cleaver close to his side. Judging by his curled fingers, he's ready to use it. Except no virtual creators or assailants have targeted him this time. I take a gander at my father smirking at me, privy to some secret only he knows.

Then, the stadium lights turn dark. Spotlights flash three times to afford momentary glimpses of Sky right before a crack of thunder startles the audience into a ripple of "*ohs*" tripping over each other. I flip the bird at Force right before laser lightning crackles and zigzags toward the bars right behind Sky. He doesn't stop. The lightning follows him, increasing in speed as if it gets closer with every bar he jumps to. If the lightning touches him, I would wager it's enough to send him falling. Given how much his body has already taken, how much sweat shines on his skin, how much his muscles strain with each new jump, I don't know if he can start again. How much more he can take?

Now, Force isn't focused on me but on Sky. Index finger curved along his chin, stroking the area just below his mouth, assessing, anticipating, judging. My nails must be carving wells into my palms as I watch Sky haul his body to the second-to-last bar. Just a few feet from the platform. Almost within reach. If he swings back as he's done, the next lightning strike will hit him. One more second passes. Sky does swing his body but not back—to the side. As soon as his hand grips onto the last bar, he swings his body right and left, out of the lightning's path, far enough for his leg to find a base on the platform. The crowd in the stadium has moved so far onto the edges of their chairs, I have to wonder how they haven't toppled down on one another. Then, Sky's other leg joins the first one, and he collapses.

The stadium erupts into ear-splitting cheers that threaten to batter my eardrums. But something's not right because the lights dim when they should shine. And my father doesn't stand. Nor does he glare in disapproval over Sky's victory.

"Well, this is an interesting development," Tristan marvels as he enhances his sprite light screen to the figure emerging onto the platform opposite of Sky. The lights are too dim to get an unobstructed view of him. What's going on?

I glance at my father the same moment the lights brighten.

"Now, that's some man candy if I do say," Tristan quips, leaning in to observe the new fighter. Force announces his trump card—this is the true final stage. A bonus match. A fight.

And Luc is Sky's opponent.

LUC

I CAN'T LOSE.

I treat every obstacle before me as if it's one of my contracts. Considering I've had to spend all my time in the Temple researching numerous levels and scoping out any areas of weakness, I've become familiar with the challenges and expectations of the course. However, training for it is something altogether. Fortunately, my father ordered rigorous training for my profession. For years, my body endured necessary trials. Ones only the elite could access. Quite similar to this. Unfortunately, my time as director left me with less time to commit to such.

But I can't lose.

Twenty-two

MoRe

BLISS

I WATCH THE FIGHT FROM MY bedroom. Detaching is easier when I'm alone. And despite how pivotal this battle is, despite how I care about each victor in a different way, despite how much I want one victor to win, I keep turning away from the sight.

Because I want to know more.

Luc is the first man I've ever spent longer than a night with. The first man who has come back. The first man to…protect me. The first man to fight for me. And the first man to open himself to me beyond his flesh and skin. Certainly, there were clients who exposed a secret or two or formed excuses for what they were doing to me—justified it by faulting and punishing me. Nothing like Luc. I never considered he would want to see my scars—the ruination of an eight-year-old child. Because he has his own scars. Ones compiled since his childhood as well.

I've never wanted to know more. All these weeks with my mother, I've never asked one question about her life after leaving the Temple. Not of her or Serenity.

"Queran?" I call out his name as I knock on his door.

It doesn't take him long to open it. I smile when I see the banquet of origami figures all over his room. He's added some new ones. Projected in the center of his room is the fight, and I find my smile spreading when Luc takes down each virtual opponent with precision and finesse. He is certainly a favorite of the crowd. But he hasn't reached the final stage yet. Once he does, he'll have to reckon with Skylar. And I cannot take sides. Not against my sister.

I remember what I came here for. Clearing my throat, I address Queran, "Where did you come from, Queran?"

At first, he gives me a blank stare and blinks just once. He opens his mouth, then utters, "Orphanage." One word. Revealing but common.

"How did you end up here?" I purse my lips after asking, rub my hand up and down my arm, hoping my questions aren't too invasive.

Queran wanders over to his desk, then retrieves an origami figure from the bottom drawer. A little boy attached to a string with two similar origami figures about the size of the original's arm dangling beside him. One has a long train of paper hair.

"You watched over the other children?" I try to guess.

Queran shakes his head before reaching up to one of the small ones and urging it toward the bigger one's arm. After wiggling it around a bit, he takes the original's arm, places it on the hair, and starts to curl it around and around.

Then, I understand. "Dolls...you enjoyed playing with dolls." When he points to each one, I correct myself. "You enjoyed *remaking* them."

One nod. If he didn't approach the desk again, I would have asked another question, but he reaches into the bottom drawer again and pulls out three more figures, but bigger this time. Altogether, they begin to attack the Queran boy. I sigh. Something creeps into my heart. An alien feeling. One I haven't known since I was a child and stayed up long nights thinking of my mother and viewing her sprite lights, practicing her movements, learning her body language, wishing every day I could be more like her. All of those add up to one thing—heartache. And it's what I feel for the paper boy in Queran's palm.

He puts the paper figures back in the drawer.

"Did Temple recruiters come to the orphanage?" I probe a little deeper, hoping the questions will keep the tears behind my eyes.

"Yes."

"They saw how different you were?"

He nods.

I'm certain it wasn't long before they began giving him the injection. Years ago, it was just in the experimentation phase. I shudder when I consider how generations past would go so far as to cut the muscle. Part of me wants to know how Queran feels about it all, but it seems too much. Whatever happened in the past, he is a professional and finds beauty in his work. In what he creates with his hands. They can never take that from him.

As soon as I turn around to return to my room, I look up at the sprite scene.

Luc has reached the final stage.

Twenty-three

Brother to Brother

SKY

"YOU'RE A REAL PIECE OF work, you know that?" I tell Luc as soon as he lands on the platform at my feet, my voice drowned out by the screaming crowd.

Suddenly, we're rendered blind to the crowd as the spotlights shift to Force, who announces an intermission from his box. It's the first time I peer up and meet Serenity's gaze. Concern creases her eyes, but I still notice her posture and how straight it is. She's proud.

"Fate is a cruel mistress indeed," Luc utters, straightening as sweat careens off the sides of his face and he cracks his knuckles.

"Yeah, if fate's real name is Force."

Before Luc can retort, a troop of drone bots surrounds us and direct us to follow them to the arena. Guess Force is still full of surprises. Begrudgingly, I follow the light beams to the arena. Virtual lasers pen us in, but at least a couple of service bots provide us with some water and chairs since intermission will last another twenty minutes. After tipping back the glass and swallowing the draught of water in two gulps, I drape a cool-mist towel over my shoulders. Could be a waterfall to me right now. Glancing over in the dim light, I watch my brother as he sips at his water like it's some fine wine.

Rolling my eyes, I stretch my arms behind my back. "Seriously can't believe we're related."

"If it helps, I didn't have a choice." I pick up on the strain in his voice.

116

"Let me guess—Bliss."

"Let's just say we both have the same reason for fighting today. I can't lose, Skylar."

I lean back in my seat, legs parting, lapping up whatever relaxation I can before the fight round. "Me neither."

"Where does that leave us?"

I glance around, ensuring we aren't monitored. The drone bots have taken position on the outside of the laser ring. Wonder if they're programmed to record everything we're saying.

Can't risk it. "They're expecting a good fight," I lead in, hinting just as the lights in and around the stadium flicker, signaling a warning the fight will begin soon. Some of the audience begins to trickle back in.

I crack my neck. "Since neither of us can lose, there's only one way this can go down." I level with my brother, pinning his eyes.

Luc nods, steeling his jaw. "We both win."

"Or lose," I suggest, hoping he understands.

It'll be ugly. We both have martial arts training, but mine's old school. Luc's is more formal and cultural, and I have no doubt he has some unique moves in his tool belt. Not about strength. If it was, this'd be an easy win for me. It's about technique. Already, I can ascertain how Luc will fight. More takedowns and clinch fighting from me. More throws, jabs, kicks, and sucker punches from him.

More drones arrive, this time with head shields to prevent neck injury. To think fighters used to have uncomfortable padded cushions on each side of the head. Technology has made everything more convenient.

After securing his, Luc takes a couple of steps until he's standing in the inner ring. Lights aren't on yet, but it won't be long now. Wonder how much our bodies will be able to take before this ends. Especially after the course tests. I've got a feeling it'll be more than I've ever taken before. We'll both need cell generators after this.

Force's voice booms over the speakers. "Ladies and gentlemen, it is time for the fight to begin. Please take your seats and enjoy the show!"

Everything goes dark just as the audience erupts into loud wallops, whistles, and cheers that swarm and ripple across the entire stadium.

Taking a deep breath, I enter the inner ring. "And here...we...go!"

The lights turn on.

Twenty-four
Healing

SERENITY

DRONES HAUL A STRETCHER WITH a bruised, bloodied, and battered Sky toward the medical bay with me following right beside him. Luc's injuries were worse, so they took him away first. I glance over at the other room and the frosted glass blurring anything but light. The process will take some time. Just like it did for me. I wonder who prepped him.

Only when the drones open the door on the opposite side of the room leading to the second CellGen do I realize who. My mother's presence is a surprise. She holds a skin-fuser, and I lift my brows as she approaches Sky, who's passed out.

"They certainly did a number on him, didn't they?" she mutters as she kneels beside him before turning to me. "Don't look so shocked, Serenity. He's the closest thing to a son I've ever had and the most important man in my life next to Kerrick."

"I figured you'd say Force," I snap, but my mother doesn't fight back. In this moment, she looks so much like Bliss. I sigh and apologize, "I'm sorry. I didn't mean that."

"Yes, you did. But I'm used to your impulsiveness."

My mother places an ice pack on Sky's head before she injects a needle into his arm. A sedative in case he wakes during the process. My mother and I work together. Since she has a steadier hand, I let her use the skin fuser, and I apply ice to his other bruises and wipe up the rest of the blood from his scrapes and cuts. Sanitary conditions for the CellGen. Obviously, he won't be getting the full Immortal Treatment as I did. No age-stalling technology pro-

119

grammed into him. Just regeneration as far as it extends to healing. For a moment, I consider what it would mean for both of us…if it *were* to happen. And what will happen if it doesn't.

"I'll stay with him," my mother announces once she's finished. "You should go see Bliss. She wants to speak with you about something. She said she'd meet you in your room."

I don't bother to ask my mother if she knows what's going on. She wouldn't tell me if she did. I kiss Sky's brow, promising to be back soon even though no others are allowed in the CellGen room.

Little wonder I haven't heard from Force. He's probably off licking his wounds since both Luc and Sky went down in the last round and didn't get up. Miraculously at the same time. Sky's doing, no doubt. Still haven't figured out why yet, though.

I work my way up the stairs to my bedroom, finding it odd she didn't simply wait at the table or in front of the fish tanks like she normally does. The bedroom door is ajar. Already sensing something is wrong, I hurriedly enter the room and notice her sitting before my vanity with her feet up on the table. Smeared all over her mouth is chocolate with a few crumbs along her bare chest and disappearing down her cleavage since she's wearing nothing but lingerie beneath her robe. She reaches for a plate to her right where one remaining brownie is left. Then, she tosses her head back and giggles—a high, scribbled-all-over-the-wings-of-her-butterfly laughter.

"Congratulations, Serenity! He made it. Looks like all your dreams are coming true." She stretches her arms out to me. "You know why he did it, right? Daddy found out."

No wonder Luc fought. Not that I ever believed he would take it this far. It can only mean one thing—Luc really does love her.

"Bliss…" My eyes fill up with compassion-steeped tears because she still doesn't know how to accept that love. She doesn't know what to make of it. It's the first time I've seen her resort to this type of coping mechanism. Doesn't seem like Bliss.

"Yes! Bliss, that's my name." She raises her finger. "So, does that mean I'm a cannibal for eating my namesake?"

"I don't know." Shaking my head, I advance toward her. I see the small bag sitting next to the plate that contains the devil-sweet dissolving patches. Bliss notices my gaze, eyes blazing in warning just before I snatch it up.

She swings up so fast the chair topples over. I don't reach the bathroom before she seizes me, but I manage to break free and get to the outer room's balcony. Just needing to get it away from her, I manage to make it to the edge so I can pitch it over.

"No!" my sister screams.

I scream louder because I didn't expect her to go after it. My reflexes force my arms into overdrive, and I manage to yank her whole body back, her belly crashing against the railing just before we both tumble to the balcony floor, panting and crying together.

"Bliss!" I grab at her face, but her eyes are just wanderlust, nothing but high spirits dancing. "What were you thinking?"

"I was thinking I could fly!" She laughs again, and I can imagine butterflies erupting from her nose when she does. Hearing a hum behind me, I glance back where a shifting of the light creates a ripple effect. Of course Force would have a shield. Even if Bliss wanted to fly, she couldn't have.

"You want to fly, Bliss? You want to fly away from here?" My hope practically leaps from my mouth, parades itself in front of her like worthless glitter.

"You're just as hopeless as him, Serenity. You want me to, right? Just like Luc wants me to feel." She taps my nose knowingly, giggles sparking again. Of course, she's never taken me at my word. All she knows is one type of man. Never believes anyone can be different.

"I'll never fly. I've got so much dragging me down. I've got a whole mountain on top of me. I'm buried so deep under that mountain, all I've got are worms and dirt. Oh, and fungus! I've got fungus all over me."

She slips her robe off and rubs her hands up and down her arms, gesturing to the skin. "Can't you see? It's growing right out of my skin! You got lightning. I just got fungus. Funny, funny world. Funny, funny—" And she laughs until she chokes. Until she's gasping and choking.

All I can see are the raised bumps on her arms, the goose flesh. Not once in my life had I imagined I'd be caring for my older sister. Even as I secure my hands underneath her arms to raise her up, stringing one around her waist while propelling her other arm around my shoulders so I can carry her to bed, I don't feel a sisterly peace. All I feel is her hurt reaching out to me, so desperate it lassos part of my heart. I wish I could dig every piece of hers out, burn the puppet strings holding it there, and put a brand-new heart in her chest. One with no memories of men's bruising fingers, our father's poison, or Temple lust. But I can't give her a new heart. Maybe no one can…but Bliss.

All I can do is tuck my sister into the sheets, then snuggle in beside her so she's not cold. But I guess she'll always be cold, won't she? The Temple has given her nothing but hate and lust, and she's sucked enough down to last a hundred lifetimes. She won't let her heart break. Around it is a stone fortress; it can't crack because if it does, then something might get through. Something…like love.

Maybe I just need to fight less and love more.

Bliss "hmms" and covers my palm with her own, closing her eyes. I don't understand why anyone would want to go high just so they can crash at the end. I kiss her cheek. It feels cold, too. I wipe a tear away with my other hand, but more come Soon, I'm weeping into her shoulder, wishing my hot tears could heal her. But they can't.

Bliss sighs. "Can't fly, sis. Even if I could dig myself out of the dirt, there'd never be enough air to get me off the ground." She giggles one more time. "Look what you did, Serenity. I'm talking like you now. Does that mean I'm going mad, too?"

Is mad better than stuck? In Bliss's case, I wonder if it can get any worse?

"You know I didn't even care until you came along. You and Luc. And he just *had* to be the one!"

I pause, hanging onto her words. "What are you talking about?"

She starts cackling now, maniacal giggles skittering up her throat like a thousand cockroaches. "All those years, all those men, night after night, I've had thousands inside me, and it never *ever* worked! Daddy saw to that. But just *one* night with Luc." She raises her index finger, jutting it toward my face. "Just one."

"What?" Confusion…and then comprehension dawns. "Are

you? Bliss…?" I trail off on her name, waiting, waiting, waiting.

"That's some pretty persistent seed of his."

Not needing any more confirmation, I grab her by the nape of her neck, force her face over the side of the bed, and jam my two fingers down her throat until she vomits every last speck of brownie out of her system. It won't dilute what's already made it into her bloodstream, but I can prevent anything else from taking hold of her. Then, I clench my fingers around her face, hands printing over her cheeks. A million different accusations are on the tip of my tongue. How could she? How dare she? It's meant to be. It's destiny. Despite our father's forced sterility, it happened, and that *has* to mean something. It's not just her choice! Luc should know and get a say. I should get a say. Mom should get a say. Force—

None of those work. None fit. Salt from her tears mingles with leftover drips of vomit along the side of her mouth. I tighten my grip around her, holding her to me.

"You can't save it," she whispers. "We're in the Temple. Everything in the Temple belongs to him. It's not mine."

I don't care what she says. When I place my hand on her naked belly, I sense a slight swell that wasn't there weeks ago. I may not be able to save my future nephew or niece from Force, but I'm sure as hell going to try.

Twenty-five

BLISS

F I GENUINELY WANTED TO, Serenity couldn't stop me. But sitting here with her, our backs up against the bedframe, her arms coiled around me like a two-strand rope like our similar DNA, I decide I don't want to. It has nothing to do with wanting. The Temple doesn't let me want. Father doesn't let me want anything. I can't want this budding life in my belly. Serenity will see in the end. His arms will hold the child first. Not its…mother. I am not a mother. I am just a vessel. Force's vessel.

"Bliss…" Serenity rubs fingers into my hair, soothing clockwise motions. "Don't you see? It's a gift. Just like we were gifts to our mother. We still are!" she tries to persuade me, words leaving her mouth with more desperation than usual.

"I am no one's gift." Even as I speak the words, I find my belief in them dwindling. Not because of Serenity. Because of Luc. Because of what he's done. Serenity has given me words. He has given me…action. So has Serafina.

Shivering, I shake my head, injecting more force into my words this time. "When will you understand? There's no love in the Temple. Just hurt and pain and disappointment. There's no love left in the world, just lust." Lust that makes up a mountain of flesh, teeth, mouths, skin, sweat, bones…bodies.

"You're wrong, Bliss." Serenity cups my cheeks, her green eyes reminding me of our father's. Same intensity. But I see something else in the creases around them. I wonder why I never paid attention to them before. The expressions she wears. Father chooses each

124

one of his so carefully. But Serenity's are a kaleidoscope. Passion, compassion, sensitivity, anger, love…she can show them all within the timespan of a few moments. "I'm going to prove it to you," she says.

"How?"

"You're wrong about love. Nothing can hold it back. You know why? Because love is dynamite, and I'm going to blow your walls sky high until you feel it."

The only action I have left is to walk away from her. She bewilders me even more than Luc does. When she talks, all I hear is our father's voice. But her words aren't his. And they're not our mother's, either. I can't fathom where they come from. Maybe a different dimension. I smirk. Maybe she really is an alien. Or some magical fairy. Whatever the case, no amount of magic can get through my mountain. The sooner she learns that, the better. That's why I will keep this child. Eventually, she will stop fighting. Eventually, Father will wear her down. Serenity will become the new Temple director. She will become Father's Yang Legacy. Once this child is born and she sees how he possesses it, perhaps that will be her breaking point.

I return to my bedroom, but Queran stands outside the door, hands folded complacently in front of him, waiting. I forget he is here to prepare me for my interaction tonight. As soon as the fight was over, Father sent word of the client booking.

"My apologies, Queran. I know I was supposed to meet you in the artisan room, but could you prepare me in my room tonight?"

In answer, he extends a hand to the door with a slight but permitting nod.

"Thank you." After I unlock the door with my barcode, I step inside and make no delay to remove my clothes while he runs the bath water for me, then gathers up skin and hair products.

I am quieter than usual. My conversation with Serenity frequents my mind like an unwanted guest. I don't know what to make of it. I don't know what to make of her. For years, it was jealousy. Jealousy of the twin who robbed me of my oldest birthright. But I harnessed that jealousy because ultimately, it was not her fault. Instead, I wrapped the jealousy in bitterness to our mother for abandoning me. But that bitterness has long since ebbed to be replaced with genuine respect and surface affection for Serafina.

When Serenity chose Serafina over me, I allowed bitterness to breed.

It was easy when she reminded me of Father.

After all, my first impression of Serenity was one of disgust. Disgust for the way she'd captured Force's heart through her defiance and life zest despite everything I'd done to please him since childhood. Now, after everything, watching her defend our mother, watching her unbridled rage when Father slit Kerrick's throat, watching her respect for Luc, what she did for Sunshine…her and Sky's faithfulness and their continued rebellion against Father… Most of all, how she stopped asking me about leaving the Temple.

She makes me wonder.

Queran scrubs my back. He must register my silence because he points to the item sitting on the decorative shelf above the bathtub—the origami swan.

"Yes, Queran. Always so perceptive. She rattles the bones, doesn't she?"

He shakes his head, murmuring low. "Sweet girl."

"Yes, sweet. Sweet and spice and salt and savory and bitter."

Where she is all flavors wrapped together, I am no flavor. It doesn't bother me—it never has—but I've never once thought about it as much as I do now. Awareness brings attention to it, unwarranted attention. And I know why. I sense her now under my skin. An annoying, persistent tickle that won't leave. And I've succumbed to the realization that…I don't want her to. Especially now that she and I share a secret.

The selfish part of me wants her to break. Wants her to stay here in the Temple. Let her become Yang. Either way, it will happen. Unless she chooses to escape without me, it's just a matter of when. But I do care. No matter how much I deny it, I care. Because she is my little sister. That is why I've worked harder than ever with her. Because she shouldn't break. If there's one person in the world who could never and should never break, it's Serenity. For the first time, I own this. I want to protect her. That means getting her out of the Temple. She shouldn't be here. She doesn't belong here. It also means relying on someone I don't even want to talk to—someone who wants her out of the Temple just as much as I do if not more.

It looks like I'll get the chance to speak to him very soon.

Twenty-six

ToGethEr

SERENITY

I'M THERE FOR HIM WHEN he wakes. Considering what he looked like just a couple of hours ago, I'm almost astonished at how healthy he appears now. The only great advantage of Temple life.

Luc is already gone.

Hoping my actions won't disturb him too much, I creep onto the bed just next to Sky and nestle my head into his shoulder. My skirt gets caught in the bedrail. It was time to change out of the gown and return to normal Serenity.

"Am I dead?" Sky mumbles a moment later, nostrils flaring as he turns and breathes in the scent of my hair.

"Nope. And neither is Luc."

"Pity."

I let out a breathy chuckle because the one word is so laced in sarcasm. So, they did both agree to the plan to knock each other out. Soon enough, Bliss will tell Luc about the pregnancy. If he and Sky worked together once, they can do it again; I'm confident they'll both come up with a plan.

"At least we're together now," I remind him, my foot rubbing up and down his calf.

Sky shifts so both his arms can form a loop around my waist just before he murmurs, "Not free but together."

"I knew you'd win."

I feel his lips brush my hair. "With what you were wearing, course you did."

Crooking a smile, I tilt my neck so I can look up at him. "Sky?"

"Hmm?" He doesn't open his eyes, just settles into me more. "What now?"

"Sleep, silly girl." Yawning, he leans down more so his cheek rests on the top of my head. "And patience."

For now, I decide not to tell him about Bliss. Whether that's patience or just my enjoying the moment, I can't tell.

I don't really care.

Twenty-seven
Learning to Fly

BLISS

E WEARS NO BANDAGES WHEN he comes. Medical drones would have warned him he needs rest. His appearance confirms it between the inflamed patches of skin still healing from the procedure to the fatigue wilting his lids and wearing down his shoulders like heavy nightmares.

"Bliss." He speaks my name. Just the one word before approaching me, hand reaching out to cup my cheek. For the first time, I try being real with him. The first time I feel I can be real with anyone. So, I flinch. Not horribly so but enough to cause him to pause.

He isn't offended. Instead, he smiles. Training his eyes on mine, he dips his chin lower, eyes begging permission, and I purse my lips and inhale. And let it out. So many times, I've held my breath, banished my senses to the furthest regions of my mind. A double-sided coin. No one is allowed to feel in the Temple. Their bodies are not their own. Only the client may enjoy anything. And...if they can't feel, then the clients can never really touch them.

But I let Luc touch me.

Against my cheek, his palm is tender, but I sense the strength within his hand. The same strength he used in the arena. For me. But without the violence. No aggression. No dominance. No *violence*. In his eyes, I find no lust, no desire. Something else. His eyes perceive more than what I am on the surface. They are sugar-dipped spears, penetrating past Yin, past the faux Swan, past the tutu girl with pigtails and every other guise I've ever worn and—most of all—past the mountain of flesh and bone. It's almost painful—the way he looks at me. It's why my cheeks ache from the subtle tears that descend their agile slopes.

I try to pull away, but Luc summons me, "Bliss, no. Talk to me. What's going on? What are you feeling?"

I lick my lips, gaze at him. "Why does it matter to you what I feel, Luc? You got what you wanted. You saw who I am. Isn't that enough?"

Luc shakes his head. What more could he want from me? My lips part to speak.

Suddenly, he touches his fingers to my mouth to stop me. "I won't let anyone hurt you again, do you see? They can't touch you anymore."

"You're the only client now," I murmur against his fingers.

"Never a client," Luc denies. "You're not a performer. You're not a spectacle. You're not a tool for anyone's purpose or pleasure. You're a beautiful young woman, and no one reserves the right to treat you like manure. And that includes you, Bliss. Don't stop being real with me. Please be Bliss. I promise you I will remain simply…Luc." He removes his hand from my mouth, then places it on his chest.

"I-I…" Struggling to get the words out, I almost choke on them because the truth feels like a thousand shards of Temple glass pricking me on their way out of my throat. Lies taste better, easier to swallow. Not so easy to digest since they've become such a part of me. Somehow, I manage to finish. "I don't even know how to be myself. I have so many masks." And a piece of the mountain behind each one.

Luc smiles because he knows how much I am trying. "Then, we'll peel them back together. One by one. Day by day. Until there's nothing left but Bliss."

"What if I can't love?" I challenge him. "What if it's impossible?"

"Guess I'll have to take a leap of faith."

"And what if I can't catch you?"

"Not expecting you to." He slips his hand into mine. "I'd rather learn to fly with you instead."

130

"I've always wanted to fly."

I should tell him about the baby, but it would spoil the moment. It would spoil all of this. This isn't about the life inside me. Whatever else is happening, he sees *me*. If I were to tell him, it would ruin that. He wouldn't see just me anymore. He'd see the parts of himself inside me.

So, I let him sweep his arm around my shoulders and kiss the side of my head.

PART
Three

Twenty-eight

AccoUntaBilIty

SERENITY

FTER WAKING AN HOUR LATER with Sky's sweat clinging onto the ends of my dreams, I decide to weasel my way out of the bed. Let him sleep a little while longer. There's someone I need to see.

Catching a glimpse of myself in one of the hall mirrors, I snigger. I look like some crazed banshee with my wild curls all over the place, some sticking to the sides of my face, my blouse dangling just below my shoulders. Good.

Once reaching the door to his bedroom, I knock once, then twice. He responds after the second knock. Dressed in a black business suit, my father cracks his knuckles but regards me with a smile and a nod. Comfortable but no tricks. Perhaps he's out of them for the moment. That's when I notice the sprite light screen up against the far wall and the figure inside it, sitting at a great desk with hands folded in front of him, almost covering the country's seal.

Of course, my timing is impeccable: I just interrupted my father's meeting with the president.

"What do you need, daughter?" The last word is soft as Chantilly lace upon its exit.

"Just a few minutes of your time when you have them."

Without another word, my father turns to the screen behind him. With one eye blink, the live feed is disrupted. Licking my lips, I try not to acknowledge how Force just hung up on the president for me.

When he swings the door open, bidding me to enter, I don't hesitate. I'm not afraid of him. But I am afraid of what he could do…if he finds out about Bliss. There has to be some way of stopping him.

"Lovely décor," I scoff when I see the stuffed swans all over the room on various pedestals. As soon as I approach one with fanned-out wings and lift my finger to touch a feather, the swan moves. I almost leap back, catching my shriek, which stops in my mouth. The swan makes no sound. Nor does it leave the pedestal. Upon leaning in for a closer inspection of its vacant glass eyes, I realize my father must have equipped the taxidermy animals with some sort of motion-sensing tech. Why he wouldn't just use sprite lights is beyond me, but then again, my father prefers the morbid and macabre.

Mosaics of moving Skeleton Flowers adorn various walls while the chandelier above my head is in the shape of a great crystal yin-yang symbol, glowing from some luminescence.

"You said you only needed a few minutes, which is preferable," Force tells me, rolling up his cuffs. "I have an appointment soon."

"I'm surprised you haven't broken all these swan's necks by now," I quip, swinging a hand toward them.

Force sighs, dropping his arms to his sides, palms open. "No amount of failures on my part could make me want to break you, Serenity. Rest assured, my zeal for *reshaping* you is stronger than ever, but I know when to accept my losses. I have had far too many wins, and it was your turn for a change. I still hold the upper hand, and you have just given me a challenge with your bulky beau. The day will come when I will be the utmost importance in your eye."

I almost snort, swallowing the words because I still need to know something first. "You'll still keep our bargain?"

Force nods, removing his necktie. "No harm will come to your beau, and he will remain in the Penthouse as your new security guard. I will have to instruct him on a few of our rules, of course."

"What about Bliss?" I remind him of our previous deal.

"Yes, yes." Force drapes the tie across a nearby chair, undoes his collar. "Luc has an all-access pass to Mara, free of any other clients."

"No, I meant the whippings."

"Yes, eight months, whip-free. But your training will contin-ue without her. Tomorrow night, we will return to the Breakable Room for our father/daughter time."

I chew on my lower lip, disgusted by how he phrases it. He probably has something else special in mind. At least Bliss will be safe during her pregnancy. Or at least much of it. I have eight months to figure out another plan to carry her through the rest of it. Or Sky will.

"Tomorrow, you and your sister will have another interaction," Force tells me just as he tugs off his socks, discarding them to the floor. I'm almost disappointed by how normal his feet look. No misshapen digits, no extra ones, no grotesque toenails. He even smells like rich cologne and appealing body odor. Unfortunately, he's also handsome. Even in his bedroom with no audience but me, Force is still beguiling from his high neck and proud chin to his cheekbones so sharp they could make a diamond bleed.

"Do you have any exhibits planned for me?" I cross my arms over my chest, eying one of the dancing Skeleton Flower mosaics off to my right.

"Would you like one?" Force grins, mimicking my stance, toy-ing with me.

I sigh, start to fiddle with my hair. "It's been a while since the last murder. I was wondering if you'd changed your mind."

"I've been considering it. As you know…" My father reaches out to catch a lock of my hair. Amuses himself with just a few of my curls before continuing, "You are my most prized possession, and the thought of losing you would destroy me."

"Get to the point," I say through gritted teeth.

"Perhaps I will arrange one soon. A safe one. An announce-ment will be made immediately, and your exhibit will commence this weekend."

I can't help the anticipation that rises within me, causing me to rock onto my tiptoes, which doesn't escape Force's notice. The thought of more crowds objectifying me, watching what should be simple, private moments, should disgust me. But my curiosity wants to know more. What costume it will be this time, what technology will be used, how long I will get to remain underwater, etc.

"Now, if you'll excuse me…" Force unbuttons his shirt more, gesturing a hand to the door where a knock occurs just a moment later. His brain interface is monitoring the hallways.

My mother's presence in the doorway shouldn't surprise me. Not after all this time, but the mere sight of her standing in the same room as my father clots the room with disgust and makes it difficult to breathe. Erratic, staccato lightning crackles pulse up and down my spine when he covers her mouth with his. Just before I leave, he informs me, "By the way, Serenity, over the winter, I'll have some upcoming overseas trips to take. I trust you and Bliss will be able to look after yourselves."

My smile doesn't shows on the outside, but I'm beaming inside. On my way out, I knock over one of my father's prized swans, hearing its neck crack. In the wake of Force's laughter, I slam the door behind me.

Twenty-nine
Flying

BLISS

"*L*UC, WHERE ARE YOU TAKING me?"

I've been blindfolded before but never for something like this. Blindfolds always come with gags and restraints and involve me never leaving my room. I'm not certain how I feel about this...Luc leading me through hallways after our elevator ride to an unknown floor. By now, Father should know I've left the Penthouse, which is never done unless he's my escort. With his interface, he can track our signatures; he'll know Luc took me outside my boundaries.

"I told you. A Temple Tour."

"If there's anything you want to experience with me, you know we have VirtuRooms that can synchronize our sensations."

I sense Luc leaning in closer, his breath hovering just above my ear. "I prefer an even closer experience."

Whatever he's referring to, the joke is certainly on me. Over the years, I've participated in just about every fantasy experience one can possibly imagine. Naturally, the VirtuRoom fantasies accompanying a private interaction cost more, so Father reserves those for foreign dignitaries and political powers. It makes me wonder if Luc considered this earlier but couldn't afford it until now—thanks to his stalemate of a fight a few nights ago—or if this is a spontaneous decision.

When he pauses, I nearly bump into him. At least I haven't tripped once. My feet have always been sure of themselves. Perhaps that is Father's doing, considering all the dance lessons and poise training he assigned to me during my childhood years. Now, I am a master over every part of my physicality. Serenity is the opposite. She's a master of her own heart. I'm learning to use mine.

A door opens before us, and I hear what seems to be wind rushing through a tube. A skyway, perhaps?

"Welcome, Director Aldaine," a feminine voice of silk-wrapped flower petals says to Luc. "Everything is ready for you."

"Thank you, Miss Maynard."

No more words are exchanged, which must be due to Luc's instructions to maintain the surprise. With his hand around my waist, Luc leads me into the tube where the wind grows intense and I can sense the drop in temperature.

Luc's other hand joins his first. "Do you trust me, Bliss?"

"Do I have a choice?"

"Always."

Licking my lips, I debate with the voices in my head united only to create a paradox. One resembles Father's voice, reminding me I don't have a choice but the ones he's given me, reminding me everyone else's choice matters before mine, which means I will never have my own. Another voice, which sounds like Luc, Serenity, and my mother all wrapped up together reminds me of their love. And if they can love me, so can I. They remind me I am worthy of a choice. And one final voice whispers in between the warring ones.

She says, *I want a choice.*

"I trust you," I finally utter. Even if I'm shaking, even if I'm shuddering, I've kept my voice steadier than all the bones inside me. Steady enough to shake them and cause them to rattle, breaking them down to allow trust and choice to root in my heart.

After pausing for a few more breaths, I feel a small flap of air before Luc takes my hand and places my palm on his chest. Naked chest. "Just so you know I stripped first." I can hear the smile in his voice right before he removes my shirt while maintaining the blindfold. It's honestly endearing he felt the need to go first and even to tell me. It's not like I have any sort of discomfort as it extends to my modesty.

He only strips me down to my underclothes before assuming hold of one of my legs and coaxing them into something soft, elastic, and form-fitting. Some sort of jumpsuit that closes at the midline of my body and encases me like a devouring cocoon all the way up to my throat. When Luc's leg brushes mine, I understand he is wearing another jumpsuit. Then, he places a thick strip just across my forehead. It sends slight vibrating pulses into my skin. After which follows something small placed in my ear.

"Now, for the harness."

Harness?

First, Luc attaches it to me. It takes a few minutes to secure around the upper half of my body. Next, he tugs me toward him so his chest molds to my back. That's when I understand it's a double harness.

"Time for the big one," he murmurs right before I hear something mechanical. It attaches itself to Luc's back because I feel the pressure and the strong stance he must maintain as it fixes to his harness.

Luc's hand brushes against mine as he raises it into the air. Seconds after, I hear a great door opening. Wind becomes a battering ram threatening to catapult my body backward, but Luc was prepared and remains strong. Panic woven with astonishment throttles my insides as I realize what Luc is doing, where I am, and where he's taking me.

"Ready?" he murmurs, soft as a sunset fondling the night.

I have never left the Temple.

There is no time to tell him I don't know before Luc leaps and we rocket onto air currents *outside* the Temple. The inertia is enough to remove my blindfold, discarding it like black smoke, which I imagine is just what Luc wanted. The open air and the cityscape swirling below me is almost too much to take. Even though the Temple has its own air-filtration system, everything inside still seems artificial. Just as I've been designed. For the first time in my life, someone is giving me something…real.

"Spread your arms, Bliss!" Luc must raise his voice to compete with the air as he sails around the great Temple city inside a scraper. Through the windows, I can see people flocking to witness the Temple flight tour. They aren't necessarily rare, but they always draw a crowd with many wishing they had the ability to afford the activity.

Overwhelmed by everything, I glance up to view the wings behind Luc.

Noticing my gaze, he smiles. Thanks to an ear implant, we can still hear one another's words beyond the wind. "These wings have been designed to most precise specifications to mimic a bird's movements. We can manipulate the air currents around us. So, if I do this…" Suddenly, Luc angles the wings to the left, launching my stomach up into my throat before pitching the wings on a plunging elevator ride back to where my innards belong. If I didn't have such a strong stomach, I'd have thrown up by now. Every sensation is extraordinary. I wonder how strong my stomach will be for this pregnancy.

"How is the pressure not affecting me?" I ask.

"Depressurization strip." He taps the one on his forehead once before asking me, "Are you going to stop asking questions now and spread your arms?"

I smile.

Luc has given me wings. It's time for me to enjoy them. To enjoy something my body can feel. The notion is so ridiculous, but I don't think about that. I think about the wind beating, my arms spreading, my heart opening, and my soul wanting. As soon as I stretch my arms to the sides, wind unleashes a steady force all around them, and I have to wonder if it feels this way for birds. For a few minutes, Luc aims for a variety. From spiraling upward to simply free-falling with the wings as a shield from the barreling wind. The suits protect us and are climate controlled, but I can still sense the gooseflesh erupting from beneath my skin like thousands of miniature rockets.

Because I'm allowing myself to feel, I have to work harder to control everything, but that doesn't last long. It crumbles like freckles escaping skin. Soon enough, I am weeping, tears forming a parade on my cheeks. A second later, I am throwing my head back in fits of unrestrained laughter. When I open my eyes, Luc's beam sails into me—a golden river coupling with mine.

His lips part, and mine follow until they arrive at a meeting point. Kissing in midair is new. Sensations form pirouetting clouds and earthy landslides inside me. As soon as Luc breaks the kiss and changes direction until we fly parallel to the Temple, sailing upward to the Penthouse, I discover I don't want to stop.

But Luc shifts to the side, swinging around the telltale curve of the Temple, remaining close to the glass. And that is when I see him. Brows sinking lower than anchors dropped in the ocean. Nostrils flaring. Anger unflattering his features like a scar. But the figure standing next to him smiles, my mother's an eerie reflection of mine. Eerie since I am so unfamiliar with the true smile I wear now. At any time, I can summon one million false smiles, but this one feels different. It feels…good.

Luc pivots the winged suit one level lower. To Serenity's room. There they are. Intertwined as they normally are. But when we hover just outside the window, Serenity leaps to her feet, knocking into Skylar as she leaves the couch, tripping over her skirts in the process. I giggle at the sight of my sister scrambling toward the window. We can't hear one another, but every part of her is giddy from her sparkling frosted green eyes to her hands curled over the glass to the zeal radiating from her beam—so great the corners of her lips have pulled tightly to each side. One hand in his pocket and a casual gait, Sky approaches Serenity from behind, nods once to his brother, and gives us a thumbs-up sign. As Luc begins to lower us, Serenity lifts both hands, waving them frantically. Lifting my own hand, I flutter it. Another unfamiliar gesture for me. Waving is not something I typically do.

Come to think of it, neither is flying.

Thirty

Need

SERENITY

'M STILL JUMPING UP AND down as they fly downward, corkscrewing through the air—a Luc and Bliss-shaped whirlwind of wings and jumpsuits and dark curls ravishing the wind.

"I still don't believe it!" I exclaim as Sky wraps his arms around my waist, breathing in the scent of my hair.

"You want to try it?" Sky's voice is more curious than anything.

I shake my head. "Tempting, but I think I'll keep my feet on the ground."

"For once," Sky finishes, squeezing me a little snugger. "Hmm." His chin lets up from my head.

"What?"

"Just a thought."

"Going to tell me?"

At first, Sky debates, head tilting to each side before announcing, "Not quite yet. Need to run it past Luc. Don't want to get your hopes up."

"Fair enough."

When he moves toward the window and braces his hands against the glass while looking out at the sunset, I can't help but admire him. The way his muscles instinctively flex, the stubborn man bun that always seems to stay bound unlike my curls, the pride leeching from his shoulders and jaw. Most of all, I love his eyes. Dark rosewood having a love affair with mahogany gold.

"Careful," Sky warns, the edge of his voice catching onto that beguiling smile I love. "Your eyes might smoke if you stare any harder, Ser."

Once he turns around, Sky winks. A moment later, everything changes. His countenance, his gait, even his crooked smile. More serious, though not dangerous, the way his irises deadpan with mine and his firm jaw still strikes a stunned cord within me. A muscle twinges in that jaw. It's not just desire. It's *need*.

Need from his fingers coaxes into my cheeks when he cups them, when he drags me closer until his lips press against mine. Hungering and warm, Sky invades my mouth until we taste each other. His hands roam the edges of my blouse, fingertips on my bare stomach, leaving sparked patterns there. I inhale when his lips slide down my neck, one of his hands sinking lower. Until his mouth rubs my shoulder, pauses on the tip of the Yang tattoo there. And then, Sky pulls away, walks the three steps to the window, and smacks a hand against it. Both his hands plant themselves on the glass. Slow but focused, Sky hunches over, leaning toward the window just as I approach him from behind, licking the taste of him from my swollen mouth.

"Sky?" I touch his shoulder.

He flinches before turning to say, "We've got to get out of here."

Thirty-one

Learning to Love

BLISS

*I*F WHAT I'VE EXPERIENCED IS an emotional high, I can't help but wonder where the low is. I keep expecting it. So much so, I'm turning my head to see if it's spying on me from around the corner, just waiting to pounce. But Luc's hand squeezing mine summons me back to reality each time, reminding me of this warmth kindling inside me. Something I haven't felt in... years.

If I am the Yin, the moon reflecting the sunlight, this must be the first time I've ever truly felt sunlight. For so long, my life has been defined by the dark side of the moon. Now, it's time to welcome the light.

Too afraid to return to my bedroom because Father might be waiting after everything that happened, I ask Luc if we can go to his instead.

"You're probably hungry after all that." He escorts me to his bedroom where he promptly orders a meal for each of us along with some strawberry scones and clotted cream. Any fresh fruit is a welcome pleasure.

I can't help but smile when the food arrives. Sushi. Father never permits me to order something this decadent. My bedroom menu is quite limited.

"I thought you would enjoy eating it as opposed to having it eaten off you," Luc points out before sliding into the chair opposite me.

He doesn't pull my chair out for me, for which I'm grateful. I

145

prefer to do some things on my own.

Just then, Luc turns to his arm and summons his interface. "Just a moment. Looks like my brother is sending me a message."

The holographic image of Skylar appears, no bigger than my fist.

"Congratulations on your flight. You're officially an owl now."

I smile at the sight of Serenity's lover strap his hands over his hips, muscles bulging as if he's trying to appear intimidating. It's rather cute, considering he's only four inches tall to us.

"Look, we need to talk," Skylar tells Luc.

Glancing to me, Luc hesitates before squaring his shoulders. "Can it wait?"

"Can getting us the hell out of here wait?"

Luc sighs, discontent creasing his mouth. Then, his brows sink lower.

Only one brow of Skylar's lifts. "Seriously? You're trying the death glare on me over transmission?"

A low rumble in Luc's throat sends my stomach on a little carousel ride. He doesn't want to leave me.

"Meet me in the security center."

"Why there?"

Sky rolls his eyes. Drops his hands from his hips. "Cause it's secure, moron." One click from his monitor and he's gone.

Grumbling under his breath, Luc rises and circles the table. "I'll return as soon as possible. Feel free to keep eating without me." He cups my shoulder once, rubbing his thumb across my bare skin there.

Smiling, I palm the back of his hand. "I will." I've been smiling a lot today. Except this one doesn't take any effort. As simple as a bird in flight. All my past ones have required effort, required practice, and have had to keep bile back behind the fortress of my teeth.

That bile rises as soon as Luc is gone and the door to his room opens to welcome my father. Because every room welcomes him. Nothing is off limits. That truth guts me again and again with the reminder that neither am I. Today was just a mirage, wasn't it? I should have known it couldn't last forever.

"You left the Temple today, Mara." Father wraps honey around his poison as he approaches me, hands folded behind his back, every vertebra in his spine tight.

"I didn't know until we were outside," I try to explain.

"And it certainly appeared as though you were enjoying yourself," he points out, swinging into the opposite chair and sampling Luc's meal, unhindered by so trite a thing as manners.

"Pleasing clients is what I've been trained to do."

One side of Father's mouth curls while his hand clenches into a fist. "Do not speak to me of training, child. Not when I gave you everything. I granted you the tools to survive in this world. Tools you lacked from birth."

Yes. He trained me how to take a beating, how to look sexy, how to smile and flirt and moan and cry and scream and bat my eyes at all the right times. And he gave me every lesson under the sun from dancing to singing to keeping me his pretty thing in a cage forever.

"The smile you wore today was not for a client," Father clarifies, spearing the table with his fork and creating squealing noises across its surface that remind me of a moaning creature. "It was for a lover."

"He is...different." To label Luc as merely "different" cheapens him, but it's all I can think to say in this moment.

Shoulders tensing, Force reclines in his seat. "Perhaps I underestimated Aldaine and his tricks. Oh, my poor Yin. You've fallen prey and wrapped yourself up in his fantasy. But you have forgotten... There can only be one fantasy for you in the Temple."

Yes, Father's fantasy. His Yin. Nothing more.

Somehow, I stand. Before I even understand what I'm doing, I'm on my feet. Taller than Father. Above him. A rule that has never been broken...until now.

"All I am is a possession to you." I steel my nerves, but my fingers itch to play with each other. "That's all you've ever seen me as."

Father rises to confront me, fork not leaving his hand. "And you think Luc is some paragon, Mara? You are so gullible. He is just a man like them all." Father circles me. His breath is hot on the nape of my neck. Hot as Sulphur strengthened by brandy. "He may share your bed, defend you from other predators so he may keep you all to himself, and take you on little flying trips, but rest assured, you are still nothing but my Yin. My dark slut. My broken whore child."

When Father cups my chin, assuming control of it, I need all my strength to jerk away. "You can call me whatever you want. It doesn't matter."

"Hmm…" He narrows his brows. "Looks like I definitely underestimated him. Perhaps it is time to remind you of who you are." Father lowers his hand to his belt. Retrieves a small compartment. No. It's his laser belt. One he uses only for special occasions.

"Remove your shirt, Mara," he directs, taking a step away to prepare himself.

I inhale, hold my breath, and revert to my method of sucking in the pain, numbing myself, preparing myself. But then I remember Luc's words. I always have a choice. No one reserves the right to treat me like this.

And I remember Serenity's dynamite love.

So, I remind myself to breathe and exhale. "No."

"No?"

I shake my head.

Father steps forward again, juts the laser whip right under my chin. It stings, warming the skin there, but it doesn't have any force behind it. Only a warning first. "Trust me, Mara, you don't want to keep testing me. I will make you bleed. Show you who is truly in control. Show you what you are if you've forgotten. That petty director and his pretty eyes have bewitched you, made you forget. But I will remind you, Mara. I will remind you again and again—even if it takes me all night and your blood stains the floor. You will never resist me again."

"She might not, but I will."

I swing around to see Serenity standing in the doorway. I sink my head because this is the worst thing that could happen. This is how he will break her. I will be his tool. Not slitting Kerrick's throat, not using her love for our mother against her, not the client interactions, not pitting Luc and Sky against each other. How could I have not seen this? My father is right. I have forgotten. Forgotten I am never enough. Forgotten it's always my fault. My sister's broken spirit will be my fault. Before, she and I shared a common goal of keeping our mother safe. We could survive Force.

But now, he will divide us.

In using me against her, Father will have the power he needs. And he will use it to twist her into who he wants her to be. She will finally fit his mold. All because of me. If I were smart, I never would've talked to her, just kept my distance like I'd planned. How could I have known she would care this much? It is why love makes you weak, why hope brings you down, every time. Now, she will understand that, but Serenity can't become a numb stone like me. She is too much fire. She will become our father. And I will lose her forever. And so will our mother, so will Sky, so will Luc, and so will everyone who has ever loved her.

All because of me.

Thirty-two

ArrAngeMents

SERENITY

"GET THE HELL AWAY FROM my sister," I order Force, fueling my eyes with as much lightning as I can.

"Serenity, just go!" Bliss cries, gesturing me away before turning to our father. "Send her away, please. I'll do as you say." She kneels before him, hands reaching up to her sleeves, ready to bare her back to his demon eyes.

"No," I refuse, shaking my head before down dropping to my knees beside her. "Stop this, Bliss. This isn't you."

"Don't you understand?" she whispers, one opal tear dripping off her cheek. "He's already won."

"He can only win if you give him the power to," I try to convince her, but Bliss isn't in the frame of mind to listen. Force has turned her into a little girl again. But I'll be damned if I let him hurt her, especially with my unborn niece or nephew inside her.

Force cackles at me, even covering his mouth and leaning over a little, so amused at my presence. I wish I could strike that smile off his face. Feed it to my shark.

"We had an arrangement, Force," I interrupt his cackling, reminding him of our deal. "Original agreement was no whipping or even speaking to our mother if Bliss agreed to take the whippings. And then, we adjusted the deal. No whippings for Bliss for nine months in return for me meeting all your suitors. I did." Lifting my chin, I begin to adopt our father's movements by circling him. "And Sky passed all your little tests, too. Training will not involve Bliss for at least seven months."

150

I glance over to see my sister with her hands on the floor, but her eyes turned up to me. Horror scrawls all over her blue irises, darkening them to a violet that reminds me of nightshade. What does she know that I don't?

Raising his fist to his jaw, Force uncurls his fingers to stroke his jaw before nodding. "Quite right, daughter. A deal is a deal. But I have neglected your training as of late and rest assured, it will commence tomorrow night. After your exhibit."

What exhibit is he planning now? I wonder, but one thing at a time. "If you're going to try to have me whip Sky, you're wasting your time. He's already felt the whip from my hand. You can't hurt us that way."

"Wouldn't dream of it, my dear." Force reaches out to grip my hand in his, jerking it up so he can kiss my knuckles. "I look forward to tonight."

Thirty-three

BrOtheR TiMe

SKY

"YOU MUST HAVE BEEN DROPPED as a baby. No wonder I was our father's favorite," Luc quips as I outline the plan.

"Stick to your day job," I advise. "You suck at sarcasm." When Luc pauses with no clever comebacks of his own, I rise to my full height and extend a hand to the volu screens before us. "Look, this can work. As long as we disable the shield, this is doable."

"And how do you intend to get the equipment without Force's knowledge?"

"Same way I got Sunshine out."

While swiping the screen and zooming in on the upgraded security of the vent shaft—of course Force put in lasers after he found out about his mole rat—I already start drawing up my virtual map of the vent and elevator shafts. Despite Luc having access to the entire Temple, I can't know if that includes the Centre. Perhaps he did weeks ago, but after everything that has happened since then, it's not likely. Unfortunately, I still need him.

Luc sighs, shifting his weight. "Am I supposed to guess or is it your intent to share this knowledge?"

"Patience, pretty boy." I launch into the program's code, then wave at my brother. "Give me your arm."

"Excuse me?"

"Just relax." I twist to see him. "I'm not going to bite it."

After rolling up his sleeve with lips tight from annoyance,

152

Luc extends his arm toward me. "What a comfort."

"Get the interface turned on," I direct, then synchronize my program's code with the interface. "There." I swipe the air in front of me, shutting down the screen.

"What was all that about?" Luc asks while following me to the elevator.

"Just hacked your interface so it gets security access now," I out him, gesturing for him to use his barcode to access the elevator.

"You realize I already had security access…"

The elevator doors open as I retort, "Not for the Centre."

"You hacked the Centre?"

"In a manner of speaking," I say proudly as the doors close behind us. "Now comes the hard part. Give Force your best death glare." I jerk my head toward the microscopic security cameras positioned in the corners. Most I can do is flip off the asshole, but Luc sports his infamous stare down. "Gotta admit, it's pretty damn effective," I commend him.

"Careful," Luc warns as I press a mid-Temple floor. "You're in danger of complimenting me."

"Wouldn't want that now, would we?" I wink and wait, already predicting how Force will react. And he does.

The elevator careens to a halt, shutting down along with the security cameras. It'll read as a malfunction to Force, that his shutting down the elevator caused a glitch that affected the cameras.

"What just happened?" I hear something unrecognizable in my brother's voice. Fear? No…but treading on the boundary of that.

"Now comes the fun part. We gotta move fast." I brace my shoes on the railing of the elevator, grip onto the small cracks on the ceiling, and hoist myself up to give the hatch the punch it needs to open. After getting on top of the elevator, I stretch a hand down to pull my brother up.

"Perhaps it's not the best time to tell you this…" Luc's voice is strained on his ascent, but my growl overlaps it as he continues, "…but I'm claustrophobic."

"A contract killer with claustrophobia." Groaning a little, I leap from the elevator to the shaft ladder, trusting my brother to follow. The ladder clangs from every footstep, and I swear the tune sounds like the funeral march. "Any other dark, unsettling secrets you want to share? Both got daddy issues obviously." I glance up to see him jump onto the ladder above me.

"Wouldn't mind one or two from you," Luc challenges, calling down to me.

Two other elevators whiz by on their journeys to different levels. We'd only be in trouble if the one closest to us started moving, but Force won't do that quite yet. His meeting with the North Korean ambassador is too important to bother with his rebellious Penthouse security.

"I got anger issues," I return, raising my voice above the whirring of the elevators behind us.

Luc pauses and breathes a few times. "Never would've guessed."

"Hey, not all of us can be smooth and controlled like their older brother."

"Half," Luc reminds me, and I can't help but chuckle.

Doesn't take us long to reach the level we need. It's not a door but another hatch, which I open with my Skeleton laser key, which can manually unlock any door with no signs of tampering.

"Time to get in the vent shaft. It'll lead us straight to the Centre skyway tunnel reserved for security."

"Crawl space, I wager?"

"See? You can be smart." I start to climb up, noting the criss-crossed lasers before the corner a few feet down from us. Already sensing their heat and humming from this distance, I wait for my brother to get into the crawl space behind me and then grab my volu screen, which is hooked up to Luc's interface—and shut down the lasers.

"Impressive," Luc remarks.

"Now that was a compliment if I've ever heard one."

"Where do you get all those nifty gadgets?" he asks as he starts crawling behind me.

I shrug as if it's obvious. "Sanctuary. Helped revolutionize a few myself. Not that I'm *bragging*."

"Be you ever so humble."

When my brother's hand connects with my leg, I turn around and snap, "Luc, if your face so much as bumps my ass, I'll turn the lasers back on and leave you here."

"I assure you, *brother*, if that were to happen, I'd likely kill myself first."

Just so we understand one another. I double check the time. We got maybe another fifteen minutes before Force is out of his meeting and comes to check on us. Up ahead, the shaft dead ends at another hatch. I reach for my Skeleton key again. Luc is more than happy to drop into the tunnel beside me, panting with a sheen of sweat on his brow.

"You survived?" I pat his shoulder twice before retrieving another couple of "gadgets" from my pack. First, I grab my brother's other wrist and slap on an electronic strip across his barcode.

"What the—"

"Barcode transformer." I motion as it starts to shift the digital ink. "Hurts like hell," I say above Luc's sudden growl and flaring nostrils. "But it does the trick. Only temporarily, so we don't have long," I add before slapping my own strip on and hissing through my teeth at the pain. Feels like a needle set on fire coming up from the inside of my wrist and taking a ride on my veins like they're seesaws.

"We'll need these, too." I slap on a small, circular object that adheres to Luc's chest, chuckling as it projects a volumetric face overlapping his own. "Just enough to get us past the entry cameras. We like to call it the camo cloak."

"Enjoying yourself?" Luc inquires while curling one corner of his lip back.

"Immensely. You look like the love child of Larke and a French poodle." Time for my camo cloak.

"Chihuahua meets zombie corgi," Luc says, attempting his own insult.

I adjust my sack, fixing it to my belt again. "Time to go. Play it cool. You're good at that."

We round a few corners of the tunnel before we encounter another guard.

Without glancing up from the reader in his hand, he barks, "New recruit training second door on the right."

"Training?" Luc glances to me when I take the third door on the left instead.

"Told you we needed to go right away. Training and initiations are the best times. Lower guard movements on the floor." I close the door behind me, which thuds with what I hope is not like a symbolic drum beat. This might be our only chance of escaping the Temple.

As soon as we enter the hallway, a white bandage in and of itself, I lead Luc past a couple of nurse's stations. No one pays the security any mind. We're here to be mostly invisible except in the case of threats.

The camo cloak thrums on my chest. "Running out of juice."

I wish we had the latest upgrades, which last longer, but the Sanctuary makes do with what it can. We need to get to the room now to turn them off so we can save the power for the trip back. Just a few more steps. After waiting a moment or two for a nearby nurse to help a patient amble down the hall with a built-in fluid injector attached to her arm, we are free to enter Maud's room. After which, I turn off the camo cloak and promptly curse.

"Whoa!" One of the startled girls nearly leaps out of her bed. Four girls total. Three I'd wager are in their second trimester.

"Wait," the brunette from the cot on the other side of the room cries, warning the first girl. "Don't you dare press the nurse's button, Calla, or I'll shave your head in your sleep!"

Luc leans over and murmurs, "Not your plan, I wager?"

Shaking my head, I resist the urge to groan as the brunette meanders toward me. Her ombré skin is healthy thanks to her pregnancy—almost glows under the light streams in the ceiling, which are designed to mimic sunlight and inject vitamin D into their bodies. Two other girls with dark hair, one curly and one straight but both with olive-colored skin, start to lose their timidity and move toward us. But it's clear the brunette is the leader. Calla, the only blonde, still remains on her bed up against the far window, hands clasped around the arches of her feet.

"Just look at them," the brunette gushes, her body swaying as she approaches us.

"Maple, you know we're not supposed to fraternize with the—" one of the dark-haired girls reminds her, but Maple interrupts her.

"Clove, just shut up! We've been stuck in this pitiful room for the past four months." She starts to rub her palms together. "This is the first excitement we've had in forever. And I never got clients like this!"

Luc steps forward. "Our apologies for the intrusion, ladies. But we are not here as clients."

Maple snorts, tossing her long waves back. "Obviously. Guards don't go to the Centre as clients. Seriously, you think they want to screw this?" She cups her swollen belly.

Clove nudges Maple's side. "Just check him out!" she croons low but enough for me to overhear.

"I know! Get a load of those muscles. Why can't the nurses look like him?"

My inner self is smiling, but a stray thought makes me consider the irony and how the roles have been reversed. In a general sense. Can't say I blame the girls.

"Please forgive our mistake and we will be on our way," Luc adds, but I have a feeling it won't be that simple. I realize if we want to get out of here quicker, it's better to just play along at this point.

So, while Maple starts talking again, I scroll through the directory on my volu-screen and search for Maud's name, discovering her room was moved. Don't care why. Our meeting will be cut short. Won't have much more time than giving her a short message and instructions for what we need.

"Calla..." Maple addresses the timid girl in the corner of the room, her voice one-part soft syrup and one-part dragon's blood—the kind that lusts after treasure. And it looks like we're the pot of gold today. "Be a dear and keep your finger on the nurse's button... if these boys don't behave, you'll press it."

"Maple, you got a Temple trouble rep," Clove informs her, but her eyes continue to shift to my brother, turning into scoops whenever they do. "If it comes down to it, who do you think they'll believe? Some Breakable?"

"No, but they'll still get in a lot of trouble. Probably suspended or fired."

In our case, it could be much worse.

Maple licks her lips as she begins to circle us. I detect the wounds behind the layer of cynicism in her eyes. For just that brief moment when she blinks.

"Don't be shy," she directs the two of us, winding around to our fronts. "Big guy first. Lose the shirt."

Shrugging, I grip my Temple tunic with one hand and tug it over my head, draping it over my arm. Out of the corner of my eye, I can see my brother, eyes so shocked I wait for them to start spinning on a top.

"Your turn, beautiful." Maple thrusts her head toward Luc. "I know Clove's pretty eager."

Luc's eyes roll to mine. By his clenched teeth, I can tell he's biting back a groan. "Is this seriously happening?"

"Only gonna hurt your pride, sweetheart," I tell him. "Just go with it." I roll my shoulders, shake out my arms, and then decide to give Maple a good show.

"Holy all things merciful," Maple gushes, waving her hand in front of her face as Luc removes his own tunic. "It's enough to give one the vapors," she remarks on the sight of my muscles flexing before approaching me and curling her fingernail across one of my biceps. As slight to me as a mouse's tail. "After I'm done pumping out this mole rat inside of me, come visit me in the Temple. You could do me for free. Well…almost free."

One side of my mouth turns up as I grin down at her. "Appreciate the invitation, but I got a girl. Pretty special one." Pretty fucking crazy one, too.

"That's a pity," she murmurs, voice like maple candies as she closes in on me.

"I'll take this one any day," Clove comments upon eyeing Luc. "Just get a load of those cheekbones, yum! They could give lasers a run for sharpness."

My brother raises a finger before Clove can swoop in with a kiss. "I…uh…have a girl, too. More importantly, she has me."

Clove just laughs, her smoke-soft dark hair diving to her waist. "There's no way you two are guards."

Maple shakes her head in agreement. "Not a chance. Guys don't "have girls" these days. Especially not Temple guards. You boys up to some trouble?" Maple winds her way around to my back, rubs a finger up my spine, and I take a deep breath and bite the inside of my lip.

"Not the kind that will hurt anyone," I clarify, flicking my gaze to Calla, who takes her thumb off the call button and starts to ease off the bed, though she still doesn't approach. Can't imagine the horrors she must have experienced from my gender. Any of them for that matter.

"Good luck, handsome."

I turn my head just in time to see Maple smack my ass. I don't take it personally. Just tug my shirt on. It's time to find Maud.

Thirty-four

SiSter TiMe

BLISS

"*I* CAN'T BELIEVE IT!" SERENITY EXCLAIMS after the device is turned on.

Pursing my lips, I watch the sprite light scene projected before me. In a way, I am jealous because Serenity sees them on the device directly over my belly. Later, I will relive this experience with our mother. Of course I would follow in her footsteps.

No bigger than plums, the twins create a yin-yang shape, but I don't reflect too long on the irony. Fingers and toes, butterfly-wing soft and so translucent they remind me of lace. Rosy veins branch out from inside their heads. So unthinkable to consider how their brains have already developed. Does one resent the other for sharing their space? No, not these two. Were Serenity and I ever curled up together this way? We certainly didn't grow up together this way. I was half her size or less throughout Serafina's entire pregnancy, only growing into the body I am today thanks to Father's medical advances. All part of my debt. Hmm…

Perhaps if I gave him just one…maybe it would be enough. Is my freedom worth the life of one of my children? It certainly was in the moment for Serafina. Then, I remember. They're not mine. Just like Serenity was stolen and her family lived as fugitives. Everyone in the Temple belongs to Force. I will never leave. We will never leave. Even if Skylar could get us all out, which is inconceivable, it wouldn't take Father long to find us this time. Not even the Sanctuary can help us.

After tapping the device screen a few times, Serenity gestures to the twins and asks, "You want to know?"

Biting on my lower lip, I hesitate for a moment. Why should I be concerned or interested in their gender either way? It's likely they're both girls. It would be just like fate to ordain it that way. But a fleeting thought has me wondering. Wondering what they will look like. Will they look more like me or Luc? Are they identical or fraternal?

So, I lick my lips and offer a tentative nod.

Serenity taps the screen once more, which signals the device to offer the information in a feminine but robotic voice.

"Fraternal fetuses. One male. One female. Eleven weeks development. Size of a kumquat. Heart has been beating for—"

Serenity turns off the information dump, smiling with her shoulders easing. Relaxed? I don't think I've ever seen my sister relax before.

"They're so wiggly..." She drags one finger across the screen, marveling at the twins as their fingers wiggle, one hand bumping the other's arm. Still, I feel nothing inside me. "Look, I think it's the boy. He's hiccupping."

I can't begin to imagine what it will be like when I can feel them move, kick, or hiccup for the first time. Sighing but saying nothing, I turn off my sprite light screen and settle into my bed. I don't ask how Serenity managed to get the Peek-a-Boo device. Her Yang tattoo gets her access to just about everything. But if Father still tracks her movements, it won't be long before he asks her about the device. Unless he has other preoccupations. Serenity doesn't turn off the Peek-a-Boo yet, but her eyes do careen toward me instead of the babies. For once.

"Have you told Mom yet?"

I shake my head. "I haven't even told Luc yet. I need...time."

"Are you okay?"

"Not as okay as you obviously." I tried to stem the snap in my voice, but I guess it didn't work too well because Serenity lowers her head, folding her lips before shutting down the Peek-a-Boo.

"We'll figures this out together."

Lifting my chin, I shake my head. "There's nothing to figure out, Serenity. You still don't understand. Serafina had the advantage of surprise. Father had no idea. He won't let it happen again."

"Force doesn't control everything. He doesn't control me. And he doesn't have to control you if you don't let him."

The past murders are proof Force doesn't control everything in the Temple. But I can't fathom a world where he doesn't exist. Serenity may have an implant in her body, but Father will always have his implant in my brain. A million different memories. A threatening whisper in my ear. Honey-wrapped arsenic words instructing, grooming, teaching, conditioning, and ordering. The sting of the whip on my childhood skin. Luc has stolen my body from Force. Serenity has helped. But I will end up like my mother. I will always return to Father. I will never leave the Temple.

"Queran?" Serenity glances from me to our preparer, who is exiting his room. Though his room opens into the hall, he'll usually go through my bedroom first. Always making sure everything is in order. Sometimes, he'll use the 3D-food printer before returning to his room.

Queran nods to us, approaching with his hands behind his back until he stands directly above me. One move and his offering palms rest before me with my familiar origami tetra-star clutched inside. Except, I recognize two tiny origami stars carefully positioned within the center.

Appreciatively, I accept the paper gift and smile.

Serenity flicks her gaze up and over to me. "How did he know?"

Nodding up at him, I allow Queran to explain.

"Body changed." As usual, he keeps his words limited. "Eating changed." He pauses, shifts his weight, and concludes, "Bliss changed."

Serenity squares her shoulders, resigned. "He knew before you did." She turns to him. "But why didn't you say anything?"

Queran shrugs and points to me, finger lingering. I understand. He let me find out on my own. Because I deserved to find out first. Not have my preparer tell me. Again, Queran's loyalty undoes me. Does he know how much I've changed? How much I appreciate everything he's done for me?

"Queran." Serenity stands, moving to put a hand on his arm. He inclines his head, focusing on it just as she continues, "We need your help."

Thirty-five
Exhibit to End All Exhibits

SERENITY

$\mathcal{J}$UST AFTER I'VE FINISHED SPEAKING to Queran, the implant beneath my shoulder begins to hum and pulse—my father is summoning me. He's only used the implant to call me a couple of times since I've lived here. Usually, he just uses messenger drones, so this must be a special occasion. It also means he wants me to return to my room.

When I arrive, Lindy is there along with a few other drones. And Neil. Both wear grins marinated in pride and over-eagerness.

My father dons a similar smile. Except he retrieves one of his folded hands from behind his back to rub his eye as if extrapolating a tear. If my father were capable of crying, I imagine his tears would be acid.

"I believe the time for games is done, my daughter," Force addresses me before cupping my shoulder. I try not to bristle when he does, especially considering I should be used to it by now. "Tomorrow night will not be so much an exhibit as it will an interaction."

At first, I tense before catching the smiles on Neil and Lindy's faces, which causes me to pause. "Just spit it out, Force."

"Congratulations, Serenity. Your engagement party will commence this Friday evening followed by your wedding on Saturday. I'm certain you and Skylar will be incredibly happy. Unless…"

I narrow my brows, already feeling my eyes darken. "Unless what?"

"Unless you change your mind." Force gestures toward one of

163

the drones, which approaches and displays a volu screen with dozens, if not hundreds, of enveloped message symbols. When I tap one, it reveals a young man extending a proposal. An ambassador from some Asian country. The next one is a prince.

"Hmm…" Neil muses, leaning toward me when I watch the prince's proposal. "Princess Serenity has a nice ring to it."

"And she would be queen eventually. Imagine…ruler of the Temple and a country," Force gushes.

Swiping the message closed, I seethe, "Forget it, Force."

In return, my father tilts his head to the side and shrugs. "It never hurts to consider all your options."

"There's only one option," I declare, trying to avoid setting my teeth. All my butterflies have turned into steel and metal, fortifying themselves.

Force resumes by folding his hands behind his back again, adopting his signature vulture persona by circling me. "Be that as it may, you will spend what's left of the day responding to each and every one of these messages and give them your undo respect. But for now, I will leave you, Lindy, and Neil to planning."

Lindy snorts behind me. "What planning? You've stolen just about everything."

"Mind your tone, Belinda Belgrave," he warns, but I know his threats are empty. Force would never take away my only friend in the Temple. Or his son's fiancé. "I am Temple director, and I take a personal relationship with anything that goes on here. Especially my own daughter's wedding. Remember…everything must be signed off on by me. Simply transfer any of your ideas and information to the messenger drone, and I will review it tonight. Invitations have already been sent."

"But how—" I start to question, but Force is already prepared for that.

"People love surprises, Serenity," he explains, rubbing his thumb against my chin. "Your beau will be announced at your engagement party, and the invitations are programmed to reveal the specifics with the announcement." He sighs, studying me before he continues, "However tumultuous this time has been, I am immensely proud of you. Yes, I certainly believe you could do better, but I cannot deny you have won your right to choose."

I shouldn't have to win anything, I want to say. *The right is mine to begin with. Like it is for every girl.* But I chomp down on each and every one of my words. Swallow them into a lump at the base of my stomach. The faster he leaves, the faster I can be alone with Neil and Lindy.

My father pauses a moment, gaze riveted on me, eyes scooping mine up. Jubilee scrawled into the irises, wrapping me up in them. Or trying to. Whatever happens, however official and public this is, it is not my wedding. Not *our* wedding. Even Force can't let me have that.

"I wish I could stay for your inspiration, but I must go handle a situation."

I can't begin to speculate what situation that might be, but whatever it is, I would thank it. At least he can't purloin this time with Lindy and Neil.

As soon as Force is gone, Lindy launches into details while cueing my mirror screen nearby. "I know we should go over your engagement party dress first, but I think I'll burst if we don't do the wedding gown."

"We wouldn't want that to happen now, would we?" Neil pats her shoulder, affection tinting his fingertips. And his smile.

Lindy starts swiping to a variety of gown collections. I recognize some of the designer's names, almost balking at the price tags.

"These are just ideas, remember," Lindy reminds me. "Your gown will still be custom made. Can you believe it used to take months to design and create one of these things?" she prattles on, and I find myself relaxing to her busy voice. "3D printing is so easy now. Whatever we pick, it has to have a lot of detailing so that way the rhodium can be added."

"Rhodium?" Raise a brow, I continue to peruse the gowns. There are far too many to choose from.

"Rarest and most expensive element in the world," Lindy explains, shoulders perked up from excitement. "Director Force plans to have rhodium detailing on the dress. It'll probably be the most expensive dress of all time. He's treating you like a princess."

No, Force could never treat anyone like a princess. However, I don't complain. It would ruin these special moments between Lindy, Neil, and me. Instead, I take a seat at the mirror screen and select a few gowns. At least Lindy stated this would be a custom piece. Flirting with a few, I discover I like the bodice on one, the neckline of another, the train of this one, and so on. Of course, Neil and Lindy interject with their favorites. Entertained by shifting the pieces around to form a new gown, Lindy rubs her hands together. In some ways, she reminds me of a child. A child with temporary bipolar mood swings with her hands as invisible friends.

"Check it out!" Lindy's eyes bulge, almost swooning.

Neil leans over, hand braced on the back of my chair as he studies the screen showing my figure adorned in the wedding gown. "It's not the first time, but I gotta say I've never wanted to be a woman more than in this moment."

Lindy shoves him out of the way. "You wouldn't last one day as a woman," she scolds, threatening finger more like a saber.

Neil bows his head to her, palm on his chest. "Sadly, I must acquiesce to your assessment."

"What do you think, Serenity?" Lindy asks, tapping the screen twice to enlarge my figure.

When Force scanned my body the first month I was here, it captured a variety of facial expressions. But Lindy always chooses my sassy one. Eyes a little pinched and sultry, one corner of my mouth pulled up in a half-smirk, and hand on my hip jutted out like a rocky crag. A pose I often reserve for Sky.

Lindy starts kneading her fingers like dough. "Force will want to add some swan detailing, Skeleton flowers will be your bouquet of course, but does it need anything else?"

I wonder what Sky would think about this. What he would choose. Inside, my butterflies cackle at the notion because I know Sky couldn't care less if I showed up after going three rounds with pigs in a muddy sty. After everything that's happened, after all my exhibits, the last thing I'd want is anything ostentatious. So, I own the picture I have in my head, wrap it up in warm wool, and store it in a special mental vault before concluding this is for them. The world.

Better make this good.

"It needs…" I begin, allowing my last word to linger a little longer, the drumroll to my crescendo, "Lightning."

Thirty-six

A Smuggler's Secrets

LUC

O, THIS IS THE INFAMOUS Maud. The woman who is responsible for those two girls escaping. The best Temple preparer in history who anyone has ever heard of. In reality, Queran surpasses her, but he is of the new generation. Because his sole focus is Yin and Yang, Force maintains his anonymity. No praise for the Penthouse preparer.

Still, I can't fathom how this woman gets out of bed in the morning. Not that she doesn't hold her liquor well, considering how lithe she is when she strides across the room toward us. An agility that reminds me of a pudgy cat. No matter how fat they get, they always land on their feet and can manage to contort their bodies into curves and arches.

"Very risky coming back to see me so soon," Maud lectures while crossing her plump arms over her chest. "No girl with you neither."

"I need something." Skylar doesn't try any small talk. Perhaps if we hadn't gone to the wrong room first, but I'm sure we're running out of time.

"Ya always do. What is this time?"

"You're the best damn smuggler the task force has ever seen," Sky praises her, causing her to pinch her lips as if she's waiting for the catch. And here it is. "Time for you to smuggle something in. You need to get it to the Penthouse. Force can never know. So, no shipping. If the wrong person finds out, I'm most likely dead."

"Get to the point, boy," she commands in a warlord's voice.

167

Sky hands her his reader. "We need these. Three of them. Two double. One single."

"Getting them in isn't the problem." Maud puckers up her nose. "Getting them to you is."

"Find a way." Never the one to mince words, my brother.

Maud eyes the reader and the objects on it. Sighing, she drops her arms and responds, "That way could cost me my position here."

"If it means bringing Force and the Temple to its knees…time for the Swan to fly away," Skylar finalizes, eyes embarking onto Maud's, toppling whatever hesitations she's had with his last words.

Maud grumbles, but everything in her body has already surrendered. "Could've just told me your girl was the Swan, boy."

"Only Kerrick and Serafina knew."

Her teeth prop themselves on her bottom lip when she nods, understanding. "Swan wants to leave?"

Skylar nods without hesitation. "She's always wanted to leave. But this is the only way."

"How soon do you need it?"

MINUTES LATER, THANKS TO HAVING once again navigated through the vents, Skylar and I drop into the elevator just as the lights turn on. As we work to contain our heaving breaths, Sky retrieves something from his pocket, uncorks the bottle, and tips it into his mouth before handing it to me.

"Pretend like we've been doing this the whooole time," he slurs. "Just roll with it."

I guess this is our alibi. For all Force knows, we've been locked in this elevator the entire time. Taking a swig, I remember how much I enjoy a good whiskey right before the elevator doors open, revealing a rather irked Force.

"And what do you think you boys are doing?" Force enters, hands casual behind his back because he's "always" in control. "Going somewhere?"

"Nope," Skylar drawls, legs spread in a wide triangle. "Just wanted some privacy so my brother and I could revel in our ultimate victory the other day."

Prickled by the reminder, Force sneers. With a roll of his eyes, he states, "And this is her chosen one. Shame you have also reduced yourself to this," Force retorts, addressing me this time.

"What can I say? We're all doomed here. So, c'est la vie!" I slur through my French before tipping the bottle back, feeling the whiskey hit me sturdy and clean.

"Clean yourself up, gentlemen," he directs us before exiting the elevator. "The next couple of days will be quite busy for you. Skylar, your bride is waiting."

It's not lost on us how Force refers to Serenity as "bride". All I know is I should get back to Bliss. Leaving her too long with her thoughts is always a bad idea, so I leave Skylar to Serenity and return to Bliss's room.

Once I enter, I discover her food is untouched. Strange, considering she was eating well just before I left. What puzzles me more is why she is standing before the window overlooking the world below the Temple. Or rather not, considering how a netting of summer clouds swathes the sky, graying it until it reminds me of the snow-capped mountains that make up her soul. Never before have I seen her more beautiful...or more mournful. Her eyes hold the weight of ten thousand coffins. Of millions of unshed tears. Damn it to hell! What happened in the half hour I was gone?

"Bliss?" I approach but don't touch her...yet.

She doesn't move. Nor does she turn to look at me. Just remains where she is, her arms holding themselves, fingers clenched into the fabric of her robe. Clinging to something. Her old life? No, not after everything we've gone through. Inhaling deeply, I remember everything I've learned over the years. How I tailored my lessons into controlling and manipulating the girls in my Aviary. I read the trauma in her eyes, in her body language. Currently, Bliss is in freeze mode. Serenity's primal instinct is to fight. Bliss' is to take flight. I only need to be there to guide her.

So, I place myself before her, directing her eyes to mine. Still without touching her, I coax as I would a child, "Fly back to me, Bliss."

And she falls. Wings too weak to continue.

Time for me to catch her.

Thirty-seven
Loving and Flying

BLISS

I AM SO TIRED. TIRED OF running. Tired of running to the mountain and hiding behind all the blood, flesh, and bones. Maybe if he'd grabbed me, maybe if he'd cornered me like Father did, even if he'd so much as begged me, the mountain would have sucked me in again. But Luc didn't. Those five words were all I needed to hear. A reminder to fly in the right direction. And it takes all my strength to do it.

As he helps me to my inner bedroom, Luc flies under me, holding me up. Pursing my lips, I stop him before we get to the bed. Confused, Luc tilts his head toward mine, breath on the verge of my lips, but it's not a hush. It's a torrent waiting to break the dam of my mouth. A dam I part for him. Luc reads my eyes, my body language, the yearning in my hands as they excavate through the buttons on his shirt to the skin beneath.

When his lips voyage onto mine, we step onto the mountain. Together. Just climbing at first. Nothing deters him. Not the mouths that have made their marks all over my body. Not the labyrinth of flesh that has shadowed mine. Luc kisses me breathless, overlapping a hundred-thousand mouths with his own—across my throat, traveling to my shoulders, stopping at the silk robe.

With swollen lips, I gaze at him and nod, swallowing any resistance that rises, shoving it down to meet its grave.

Closing my eyes, I go deeper into the mountain. The first layer. When Luc removes my underclothes, the bones rattle more. As his lips collide with the base of my throat, most break until

170

there's nothing left but dust. First layer of the mountain removed. His clothes join my dress on the floor, the fabrics making love in their own still way.

Time for the second mountain layer. Flesh. Luc's fingers seek my skin, exploring slowly. Pressing, touching, fondling every curve and straight line, every dip and indent. The warmth of his touch melts the flesh inside me. Tender, Luc cups me—my innermost regions.

I tense, my breath swifter than the ocean tide.

Luc whispers in my ear, "Lean in. Don't resist. Feel it...for yourself. Let me give. You receive."

So many years, so many faceless men with vacant rooms for eyes shoving themselves inside, injecting their own holes of souls inside me. Left in tatters and pieces. With his breath on my outside and his fingers tasting me, Luc warms the remains, repairs them. And the flesh mountain liquefies, decays. All that is left is blood.

Something new rises within me, something that should be familiar, but it was always something I had to swallow, coat in bile, and shove into my stomach where it belonged. Because my own pleasure was forbidden in the Temple. Only theirs mattered.

Luc pauses.

"What?" Opening my eyes, I breathe a disappointed exhale.

Coiling a hand around my neck, he draws me closer and murmurs, "Not yet," before overlapping his body and mouth onto my own.

Blood is the strongest. It's everywhere. Infected, dissolved, and fused into mine. But Luc threatens their blood by injecting his own. Stronger than the rest of them. Powerful enough to drive them out. With every kiss, every touch, every thrust, their blood retreats in the wake of his.

And I join him.

That something builds inside of me again, rising like a long-slumbering Phoenix shaking off frozen ashes, rearing her head. One more powerful thrust from Luc, and she catches fire and blazes. I lead the way and take Luc with me, discarding the blood, flesh, and bones until they are nothing but rotted memories. They will always be a part of my past, but I refuse to carry

171

them into my future. They don't define me anymore.

Only one remains, but he is standing in Luc's shadow now.

And we are the warmth of Luc's bed.

I am no longer Father's Yin.

Now, it's time.

"Luc…" I murmur, parting from his mouth for a moment.

Eyes closed, he breathes against me, long, slow bursts of exhales. "Bliss…"

"You're the one."

"I want to be." There's a hint of a smile in his voice as he opens his eyes, granting me the sight of an underwater world of blue dreams and deep secrets.

"You are," I emphasize, summoning the secret inside of me. "The lives growing inside me are proof."

Luc blinks. Once. Twice. Three times. Then he kisses me deeper than the waters in his eyes could ever fathom.

Thirty-eight

EngAgeMent

SKY

SHOULDN'T BE SURPRISED FORCE WENT all out for the engagement party. Wish it were five hours from now so Serenity and I could be alone. Thanks to Force's little assignment, Serenity has kept busy responding to her hundreds of proposals. From the low-income laborer— "thanks but no thanks"—to the Glass District manager—"go to hell"—to the foreign prince with a harem—"no, really, go to hell," Serenity quoted quite a few colorful phrases I hadn't even heard yet. So, I left my girl to it and handled the security functions for the engagement party. At one point, I saw her down a few floors on the security monitors. Took a break for some self-care with Sharky before mustering the gumption to handle the rest of the proposals. When I discovered her working late into the evening until she was nodding off in mid-response, I arranged for generic "fuck off" responses to the rest, carried her to bed, tucked her in, and climbed in beside her.

Now, I stand beside Serenity as we enter the party hall. All eyes feast on her, but she only cares about mine. Lucky man that I am! With what she's wearing, it's no wonder. A backless platinum-and-diamond-encrusted gown. Spared no expense from Force and a precursor to her wedding gown. From what she's told me, it'll be earth shattering. Sure can't wait to see her in it. Or out of it. Not that I'm trying to entertain any lustful thoughts. Considering I don't have any intention of acting on them, it's useless to entertain them. At least until we get out of here. We've both made that quite clear. What's on paper doesn't matter. What's in our hearts does. And her heart would break if she lost her virginity in the Temple.

Tonight, I'll finally get a moment alone with her. Need to tell her about Maud and how escape is closer than ever. By the time Force discovers we're gone, he won't be able to interfere.

Resisting the urge to grab at the collar of this stuffy suit, I focus on the crowd before me, remembering I'm not just a half the couple of the hour but also Serenity's security. With the contact lenses I've donned for the evening, I can monitor the crowd more effectively. Anybody can be scanned for heart rate, change in body temperature…weapons. Not that Force would allow weapons into the party with his drones searching every partygoer. Unless they had some inside connections and knew how to procure a weapon.

After Force announces Serenity's engagement and says a few words, he allows us to mingle. Good thing his speech didn't last long. With his hands cupping her shoulders like that, I was close to busting his knuckles.

As eager strangers flock toward Serenity, battering her with questions—both young men and women—I scan each. No signs of ill will or weapons. I recognize my paranoia, but she's my girl. Paranoia is permitted.

With each new lineup of party guests, the questions launched at Serenity begin to recycle.

Will you have any more exhibits after your wedding; where will you honeymoon; what are your plans after your wedding; will someone else play the Swan; does he have any brothers?

Sure, that last one was my favorite. Mostly due to the humor and the irony. Another thing Serenity and I have in common—we both had blood relatives we didn't know for years. Well…I guess I knew there was the potential. Not that I gave a damn before the Aviary.

Enough time has passed not to be rude. Judging by the tension in Serenity's shoulders and how her hairs are standing on end, it's time for me to jump in. Scooping up her elbow, I excuse us from any further questions and suggest people enjoy the cocktails and hor d'oeuvres. Most were all too enthusiastic and began to extend the lines of the tented bars, tents forming the shape of a swan, of course. All across the walls were sprite lights of swans on repeat, circulating between flying and landing.

A thread of silver escapes Serenity's curled updo as I escort her to the head table. Force's idea to have actual silver woven into her hair. While everyone else must wait in line for their signature cocktails unless they opt for simple champagne punch bursting from one of many swan-statue fountains, Serenity and I are served immediately. To my surprise, she just orders champagne. I figured she'd be milking this for all it's worth. Maybe she's saving that for the wedding, but when I see her eyes droop a little, I understand. Hopefully, the night will pass by quickly for her. She needs her rest, considering the wedding is tomorrow afternoon.

A server brings us our champagne. Flecks of gold decorate the glass while pinky-tip-sized pearls nudge one another at the bottom. One of many favors from the evening, I'd imagine. I drink mine slowly, needing to be sober.

Serenity drinks hers much more quickly.

The table strategically rests underneath the enormous moving crystal chandelier. It's not until Serenity shifts at just the right angle that I understand why. Each crystal has been precisely cut into the shape of a swan. So hundreds of miniature swans start dancing along Serenity's face, waltzing along her cheekbones and frolicking on her neck. The effect is transcendent.

In no time at all, Force joins our table and announces the beginning of dinner. Wouldn't be surprised if we were having roast swan, but something tells me if he pulled a stunt like that, Serenity would turn the table over.

Unfortunately, I don't get a chance to look at the menu. Only halfway through my champagne, the room begins to swirl and the chandelier above my head has caught on fire. I blink a couple of times, trying to steady myself, but it doesn't do much good.

"Sky…"

Sensing something is wrong, Serenity touches the back of my hand where my fingers dig into the table. Her hand is more lightning kiss on my skin than anything else. My stomach rolls again.

"Why, boy, you look positively ill," Force comments with a bit of a smirk. Did he put something in my drink so he'd have more time with Serenity? One last attempt to undermine me before our wedding? Wouldn't put it past him, but it seems uncharacteristic since it was his idea for the engagement announcement. When it comes to me, he's played all his hands. And I topped him. *We* topped him.

"I'll be right back," I excuse myself, swallowing a groan before making like a bullet for the bathroom. One thing I didn't consider in all my security protocols was the tampering of my drink. Of course it'd be mine. Serenity's the real target. I'm just the one who's in the way. Jealous admirer. Some wounded rejection from previous days. Either way, they did a sloppy job. Maybe if I'd drunk all the champagne, but my saving grace was sipping it slowly. And now, I can take it back to the security center and have it analyzed.

Just have to regurgitate it now. As soon as I enter the bathroom, I understand why the attempt was so sloppy.

"Lights on," I demand in a growl, but the bathroom system doesn't reciprocate. And before I can get to the toilet to empty the poisoned contents of my stomach, the attack occurs.

I see red. Even though it's all black in here, I see nothing but red when he attacks. It's not his strength—it's his precision. He knows just where to apply pressure so I'm already blacking out. Amazing to think it could get darker. Like I'm diving headfirst into an ash pit. Can't let this happen, though. Can't go unconscious. Shifting my weight, I plant my feet, bending by knees into a firm squat, then hurl my attacker in an arc over my body, slamming his back onto the floor. A smart man knows when to run, knows when to pick his battles and where. For all I know, this was the first attempt and the man could have a weapon as backup. Not to mention the adrenaline is wearing off, my body reminding me of the poison in my belly. Whatever the case, I'm not sticking around to wait for him to kill me. I'm not my brother. I don't kill with such ease. Especially since I've never killed before.

So, I escape the bathroom, vomit into an obliging plant, then return to the table.

I don't say a word to Serenity about anything that happened.

Thirty-nine

LeVel TwO

SERENITY

*A*FTER THE ENGAGEMENT PARTY IS over, it's past midnight. I barely have any strength left. Perhaps that was my father's plan all along. No rest for the wicked. Back in the Breakable Room again, I hold onto the kiss Sky planted on my temple right before we parted. I hold onto the reassuring way Bliss relaxed into Luc's arms when I visited her right before coming. I try to forget the traces of concern and melancholy etched in her eyes.

Force enters behind me, whip already in hand. Any second now, I expect the door to open for him to usher in some new victim for me, but none comes. Perhaps he wishes to monologue first. Then, I notice how the whip is a beginning one. Nothing high-tech about it. No electric pulses, no heat sensors that trigger when more force or strikes are applied. Softer leather and not as likely to break the skin. What on earth is going on?

"After tonight, your training will be complete," Force opens, tapping the whip against his palm. The curled edges of the leather flirt with the crisp white shirt he wears. Neither of us have changed from the engagement party. But my father had removed his jacket. "From now on, you will choose your own whip. And you will punish Temple offenders."

Maybe Sky will have more insight on what that means since I have no desire to ask Force. Off the top of my head, all I can think of are security guards who steal.

There is no more time to ponder. Not when my father unbuttons his shirt, jerks it off his shoulders in one smooth motion, and lets it drop to the floor. Silent and white as a fallen dove. But to me, the sound is loud and ominous as a warning horn. All sorts of alarms go off in my head, along with a radar pulsing in my veins.

"What are you doing?" I demand, setting my teeth as Force reaches for my clenched hand, his fingers uncharacteristically tender when he urges my own to open so he may place the whip inside.

"It's time, Yang."

He blinks once, regarding me with that same affection he had when he announced my engagement. Underneath the surface, I'm sure he's still sporting the same sinister smile. That murky pleasure that defines all bottom feeders.

When he turns around to exhibit his back, I stare at the ceiling, aggravation creasing my lips and sending a fire trail from the whip directly into my arm. Inside my blood, it writhes, latching onto veins. A precursor to my lightning. What is my father trying to prove?

I ask. "All this time, you've had your agenda of showing me you're in control…and now, you're just giving it up? I don't buy it."

He makes a sound almost like a sigh, though he turns for me to see his crooked smile.

"You still don't see it, do you?" Force approaches me and cups my cheek, gazing at me with eyes so earnest it's almost terrifying. And then he weaves his arms around me. I want to resist. I do… for almost three seconds.

"All this time, you've tested your boundaries." His voice coddles me, pride built in his hands as they stroke my hair. "You came out swinging, but I showed you who was dominant every time. Up until now."

Then, I pull back. "What do you mean "up until now"?"

Force shakes his head, sniggering. "You've earned everything, Serenity. I'm giving you what you want most now. I knew you would triumph through each one of my tests. Even down to your engagement party. You've earned your relationship with your sister and your lover, and you've earned the right to cancel all your exhibits. And now…" Force drops his arms to the sides, palms open to continue, "You've earned the right to do what you've wanted most since you walked into the Temple. No, since you first laid eyes on me. So, I surrender." He turns around once again, then does something I never thought I would ever see. The devil kneels before a human girl. A pimp capitulates to his stable woman. The abuser submits to the child.

My hand burns all the more. Lightning quivers, rocking my skin with goose bumps. And I lean my wrist to one side, the end kissing the floor—even it seems to desire this, to punish the tormentor who has caused it to torment others. I slam my eyes shut, struggling against the urge rising inside me. But more rises. Memories I've tried to submerge, but each drifts up, flaming hot as an ember to scorch me.

The sight of Bliss's back bathed in scars, blood dripping like melted rubies. The pages of my mother's journal and the picture of her as the Unicorn. The crimson smile he created in my true father's neck. The tempting prison he kept Sky in, the countless suitors he forced on me, the way he kept us apart. Each and every one of his poisonous games. All the exhibits. Sunshine. And the thousands upon thousands of girls, past and present, trapped in the labyrinth of lust that is the Temple. One girl I care about most. I struggle for breath as one last image quickens the lightning in my blood. My niece and nephew. Curled up as a plum-sized yin and yang. I'll be damned if I let him take them away from Bliss. Away from us.

I'm already damned.

My lightning ignites. And I use it. One thrust of my wrist. One crack down the center of his spine. One weeping line of flesh.

I fall.

Ferocious tears are molten lava, but I can't get them out fast enough. The lightning is still here, and I can't harness it. My butterflies shake and twitch as if in a seizure. One second later, I'm doubled over and vomiting everything on the floor. I vomit Force out of my blood, out of my body, out of my mind. But then, he's patting me on the head— "there, there"—his touch so familiar I recognize the perception in his fingertips, the concern in his voice. It's my own. The way I've spoken to Bliss. Force's signature has been etched on my heart since the beginning. All this time, I've denied it. That I could overcome my blood, the damning DNA he passed onto me. But I can't. And I might not ever.

Force squeezes my shoulder. "You will get there. Power is overwhelming. I remember my first time. I have my methods of... release. You will, too."

I know what his methods are. My mother knows them better. Bliss knows them best.

And I am closer to them than ever.

Forty

ForGiveneSs

LUC

WHEN SERENITY BARRELS INTO THE main room, Bliss and I are sitting at the table enjoying some midnight refreshments. At first, I assume she's here because we did not attend the engagement party, but Force was specifically clear Bliss is not for public view. My personal conclusion is he simply wanted to shower all his attention on his youngest daughter, and he's none too pleased with mine and Bliss's relationship.

However, judging by the onslaught of tears wreaking havoc down Serenity's cheeks and the way she throws herself right onto Bliss's lap, I know the engagement party is nowhere near her mind.

"I'm sorry, I'm sorry, I'm so...so sorry," Serenity cries, words muffled by Bliss's shoulder.

Bliss almost surprises me by how she handles her sister. How she strings one hand around Serenity's waist, then pats the back of her head with the other. "Shh..." she coos, saying nothing else, but her eyes hold an understanding that mine do not. Did something happen with my brother? I turn to the door, nearly expecting him to come running behind her, especially given how rare it is to find them apart.

"You were right about everything," Serenity unloads, breaking from Bliss's shoulder to look up at her. "Right about Mom. About Force. And...about me," she chokes out. "I'm just like him. I've always been like him."

I sigh. So, that's what this is all about. It's tempting to intervene, but I let Bliss, as her older sister, handle this. It's not my

181

place anymore.

"Serenity…"

Bliss scoots her chair out to make more room, staring down at her younger twin. Her eyes turn deep. Like frosted crystals just unearthed in the depths of a dark cavern; she's saved this most cherished gaze for her sister—for when Serenity needs it—because up until now, Serenity never has. Invested in Bliss's eyes is more love than any of the times she's regarded me. Perhaps it took her longer to surrender to it, but the bond between sisters, between twins, does not ever truly break.

"Listen…" Bliss licks her lips, then takes a deep breath before cupping each of Serenity's cheeks. I can read how hard this is for her. Showing love and accepting it may always be difficult for her. "You are *not* Father. You are my *sister*." She pauses between each phrase as if they are quicksand and she's allowing Serenity to sink into them. "You help. He harms. You fight and defend. He warmongers. You *love*. He *lies.*"

Serenity shakes her head and lays her cheek against Bliss's leg, so only one side of her face is showing. "I've hurt you."

"I've hurt myself far more than you could ever hurt me," Bliss denies, and I refrain from interrupting, from growling how Force is the ultimate one who has hurt her. But it won't do any good to recount what she already knows. This is her moment with her sister.

"I've played right into his hand. Even with Sky." I recognize the weakness in Serenity's voice. These are but fragile excuses. Lies she's believing from Force. Bliss knows his lies better than anyone.

Bliss's chuckle launches from her throat like glitter from a cannon. "Trust me, Serenity, Force never would have chosen Sky. The wedding is his last desperate attempt," she explains, prompting Serenity to pause and look up. "He is still serving himself. Convincing himself this was his plan all along. He had to believe it first in order to get you to believe. He did the same thing with me when I was a child. If I ever won a game, if I ever excelled at a lesson, he could never let me take the credit for it—it always had to be his plan to let me win."

"But then, I—" Serenity folds her lips together, pulling away as if her very body could sting Bliss. "I struck him. With the whip.

Just once, but—"

"Just once?" Bliss interrupts, indigo eyes prevailing against Serenity's. "That's surprising. Your control...it..." She nearly fumbles, but I smile at her.

I continue, assuring Serenity, "I've fantasized about whipping him until there is so much blood and flesh oozing that a cell generator could never repair it." Of course, one of my exploding-bullet guns would work, too. Fitting end. I wonder what Skylar would prefer. Good old-fashioned strangling perhaps?

Bliss takes Serenity's hands in her own, then kisses the back of each one. "Your hands are nothing like his. They don't create pain. They take it."

"I never should have whipped you. What I did to my own—"

Bliss shakes her head, eyes bordering on ferocious. "Stop punishing yourself. We both made the decision. For our mother. Father wouldn't have stopped. She's his Unicorn. The Unicorn belongs to him and no one else. Serafina wouldn't have been able to go to the cell gen. Not like me. I had other clients. He would've kept opening and reopening wounds. We both did what we had to do. You had no other choice. And I...I forgive you." When Bliss laughs, it seems to do the trick because Serenity smiles for the first time and starts to wipe her cheeks.

Then, Bliss winces and stands, clutching her stomach. "Excuse me. I think...I think I'm going to throw up."

I smile at the thought of my children growing inside her. Our children. No, Bliss and Serenity do not have hands that can cause pain. But I will use mine against Force if he ever threatens Bliss and my children.

"Go to Skylar. I'll stay with Bliss," I direct Serenity as I prepare to join Bliss in the bathroom.

Serenity touches my arm, causing me to pause.

"You're good for her," she says, chewing on her lower lip, unsure of what else to say.

"She's better for me," I add, squeezing her shoulder before walking away.

Forty-one
Morning Sickness

Bliss

 REGNANCY SUCKS.

Forty-two

AlErt

Sky

EVER SINCE THE ATTEMPT ON my life, I've stayed alert. Even after the party is over. I never take alone for granted. There's no such thing in the Temple. From now on, the only food I'll eat will come from 3D-food printers, and I'll check the specs prior to make sure they haven't been hacked or tampered with.

For the third time tonight, I return to Serenity's bedroom and do a perimeter sweep. Still waiting for Force to finish whatever training he has planned. At least this is the last one. And it won't be too long until we get out of here.

I head upstairs to check her bedroom. She left a couple of sprite light scenes on from before the party. Can't fight a chuckle. One is footage from the obstacle course. The other is her swimming with Sharky. Side by side. Yes, we have had some good moments in the Temple. Few and far between but good all the same.

A few minutes later, I hear the door opening downstairs. Tensing with hairs on the nape of my neck primed, I exit the bedroom area and step out onto the balcony, surprised to encounter Force.

"Where's Serenity?" I demand, voice bordering on barking as I descend the staircase.

Force waves a hand, turning his body just enough to grant me a glimpse of his back where one long streak of red stains his white shirt. What the hell?

"She'll be along shortly. Went to visit her sister. It will give you and me a few moments to talk."

I reach the base of the stairs and cross my arms over my chest, flexing my muscles for good show. By the way he grins, we both know I could end him with one solid punch. Force respects me for that...but nothing more. Beyond the fact he contributed part of his DNA to the girl I love and her sister, I don't have to respect him for anything.

"You are marrying my daughter tomorrow." Force keeps his hands united behind his back as he approaches me. "And you will remain my head of security as well as her personal guardian. Luc is still tasked with investigating and tracking down this killer if he ever rears his head again." He approaches me and raises one finger, not condescending but in a promising manner. "But you can trust if anything should happen to my daughter, I will personally throw you over the side of this Temple and revel in watching the vultures feast on your remains."

I smirk, setting my hands on my hips. If I were Luc, I'd be able to stare him down. Only time I've ever been jealous of my brother, but I hold my own, considering my shadow can feast on the width of Force's. "Pretty pathetic, isn't it?" Force does nothing but stares dead-on at me as I finish, "You try a desperate threat because you finally figured out you could never be the number-one man in her life?"

"Don't test me, Skylar," Force warns, eyes creasing together because he still knows he can't touch me. "Accidents can happen in the Temple. You should be careful not to underestimate me. I am still her father. And she will fulfill her Yang role once your honeymoon is over."

No matter how much I may want to, it's pointless to add a quip like "glorified sperm donor". It seems like Force would get a clue—not once has Serenity ever called him "father".

"By the way," I add just as Force walks away. "You wouldn't have to throw me over." I jut my jaw out and finish, "If anything ever happened to Serenity that resulted in her death, I'd gladly jump."

Forty-three
The Night Before

SERENITY

UST AS I START TO leave, I decide to tap on Queran's door. Tomorrow, he'll act as one of my preparers. And I need to ask him for something…special.

He seems tired. Deep shadows under his eyes. And when I see the unmade bed, I register I must have woken him.

Embarrassed, I flush and apologize. "I'm sorry, Queran. I forgot how late it was." Ironic, considering how tired I was before the Breakable Room.

Queran holds up one hand, excusing my intrusions before extending it toward me. His way of asking what I need.

"Could you make something for me? It can count as my "something new"."

In response, Queran swings the door open and invites me in. Approaching his desk and the numerous origami figures he has there, I search for one that is similar and discover it.

I pick up the Skeleton Flower, then raise it up to him. "Not this one but another flower. A simple one. *Two* simple ones," I add to clarify. Paper flowers in the attic. "How long will it take?"

Queran blinks a couple of times as if forming the objects in his mind before he retrieves a few pieces of paper and sets to work at his desk. His fingers are careful, precise, and strong as they work. The fingers of an artisan. From birth, he was destined to make beautiful things. And to make things beautiful. Tonight, these are special. I don't care if Force has already chosen our wedding cake toppers. These will be our real ones. For Sky and me to

187

share tonight.

When Queran finishes, he holds up the flowers. They are perfect. One is slightly larger than the other, and I understand he's captured the vision of Sky and me perfectly. Just before giving them to me, he weaves the stems together, but I touch my hand to his to stop him.

"Um…no, that's not…" I bite down on my lower lip, trying not to blush. "It's not necessary. Um…not yet."

"Tomorrow?" He presses them to my chest, then points to my hand.

Shrugging, I accept the flowers. "Only sort of. This wedding… it's Force. It's not us. Nothing is…real."

Queran gestures to the flowers and tilts his head to one side, eyes curious. Recognition of his silent question suddenly dawns on me.

"Oh yes! We're together. But not *together* together. Not until we leave the Temple. Someday," I finish a little softer, a persistent ache pushing against the lining of my heart. In some ways, it will be harder now. For both of us. Because of the wedding, we'll have all the excuses in the world. But I don't want it here.

When I return to my bedroom, Sky is already waiting. Showing him the paper flowers, I ask him what he thinks.

Sky sifts a hand into my hair, cups the side of my face, and smiles. "They're perfect. I was worried about you. Force paid me a visit."

I lower my head, eyes on the floor. "What did he say?"

"Nothing important. But I did see his back. Was that you?"

"He…he let me whip him."

Sky heaves a sigh and pressures the side of my face just a little, enough for me to raise my chin toward him. "Doesn't look like you did too much damage, Ser."

"I…stopped."

"Good girl. I wouldn't have. You okay?"

That's when I fall into him because we both know I'm not. Even if he wouldn't have stopped, Sky has different motivations, different intentions. Protection instincts. Not the violent killing type.

He groans before scooping me into his arms and carrying me

up the stairs. Wrapping my arms around his neck, I giggle and remind him, "Hey, I thought the groom wasn't supposed to carry the bride across the threshold until the honeymoon."

"And when have we ever followed the rules?"

Just as Sky reaches the top of the stairs, he kisses me. Mouth sinking deep onto mine, lips opening to urge mine apart so he may taste me. All the while managing to keep his eyes closed and walk across the room to lower me onto the bed. By the time I sink onto the pillows, I'm already breathless. For the second time, I consider telling him about Bliss's pregnancy. Everything's been happening so fast. But this is our last night before our faux wedding. Our last night to be just Sky and Serenity.

I'm not going to wreck it.

Forty-four
Wedding

SERENITY

O F COURSE MY FATHER WOULD outdo himself. Neil adjusts his bow tie as Lindy swipes the sprite light scene to show me the ceremony level where hundreds have gathered and begun to take their seats. The ceremony will be televised, including my entrance.

"Just wait until you see the reception," Lindy exclaims while double checking her work in the mirror.

I steel myself to reassure her, "Lindy, everything's perfect." I stare at the white siren in the three-way mirror. No, a siren would lose her voice if she saw me right now.

"You're a goddess!" Neil announces with a more appropriate adjective while approaching us and offering Lindy a white-rose corsage, embellished in Skeleton flowers. "But I prefer the goddess's preparer." He bows just a little.

Lindy is a vision in the gold, strapless ensemble, which hugs her hourglass curves and shows off her plump but peaches-and-cream skin tone. Printed into the fabric are real gold-leaf elements.

"You're not so bad yourself." She straightens his tie, then gives him a little peck on the mouth.

"I'll put a baby in you tonight." His eyebrows do a giddy jig as he leans over and showers kisses on her neck, causing her to giggle.

Encouraged by their playful banter, I turn back to the mirror only to feel my shoulders sink. This is supposed to be the happiest day of my life. And I have the most expensive gown and wedding in the world. So, why does it seem so ominous?

For the last time, Lindy arranges the waterfall of my veil in a direct line with my train before excusing her and Neil to give me a few minutes alone. The earpiece Force imparted to me earlier will do a countdown to the five-minute mark.

I wish Sky were here.

"Breathe…" His familiar voice drifts into my ear, breath curling on my neck right before he cups my shoulders. But his palms are not possessive as they were before, his tone relaxing and encouraging instead of seductive.

Sighing, I purse my lips. "Thank you for coming."

Luc surveys me in the mirror for one moment before pronouncing, "You look breathtaking."

Everything is ready. *I* am ready. My makeup printed to exact specifications, never-ending for the evening. A tornado could occur, yet my lipstick wouldn't smear and not one eyelash would suffer from a loss of mascara. The neckline is just as I selected. Broken. Not seamless but with decorative swan-like curves, which make up the rest of the dress. Despite the neckline plunging to the center of my chest, no cleavage is displayed. That was my favorite part. Not one part of my breasts is exposed for my most important exhibit.

"You chose well," Luc commends me on the gown, remarking on the way it would be a simple mermaid form to accentuate my curves, but for the sweeping, sinuous skirts branching out from each side of my waist and trailing far behind me. Naturally, Force followed through with his rhodium-infused embellishments all along the gown and in the back to create a feathered and winged effect on each side of my spine, which sweep down to meet the rest of the fabric.

I touch the wide rhodium choker with a thumb-sized swan-shaped diamond at its end. "The gown is heavy."

Luc gives me a one-sided smile with a breathy chuckle escaping from his nostrils. "Given that you have what far surpasses a chapel train, I'm not surprised."

"I'm just happy it splits apart for the reception," Heaving a sigh, I stare at the floor again.

"Hey," Luc consoles me. "I know this was not your idea. Or my brother's. And trust me, he's just as uncomfortable by the whole thing. Bliss is settling him down since I wasn't doing the greatest job," he mutters under his breath, and I can't help but laugh at the notion. "Yes..." Luc laughs with me. "The irony that the one thing Bliss and I have in common is we seem to do better at calming our sibling's significant other rather than our own blood."

"You have two other very important things in common," I remind him.

Luc smiles. A smile so tender I'm sure I'll always treasure it when I remember this day. "Yes, but this day isn't about Bliss and me. Remember..." Luc positions two fingers beneath my chin to raise it. "You can make this your own."

"How?"

"Strip off every mask you've ever worn, the Skeleton Flower, the Swan, Yang...and you're left with Serenity. And that is all my brother will ever see." Luc nestles one kiss on the side of my head before lifting a familiar item to my eyes. "I once gave this to you. You returned it to me after we left the Aviary. Consider it your something borrowed."

"Borrowed?" I smile, accepting the swan charm. Luc helps me tuck it just behind the diamond-and-rhodium Swan combs in my hair.

"Bliss has a love of sparkly things. She's taken a shine to this one."

I was right after all.

"And I have your old and blue." My mother's voice interrupts our meeting right before she sweeps her way toward us. I wonder if the indigo-blue gown with silver detailing was her choice or my father's. Whatever the case, she looks beautiful. More enchanting than me. Today, I am far higher than enchanting.

I don't have time to say anything before my mother reveals an item from my childhood. The butterfly once pinned in a frame. Now, she's free. Serafina even had her lacquered in silver to preserve her more. Her wings are still so delicate I'm afraid she'll be crushed.

"Thank you." I clasp the butterfly a little longer than necessary, a tear crossing the border of my eye. Why do my butterflies seem farther away than ever? While my lightning quivers just below the surface of my skin, waiting to strike? Perhaps because this is still all my father's doing. But I try to follow Luc's guidance and remember…I am Serenity.

"I am proud of you." My mother squeezes my hand. "Both of you."

"Tell the truth, Mom. We all know you're prouder of Sky."

Serafina shakes her head, but she doesn't allow her smile to fade. "You are my daughter. Skylar can never say that."

I read the hidden subtext—*Yes, Skylar is your better half, but I will always love you more than him.* I'm not offended by it.

The countdown begins. I take Luc's arm so he may escort me for part of the distance. Security drones monitor us the entire journey down the walkways and moving staircases my father installed for this occasion. With the length of my gown, the elevator was not an option.

"Will Bliss be there?" *Of course she'll be there,* I ridicule myself. She's my maid of honor.

"We will both be there, but Bliss will be masked. Force doesn't want any detractors from your *special* day," Luc clarifies in a loathing-tinted voice.

Hopefully, Force will be too preoccupied with me to notice anything amiss. To notice Bliss won't drink champagne or if she chooses not to eat or excuses herself to use the bathroom more than usual. It dawns on me how impossible it could be to keep this from Force. I want to dwell on it, come up with a solution, but there's no time. I've reached the wedding aisle. Or, rather, the floating staircase that is the beginning of the aisle. It descends two levels to where the ceremony truly takes place. From up here, all I can see is a few feet of the level path at the base of the stairs leading into the ceremony.

Luc kisses my cheek, then says two words that, a year ago, I never thought I would hear from him. "Be Serenity."

A moment later, he disappears the way he came. Ten-second countdown. Only one security drone behind me. Now, volu-drones ahead of me capture every moment for my televised entrance. All pre-programmed for production perfection.

Ten…when I step down, music begins to play. *Nine.* I'm so glad Force let me skip the shoes. *Eight.* These barefoot lace sandals—like fingerless gloves—will help prevent me from tripping. *Seven*. Obviously, Force had to add his personal touch with diamonds and pearls sewn into the lace. *Six*. Oh well.

About halfway down the floating staircase six swans appear, swooping in from behind me, trained to fly in waltz-like movements all around me. The closer I get to the bottom, the louder the music gets. Just as the swans swish past my sides, I reach the bottom step where the aisle runner greets me. Rhodium-infused fabric. The double frosted French doors of the ceremony site swing open, giving the swans access so they can fly all the way up to the perch on each side of the altar. No surprise the altar is two giant marble swans curved in a heart-shaped beak kiss.

The music pauses for a moment, and my father's voice resounds in the great hall.

"All rise!"

Hundreds of guests stand at attention, all eyes rooted on me. Above my head on all sides are multi-level balconies packed to the brim with people. All watching. All waiting. Dozens of naked trees surround the edge of the hall.

I exhale. Look up to see Sky standing at the end of the aisle underneath one swan beak…eyes searching for mine, to steady me.

The light dims, canvassing the entire hall in a darkness with the trees glowing an iridescent silver. Force really spared no expense.

After what feels like an eternity, I take my first step onto the curtain of swan feathers and Skeleton flowers brushing the bare soles of my feet as the music begins again. Hundreds of meaningless smiles. Only one expression matters.

When I focus on Sky, it all seems to fade. The fog eclipsing the steps leading up to the altar. The fairy-tale forest on all sides of me. The spectator audience I don't even know. And even my father, who stands in the center of the altar because some bylaw gives Museum directors the ability to perform marriage ceremonies. Much like the captain of a ship or something. I'm just thankful he can't give me away and perform the ceremony at the same time. He's never had the right to give me away.

My feet find the last step, and I take my place opposite of Sky with most of my train sweeping down the generous aisle, overshadowing the feathers and flowers like a waterfall made of lace, chiffon, and rhodium. Bliss takes my bouquet of Skeleton flowers with rhodium-lacquered feathers, eyes smiling at me from behind the mask. Though I know I can do this without them, it's still encouraging to have Luc and my sister standing up with us.

Sky is more handsome than ever. The tuxedo has softened his muscles in just the right way. With him clean-shaven and his waves gelled and pulled into a tight ponytail at the nape of his neck— at least my father let him keep that—I need to keep myself from launching for him right now.

"Dearly beloved…"

My father opts for something more traditional, which is almost surprising, except I remember—he must keep up appearances. It's likely the Temple board of lower-ranking Syndicate members are here. Force will appeal to their antiquated bloodlines and palettes. For the first time, I consider what it would sound like if Sky and I did write our own vows. Somehow, we'd work in the thunder and lightning bits. Water and mountains, too. Those will always belong to us.

By the time the audience stands to applaud with the closing music in the background, I've already forgotten every one of Force's words. All I needed to do was stand there, say "I do," let Sky place the ring on my finger, and light a rhodium-gilded candle. That was it.

No relief yet. I brace myself, pace myself. We still have a whole reception to get through.

NOT WANTING ANYTHING TO BE amiss for my "most important" day, Force has left nothing to chance. Since there was no time for dancing lessons—and thanks to advancements in technology— Force attaches a device that grants mine and Sky's bodies the ability to perform a perfect waltz. The only relief was when the enormous train and sumptuous skirts on my gown were removed to leave the mermaid silhouette in place, granting more ability for me to move. Due to the makeshift lake my father erected for the reception, which takes up half a level, our dance is the stuff of fantasy legends. A dance they will play on billboards throughout the country to advertise the Temple. A dance that Hollywood directors will try to mimic. A dance that engaged couples all over the world will try to emulate.

With no care the entire world is watching, I stand on my tip-toes and kiss Sky long and hard on the mouth until Force clears his throat.

His warning is clear behind his proud-papa smile. "Save it for the honeymoon, Serenity. It's time to greet your guests."

For once, I don't fight my father. Even if it's much harder than any of my past exhibits, even if I'd rather be swimming with my shark or even in the Skeleton Flower exhibit, I muster through welcoming every guest. All the important ones my father has stip-ulated I make an effort with—his shareholders. The less important guests are in the nosebleed section on the second and third levels. Through it all, Sky stands sentry next to me—my faithful guardian angel.

Finally, it's time for dinner. I am famished. The table decora-tions boast of a floating six-foot high display of a swan with Skele-ton flowers pirouetting in a figure-eight motion around it. As I sit, I notice the trained swans from earlier now swim contentedly in the lake a hundred yards away from the bridal table. My father sits at the head with Bliss on my right and Sky on my left. Above our heads is an overhanging canopy swathed in pearls and diamonds. Nothing lacks in finery, and I shudder at the thought of how many slaves have been trafficked at the expense of it all.

Sky must notice me tensing because he plants a soft kiss on my neck, then murmurs, "You'll be fine. By the way," he adds before finishing, "You look like lightning on water."

My butterflies leap in mid-flutter. It's the most beautiful com-pliment he could give me. Tonight, I need to tell him about Bliss and the twins.

The rest of the reception goes smoothly. Even when Force has me greet one latecomer.

"Congratulations, Skeleton Flower."

Jade's words are disguised as a compliment, but I can pick up on the notes of revulsion underneath them. No doubt she couldn't miss the wedding of the century, the one to make history books. I notice how her nostrils flare when I touch the back of Sky's hand.

"And you as well, *Kyle*," she almost hisses, trying to bait Sky by referencing his Shed name.

He refuses to answer, but there's a hint of a grin creasing one corner of his mouth because he doesn't have to.

I don't bother addressing the comment. It's not worth it.

"I am absolutely thrilled to see my Garden exhibit represented here," Jade notes to Force, who chuckles in response.

"It seemed the Skeleton Flower created a lasting impression. Despite the Garden's remote location, rumors do spread."

I roll my eyes. Everyone knows once I was in the Temple, Jade released all footage of my time in the Garden. For a price, I'd wager, but she released it all the same.

"*Sky*, I think it's time to cut the cake." I draw out the "y" in Sky a little just to revel in the way Jade's brows sink low from derision. If she'd had her way, she would have auctioned me off to the highest bidder and Sky would have become one of her soiled seedkeepers. Fortunately, the "highest bidder" turned out to be Neil.

"A pleasure to see you as always, Jade." Force kisses the back of her hand before following Sky and me to the cake table.

I fight the urge to shake my head in disbelief, but I do take the time to guffaw at the creation. It's not one cake but seven. An enormous floating creation of seven swans. Four have their wings spread. The highest swans meet in a symbolic kiss with gold-and-rhodium crown cake toppers on their heads. Skeleton flowers, diamonds, silver, and gold decorate the rest of the confectionary creation. It tastes just as beautiful as it looks. Even if some of it ends up on my chest. I'll never forget what Sky looks like with cake in his eye.

Somehow, I manage to keep the bile inside my butterflies when it's time for the father/daughter dance. It helped to see Sky dance with my mom. Even if she's not his true mother, she's always been there for him, so it counts. The line of men wanting to dance with me wraps all the way up to the second level. But Luc and Neil are first.

"Ya knocked 'em dead, goddess," Neil proclaims, commending me. "What's the plan now?"

Staring at the endless line of dance requests, I reply with one word.

"Pray."

Forty-five

The Wedding Night

SERENITY

BY THE TIME THE WEDDING is over, my feet feel like they're ready to fall off. At first, I think we're going to my room, but Sky squeezes my hand in the elevator, leans over, and announces, "I have a little surprise."

"I don't know if I can handle any more surprises." I yawn, pulling the diamond-encrusted pins out of my hair one by one until all my curls grace my arms and shoulders again.

"I think you'll enjoy this."

Sky leads me off the elevator into the tank room where Sharky is kept. It is a pleasant surprise to get to see my shark on my wedding day. If it'd been up to me, he would've been my ring bearer. Then again, he'd have looked awfully cute in a white tutu for my flower boy.

Then, I notice something floating on the edge of the tank. A thin, bubble-like sphere. Taking my hand with the ends of my dress swishing across the stone steps, Sky leads me up to the tank platform.

"It's new technology. And the best I could come up with for a wedding gift." Sky shrugs, one corner of his mouth tugging to the side. "Figured visiting a snow globe would be better than giving you one this time.

Dumbfounded by the sweet gesture, I press a hand to my chest and marvel at the device. Nothing should come as a surprise in the Temple when it applies to tech. Besides, Sky would know it all. I don't hesitate to start climbing inside, hearing Sky's throaty

198

chuckle behind me. As much as I enjoy swimming with Sharky, I'm not in the ideal dress. Plus, this will be the first time Sky will get to share this with me. I can't wait.

Two seats jut out from the base of the *water* globe, and I start strapping into the left one. Sky gets in next to me, then cues up a volu-screen with some sort of control. Sharky approaches the sphere, gray body skimming through the water, stirring up a torrent of bubbles in his wake. Too distracted by my pet, I don't notice what Sky's doing until the globe begins to sink into the water. Excited, I part my lips and plant my hands on the sides of the globe. It's thin, flexible enough to roll with the water but strong enough to keep us encased. Whatever volumetric technology is inside, it also maintains the temperature to keep us warm since Sharky's environment is like fresh-melted seawater icicles.

"Whoa!" Sky exclaims when Sharky swoops by, his tail swinging against the globe and launching it to the right.

"Who's a good boy?" I croon to my fish, marveling at his sleek body, the dark pewter gray of his skin. "Thanks for this," I say, leaning my head on Sky's shoulder as he maneuvers to the left.

"Only thing that would complete it is snow, but—"

"It's perfect."

He shrugs. "Not like we can have a real honeymoon. Thought this would be a good substitute."

"We'll have a real honeymoon someday." I squeeze his hand.

Sky's gaze rolls across me, muscle twinging in his jaw. I can't help but grin because I know what's going on in his head, but when I do, he blushes.

"Sky," I scold, poking his bicep. "I'm officially your wife. Your eyes are allowed to undress me."

"We haven't talked about it much."

"Sex, Sky. You can say it."

"Not just sex," he disagrees, shaking his head. "It'll mean more than that. But you haven't really talked about how you feel about it. Not since your armor."

Sharky swims around us once more, and I blow through my nostrils. No wonder Sky is curious, given our history. Given I vowed I would never to go there. Growing up on the outside looking in, hearing all the stories, knowing what Force did to my mother…it all cheapened sex. Ruined the thought of it…for a long time. Not anymore. Not when I look at Sky. Not when I think of all he's done and does for me. Not when I think of us together. And especially not when I undress him with my eyes, my irises practically burning a hole right into his muscles.

"I love you, Sky." I lean over. Plant a gentle kiss on his neck. "We'll figure out the rest together. Practice and all that."

"Soon."

He says that like he has an idea. But Sharky swipes at us once more, diverting the conversation, and Sky docks. As he helps me out, I decide to wait until we reach my room.

Except I didn't count on…

"What the hell?" Sky yells as soon as he turns over the body, her familiar silver-bullet eyes now lifeless and her albino skin even paler…with a swan symbol carved into her chest.

"Sky…" I motion to the piece of paper she's clutching. "Her hand."

Sky uncurls Jade's fingers until the small note tumbles to the floor. I snatch it up, unfold it, and show it to Sky.

A wedding gift.

Forty-six

YaNg

SERENITY

*B*YNOW, LUC HAS INSPECTED the corpse, and Jade has been carted away. Sky's gone over every inch of the security cameras, but I overhear his conversation with my father. Nothing visible from the cameras. As if the perpetrator understands all the angles and how to thwart them. I pace about in the main room, the door cracked for me to hear the conversation between the three men.

"There is no need to be concerned...yet." Luc, the voice of reason.

"Like hell there's not." Protective Sky.

"This is our killer's first act in weeks," Force declares, voice rigid. "And no trace anywhere."

I rub up my arms as I listen to them confer.

"I'll see if I can track Jade's whereabouts during the wedding. See who she interacted with," Luc assures the other two men. "Just remember, our killer has no ill will toward Serenity. His profile is an admirer. This time, he left a note. Yes, it's his way of upping his game by choosing a more personal target, but it's the first time he's tried to communicate with Serenity directly. Any extra clues like this will only work in our favor."

"Twenty-four seven," Force interrupts, tone bordering on violence, but it's that dictatorial voice he uses when barking out orders. "You eat with her, you sleep with her, you accompany us to any appointments, and if she goes to the bathroom, you're there. Understand?"

201

"I won't violate my wife's privacy...unlike others," Sky proclaims, seething. "But I'll make sure she's safe."

"Go," Luc directs him. "We know she's waiting for you. And eavesdropping," he adds, and I hear the smooth smile in his voice.

I start walking away as Sky enters the main room, fully expecting him to follow me up the stairs to the bedroom. All I want to do is change out of this gown, which follows me like a lace-wrapped cirrus cloud, but it's the wee hours of the morning and I don't think that will be happening anytime soon. It's time to stop beating around the bush. Sky has to know what's going on.

So, I let him kiss me just once. Because this kiss is what we both need. The all-consuming type that involves depth and angle-changing, warring tongues, and stolen breath. I try popping the cloud that's hanging over us, but I imagine there's no silver lining behind it. Just thunder and lightning, and that works for us. It has always worked, and I shouldn't toy with the status quo. Some couples operate better off black-and-white emotions like love and war. We can't function in shades of gray like Bliss and Luc.

"Sky..." I stop him before he can continue by placing my hands on his chest. "There's something I haven't told you yet. Everything happened so fast after the engagement party. And I didn't want to spoil anything else."

Plopping down on the bed, I start to chew on one of my fingernails. Sky tugs my hand down right before pounding on the bed next to me, sinking deep into the pillows and folding his hands behind his head. When he sighs and closes his eyes, I take it as a familiar signal he's listening, waiting for me.

"Bliss is pregnant."

One eye opens. "Come again?"

"She's pregnant with twins. Luc's twins."

His eyebrows shoot up, eyes wide, and he sits up, but there's something unreadable in his expression. Not tension...but not appreciation, either. His eyes start flicking back and forth like they do when he's working on a puzzle or a hack. What is he trying to figure out?

"How far along?" is the first thing Sky asks, hands flexing on the bed.

Not quite the words I was expecting to hear from him. "About two months."

The sound he makes is halfway between a groan and a growl when he grips his hair, yanking the waves loose from his bun. Touching his shoulder, I lean into him.

"What's wrong? We're going to be an aunt and uncle. That's pretty exciting."

"Trust me, Ser. I'm not mad. I'm just..." He turns to me, smiles, and brushes his knuckles across my cheek. "Gonna need to postpone our plan. Our escape plan. It won't work now."

I dip my chin onto his shoulder. "But it'll still work later?"

He nods. "Can't tell you. Need you to stay in the dark."

"I'm good at that."

Sky tilts his head toward mine so our hair tangles. "Only way for your lightning to shine." Then, Sky does tense, head flicking up. I reach for his hand.

"What's wrong?"

His eyes remind me of a dark sky before a storm. I can't see the details of destruction, just recognize the violence brewing there.

"Force said you're ready to become Yang. You're going to take on responsibilities, Serenity. He's training you to become Temple director. To become him."

My mind scrambles with the possibilities. What does that mean? Other than what goes in in the Penthouse between his family, I have no basis for what Force does. How he runs the Temple. Yes, he signs off on exhibits. Meets with his shareholders, board of directors, and some foreign dignitaries, but what else? What could he possibly expect me to do?

"What are you prepared to do, Serenity?"

Sky's question stuns me. Lightning striking the beach to create glass and then striking it again, leaving me standing in the burning shards. If I become Yang, if I play my part to perfection, it would draw attention away from Bliss, away from the beauties growing inside her. Bliss has always been Yin, the secret-keeper. But now, she will have Yang to bear the secrets with her and to ensure they never see the light of the sun.

Horror paralyzes my butterflies. A new evolution metamorphoses them. Each butterfly wing sparks, each antennae, thorax, and vein quickening and transforming into lightning. What did my mother say? My lightning can be used for good or evil. Now, it will be used for both. And I will become the monster my father wants me to be…for Bliss, for my niece and nephew, for my family.

Whatever I need to be, I will become.

So, I am not just Serenity anymore.

I am Yang.

PART
Four

Forty-seven

DisTraCtiOn

SEVEN MONTHS LATER

SERENITY

HE CALLUSES ON MY HANDS will heal soon. Just like they
always do.

This time, it's a member on the Temple's board of directors
and a high-ranking shareholder. He's been selling company secrets
to a Museum director on the West Coast. A public whipping at a
board meeting is Force's preference. And Yang is all too delighted
to oblige.

His half-cry/half-scream infects the air for the sixth time. I
crack the whip for the seventh, lightning funneled from my wrist
and hand into the handle. During the brief moments I pay attention to the other board members, I notice winces, squeamish arms
constricting chests, color in cheeks leeched out. So pale they remind me of the inside of a coconut. I come up with new likenesses
each time. A winter mountaintop, angel wings, sugar cubes. No
matter the audience, their cheeks are always white.

When I pause too many times, my father takes over and finishes the job. This is my third whipping in a row, so I'm more tired
than usual. He explains Yang has other important business and
dismisses me. My crimson cape—Force's idea—becomes a spill of
blood behind me. The sound of more whip thwacks followed by
screams pricks my ears as I retreat.

I don't wince anymore.

Queran meets me in the preparer room to help remove Yang
from my skin.

Sometimes, his silence is infuriating.

206

I should be used to it by now. I wear Yang, but all I feel inside is Serenity. So…it hurts every time.

First, Queran removes the gold details from around one eye. And then sets to work with the gold-and-ruby gown that is more a second skin. It's similar to my last interaction gown. Thanks to Queran's preparation and outfitting Bliss with voxel-disguising tech, it was enough to fool Force and the participants.

And thanks to all my involvement as Yang, it's proven to be a worthy distraction from Bliss's pregnancy. Since all her "client" appointments were canceled due to mine and Force's bargain, he hasn't bothered to monitor or check in on her. Everything has worked out well.

Too well.

"Thank you for your help," I tell Queran, my voice soft as the liquid he slips underneath my navel to remove the gold there.

Next, he unrolls the choker necklace of multiple strings of rubies. I tilt my head to the side, exhaling in relief. I swear each one of the gems has the weight of a snow globe. After the gold on my legs and arms is gone, Queran's hands move to the lace corset strings. But everything is taking too long. I'm so done with this. So, I start ripping the lace until it's in fragments—bits and pieces of Yang's radiance.

Queran starts the shower for me. As I slide into the water, which is a combination of water and a special type of soap that will remove the paint, I notice him pick up the lace scraps and place them in a neat little pile on the table. If my father decides the costume is warranted again, Temple tech can easily print out a new one, but I know Queran prefers to simply repair costumes.

He has a thick cotton robe ready for me when I emerge. Once I'm settled inside its plushness—take a moment to sit and breathe as is my routine—Queran holds up a finger and motions to the two origami figures on the table in front of me. He always uses a swan for my symbol, but he's created a new one…a Yang symbol. With one hand, he takes the paper Yang and positions it on top of the swan.

Giving him a little smile, I shrug. "No, Queran. Yang isn't swallowing me. I just wear her when I need to."

He then retrieves another familiar paper design from his

pocket. The tetra-star.

"For Bliss, yes," I confirm, pursing my lips. And her children.

"Ultrasound," he informs me, pointing to Bliss's room. "Dr. Moby."

I grin, the news injecting new energy into me.

I wouldn't miss it for the world.

Forty-eight
KeEpIng DeAls

Bliss

M Y SISTER'S FACE ERUPTS INTO the same glow I've grown familiar with when we hear the heartbeats, since the apple doesn't fall far from the trees. Almost as incandescent as Luc's every time he looks at me. I don't know what to make of it. Both their eyes resemble a sunrise on a frosted morning. For them, everything is crystallized, a new world of beauteous patterns and intricacies. For me, I still don't recognize my body even after all these months. I'm certain Father wouldn't either if he saw me. Serenity's plan has worked in our favor. If he's not preoccupied with training her, he's tending to international relations, preparing his Temple for her.

Somehow, Serenity has managed to halt our joint interactions, giving us as much time as possible to hide my condition. I haven't asked how she managed it. I don't want to know, though part of me has to wonder if our mother's absence has something to do with it. Father decided she should accompany him on his overseas rendezvous, which is the only reason she is not here to join us.

"Listen, Bliss!" Serenity glories in the rapid *thump-thump-thump* of the twins' heartbeats. The way they nudge each other on the Peek-a-Boo. Their tiny alien shapes. "Are you sure you don't want to talk names?"

I don't even bother to look down at my swollen belly. "What does it matter?"

At first, she seems hurt, but it doesn't take her long to regain her smile. "What about you, Luc?" she asks, grinning at him

209

where he sits across from me.

He smiles back at her. In some ways, they are living this for me. I'm experiencing it through their eyes, though not feeling it for myself. I've continued to keep a…distance. Luc and Serenity are naïve to believe Father will never find out. So, whenever the twins kick or roll over or hiccup, I try to remember they don't belong to me. They don't even feel like mine. Nothing has ever felt like mine.

"If Bliss prefers to wait until they're born, then I will, too," he vows, seeming satisfied by the mystery of my choice.

Serenity huffs just as the Temple Peek-a-Boo starts recording the twins' weights and health. We've been lucky. I haven't needed any nurses or doctors. Once a month, Skylar manages to hack the Peek-a-Boo system to send the updates to Dr. Moby. Everything has checked out.

Before I can turn off the Peek-a-Boo, Serenity frames her hands on each side and leans over to press her lips to the screen, kissing each twin. I hold my breath a little, trying not to cringe. With the way she's acting, I'm surprised she hasn't managed to get knocked up already, especially since she and Sky have been virtu-ally inseparable for the past seven months. But I remember the conversation we shared over Christmas when she felt the babies kick for the first time…

"That's incredible," she'd exclaimed as we snuggled next to the fireplace together.

Serenity has worked much harder over the past few months to get closer to me, adopting a possessive manner. Luc is more protective, but as far as Serenity is concerned, she wants to own every little kick or nudge. And I let her.

"What about you?" I'd asked. "Is this how you will be when you have your own?"

She'd shaken her head. "I'm not having my own. Ever."

I had to admit I was a little surprised. "Why?"

"I don't like change."

"You don't like responsibility."

"I took responsibility where you didn't." I'd picked up on the disdain in her voice.

"Because it won't matter. Eventually, he's going to find out.

My avoidance and loose robes won't fool him forever. What do you think is going to happen?"

"He won't hurt them," she'd denied, resolute, shaking her head and turning to the fire. "He won't hurt anyone I love again."

"Is that the real reason you don't want any of your own?"

She hadn't responded, but I'd read her expression because there'd a shocking lack of anger. No compressed lips, no heated eyes stirring lightning. No, what I'd seen instead was pure, untarnished fear. Fear in the way she squeezed her shoulders together and clutched the blanket as if she'd suddenly turned cold, fear in the way she bit down on her lower lip and then pursed her lips together, fear in her furrowed forehead.

"Serenity?" I'd dropped my blanket to touch her shoulder. "You're afraid of yourself, aren't you? Because there's so much of him in you."

She hadn't answered, just dipped her chin onto her raised knee. It had been enough of a confirmation as any.

"You will be a good mother if you give yourself a chance," she'd pressed, turning the discussion back to me. "You have more of Mom in you."

I'd just shaken my head. "That's not true."

"Yes, it is!"

"No. Serafina has always been worth more."

"You know Luc doesn't feel that way. Or me." I'd pinched my lips as she continued. "I thought you were past all this."

"It takes…time. You know I love you and Luc. But I can't love these children. Mother could love you because she escaped with you. But lightning can't strike twice, Serenity," I'd said, stifling the tears.

"Sky has a plan. But you have to want it, Bliss. You're worth more to Luc and me but also to these babies. You're their mother. You're the one carrying them."

"I tried to kill them," I'd almost shouted, reminding her of that night with the brownies when I first discovered the truth. "They don't belong to me. I'm only doing this for you and for…Luc." I'd swung the blanket back to show her my protruding stomach. "But this…it's too much for me. I can't be their mother. Not when she's doomed to turn out just like me. Or he will turn out just like

Father. I can't watch that. I don't have as much…hope as you do. Or love. I was always the weaker twin."

"Don't let him rob your hope. Or your love. You've spent too long doing that." She'd squeezed my shoulder. "Bliss! You have so much love to give. Maybe you were never the weaker twin. Maybe you let me grow strong and healthy. Maybe you took the punishment because you could endure it. Just like you took the whippings for Mom."

I'd pondered her words for the first time, allowed myself one moment to believe they might be true because I knew it would be the only way I could make it through this.

SERENITY DOTES ON ME LIKE a mother hen even more than usual since I've grown larger and will be due soon. Even with Luc in the room, Serenity isn't ready to leave until she's made sure I don't need anything else. Her fussing becomes annoying, but I still can't fault her for it. I've determined these babies are more hers than they are mine with how much work she's put into taking care of me.

Finally, Luc grips her by the arm and stops her in her tracks as she prepares to bring me another glass of water. "Serenity…" When he hardens his tone, she pays attention. "Go to bed. You're exhausted. And you have more duties tomorrow night."

"But I—"

"Go to bed!" He raises his voice right before taking stock of her wounded expression, like a defeated gazelle before a lion. Softening his eyes, he gentles his tone. "I will take care of her now. It's not only what I need to do, it's what I want to do. Will you let me do that?"

Appearing properly chastised, she nods. "I'm sorry."

He leans over, tenderly kisses her cheek. Nothing sensual whatsoever. More like a brother to a sister. How things have changed over these past months.

Once she's gone, Luc approaches my bedside with the water, pausing to look down at my bulging stomach. After handing the glass to me, he tucks the sheets around my frame and secures an extra blanket on top of those. This is his routine every night. Except he normally comes in after Serenity has left. Tonight is the first time he's thwarted her. Perhaps it's because he felt like he owed it to her after everything that happened, but tonight, I see more than just the steadfast man who has come to me every night, who helped me break the mountain. Tonight, I see a father in his careful eyes.

I work up the courage to tell him as he prepares to turn off the light, "You don't have to sleep on the couch."

He scans the room, almost teasing in his reply, "Would you prefer the floor?"

I don't have to work at the smile. It's genuine for how I feel toward him. Then, I pat the spot on the bed just next to me. Ever since he learned about the twins, our lovemaking has taken a backseat.

Luc pauses but doesn't require more encouragement than that. He doesn't turn down the covers to let himself inside and close to me. Instead, he positions himself on top of them instead. Months ago, he changed his tactics. No less affectionate but in a different way. He's taken to surprising me when I don't know he's there— like slipping his arms around my waist from behind or placing his hands over my eyes and kissing the nape of my neck. Other touches are more purposeful like when he senses I'm cold and wraps me up in a blanket because it's still unusual for me to wear anything besides lingerie. Over the winter, I found myself colder despite the climate-controlled Penthouse. Luc would fasten on my socks, pausing every now and then to brush his lips across my stomach. Every motion and gesture has been endearing. I don't know what to make of it. Sometimes, it still doesn't seem real. That I'll wake up and Luc and this belly will be gone, replaced with the bones, flesh, and blood of my past.

But every time I wake up, he's still there.

So, if there were any doubts in my mind before, they are all gone now. These twins may not belong to me, but they definitely belong to Luc. And so do I.

Forty-nine

Keeping Up Appearances

SERENITY

VERY NIGHT WHEN I RETURN to my bedroom, Sky is waiting for me. The rolling water sprite lights on all the walls. Some new chocolate confection on the table. Each time, Sky retrieves my hands and kisses my callused palms. My hair is still damp from my shower earlier. Tonight, Sky decides to braid it while I sit at the table. Chocolate butterflies. I smile. It's a reminder.

"Who was it tonight?" Sky asks, able fingers parting my hair in three ways.

"Board member. Was selling secrets to the enemy." I examine the chocolate staining my fingertips because I'm still holding the butterfly, but I can't bring myself to eat it...yet. "I whipped him ten times. After the tenth, I couldn't stand the blood stench, so Force took over. You'd think I'd be used to it."

Sky tugs my head as he continues braiding, unhindered by my words. This room has become my confession box, and Sky... my priest.

"You still won't whip the girls," Sky tries to advocate for me.

I shake my head. "He tried. Last week. One of the girls on level 127 was *insubordinate*." A fancy word for 'she defended herself when one of the guards tried to rape her'. Glowering, I devour a butterfly. "I threw the whip at Force and stormed out."

Sky finishes by securing my braid with an automatic hair tie. When he tosses the braid's end over my shoulder, I catch the hair tie to finish its fourth loop. NAILS could easily braid my hair, but

214

Sky enjoys doing it himself. Sometimes, he'll give me a foot or back massage. Other times, he'll have a bubble bath waiting for me. Another time, he arranged for me to go skinny-dipping with Sharky. On Christmas Eve, he took me down to the Winter level. We got to stand in a virtu-globe under a snowfall with fir trees lit by twinkle lights all around us. Every gesture he's ever performed has wrapped a protective coating of ice around my heart. Enough to contain my lightning, to keep it at bay. Any day, I wonder if that coating will break and I'll finally snap and truly become Yang inside and out. According to Force, I was born Yang. She will always be inside me.

Sky leans toward me, kisses the top of my head, and whispers, "Proud of you, Ser."

Then, he helps himself to a butterfly and sits down opposite me, shoves another one in his mouth. "Bliss is due in just a few weeks, right?"

"Three," I confirm with a nod. "Growing babies takes forever!" Sure, these things take time, but nine months seems a little extreme. Since the birth rate is so low, the Centre started harvesting eggs and speeding up the fertilization and development process. By now, they've just about perfected it. Which means another round of perfected baby girls destined for the Temple.

"Won't be long now. You've done well at keeping Force distracted."

I arch my neck back, my braid taking a nose dive. "Do you really think he's not going to find out? When she goes into labor, she's going to have to go to the Centre."

"And if all goes as planned, history will repeat itself and Bliss and her children will be gone by the time Force arrives." Sky pops another butterfly in his mouth.

I break a dark chocolate wing in half. "You enjoy keeping secrets from me, don't you?"

Sky grins, rolls his masticated butterfly to one side of his mouth, and replies, "It's pretty fun."

"Licking your wounds, Serenity?"

And just like that, the butterflies on the plate seem more like mud pies.

"Ahh...speak of the devil," Sky insults my father, reclining in his seat and folding his hands behind his head. "Never mind, aspirations are too high. Devil's kiss-ass is better."

Force's lip curls in revulsion. To him, Sky might as well be something he scrapes off his shoe, but he still knows he can't touch him. Not Yang's husband.

"Your performance tonight was adequate, daughter."

It's a disappointment-wrapped compliment.

Force paces the room, gait more gradual because I recognize he's leading up to something. Words waiting just behind his lips, ready to pounce. But only for me.

"Sky…" I hint, flicking my eyes to the door. We both know my father will wait us out if we try to play his game.

As soon as Sky is gone, Force gets to the point. "You seem tired." He studies me, eyes prodding mine while his arms cross over his chest.

I blow out a breath, a few of my curls kicking the air. "Over the past seven months, you've had me shadowing you everywhere, whipping anyone from the journalist who writes something nasty about you to a corrupt shareholder. When I'm not doing that, I'm combing through the history of the Temple and its architects and directors and studying everything about each level and exhibit and security guard and preparer and—"

My father raises his hand, interrupting me. "I believe I understand, daughter. You've been working extremely hard." He draws his hand to his chin, stroking it as he would a baby bird. "Too hard."

Apprehensive, I worry my lower lip with my teeth as he begins to circle me.

"Your transition into Yang has been quite smooth. Up until now, I haven't questioned it."

"So, don't."

I walk away, approach one of my water walls, and sweep my fingers into the stream. Amazing how the technology responds, droplets interacting with my hand, some splattering and others reuniting to form a new current below my hand. I smile.

"That is what surprises me," my father concludes, finger brushing the side of my cheek right before the corner of my mouth falls in response. "Your happiness. One could attribute it to the honeymoon phase, but we both know better than that." Force leans against the wall next to me, upsetting one whole water stream so it sluices around him. His mouth curves into a mocking grin. "Don't we?"

I don't care if he knows I'm still a virgin. But I do care he feels my intimate life is any of his damn business. Even after marriage, why should I have expected that to change?

"You should be thwarting me. Testing your boundaries. Fighting me at every turn." Force cocks his head like a vulture surveying a smaller of its own species, curious but non-threatening. "Why, why, why?" he singsongs, tapping the apex of his chin. Then, the vulture closes in, beak pecking beak. "We both know you're not going to tell me, are you?" Force bumps noses with me. "Your sister will be more obliging."

My brain short circuits. He hasn't visited Bliss in weeks. The last time he had, it was planned. Thanks to Queran and Sky helping with preparation and illusory tech, Force had spoken to pre-maternity Bliss as far as he'd been concerned. If I try to stop him, it'll urge him on all the more. A deflection will have the same result. So, I choose a different option.

"Yes, Bliss will tell you everything. Just like my mother." Frowning, I add, "Because you control everything in this Temple, except for me." Looks like I've learned more from my father than I thought—like the art of dropping a subtle hint while propping his ego up in a backward, mocking sort of way. I just hope he doesn't pick up on it.

"Not in all respects." Force straightens, adjusts his vest, and grins, saluting me. "I look forward to dinner later."

As he exits my bedroom, I count the steps he takes on my winding staircase. Staccato rhythm, a spring in his step. A new challenge always does that. Sky's footsteps replace his, overlapping just at the edge. When he enters my room, I glance at him, brows anticipating as much as my eyes are.

"Which way did he go?" I hold my breath.

"Toward Serafina's room."

For the first time...

Serenity, one. Force, zero.

Fifty

BlOod

BLISS

IT'S ABNORMAL FOR ME TO visit my mother at this time of the day. Up until now, I haven't spoken to her much about labor. We've discussed every facet of pregnancy and how hers differed from mine. My morning sickness hadn't been as aggressive as hers. But the twins kicking and vying for room in my womb is.

"What would you have named me?" I ask Serafina as we sample on fresh, 3D-printed scones.

Our styles are similar. Except she prefers dresses. My mother wears a lacy white dress with capped sleeves that frolic along the skin of her arms. These days, I simply prefer nightgowns. Since I don't spend much time outside my room and I sleep a good amount, it makes sense.

Serafina finishes her sip of tea and then sets her cup down, pursing her lips. "Bliss suits you," she declares, giving me a non-answer.

I open my hand on the table with a sigh. "Mother..." I'll never tire of calling her that. Serenity may shorten it to the ever-common "Mom," but I prefer the traditional term. Or Serafina.

Easing her head back a little, my mother chews on one side of her lower lip and debates. One gesture she passed down to Serenity. Finally, she levels with me. "For the first five years of your life, I didn't know your name. Whenever Kerrick and I...spoke about you, I called you Verity."

"Verity..." I say the name a couple of more times, enjoying the sound of it. "So, for years, you searched for verity, for truth."

218

"And the truth did not disappoint," my mother confirms, her hand reaching over the table to cradle mine. Her eyes become blue pockets, the kind people hide and store things in just as she has stored my secret all these months.

By now, the twins are nearly at full term. And both are equal in size. Whatever condition affected Serenity and me was not passed down to my twins.

"If you're looking for boy name ideas," Serafina goes on, retrieving her hand, "I think Kerrick is a good one."

"Oh, come now, Serafina."

At the sound of his voice, a million ice shards impale my spine. And root there. My chest begins to heave as my father circles the table, gazing back and forth between the two of us right before his hands lunge for my shoulders, nails goring my skin.

He descends toward me, breath venomous just like always. "I think I can provide one or two ideas, don't you think?"

THE LAST WORDS FORCE USED before dragging me to my room was a promise he made to my mother, too. A promise to deal with her later for keeping this from him.

First, he'll deal with me.

Once we arrive in my room, Force dismisses Queran—the one I normally eat with. If I had, things may have turned out differently since I entrusted the illusory device to him. The last time my father visited, Queran used it to manipulate the light fields along and around my body while emitting a substitute spright light of my pre-maternity body, overlaying it across my present one. But I ate with Serafina today. Not Queran.

Just before he closes the door, Queran's eyes brush across mine, compassion engraved there. Just as it was when he first prepared me years ago, when he first observed the whip scars on my back.

Like always, I stand in the center of the room, submissive hands placated in front of me, except now my belly interferes, pushing them outward more.

Father strokes his chin, lips compressed, eyes deviating between fury and skepticism. "It seems I underestimated you, Mara. Your condition explains so much regarding your sister. But you...I hardly know what to believe. Serafina's influence, no doubt."

When he pauses, it's my turn to speak, especially when his shadow overlaps half my body.

"Nature cannot be controlled, Father," I say, trying the safest option.

He grips my jaw. "Of course it can. You should have come to me. We could have settled this quite easily. What were you thinking? Did you honestly believe I wouldn't find out? That you could play your mother in *my* Temple?"

I shake my head, lowering it. "No, Father." I never have.

Force sighs, dropping the hand gripping my jaw to rub a few of my curls instead. "Serafina's influence. Serenity's doing. Perhaps we can remedy this unfortunate business. Redeem it."

When he presses his palm to my belly, something strikes a chord in me. It's not lightning. Nowhere close to that. But it does burn. And it lingers. I can't extinguish it. A slow-burning flame. A mini-forest fire in a bottle. All I want to do is push his hand away. Because it doesn't belong there. Just like they don't belong to him.

"I assume a boy?" he wonders, neck angled, eyes anchored on my belly.

"One of each," I respond, voice softer than a ribbon because it takes so much for me to get the words out.

My father rears back, routine cackle following. "Oh, this gets better and better. What to do, what to do..." He begins to pace, hand cupping his jaw right before he rhythmically slaps both his cheeks as if to jar his thoughts in the right order. "You will birth these twins, but that is all. Do you understand? Serenity will be their mother. Skylar will act as their father. And I will be their doting grandfather." Which is code for 'he will raise them both'.

The door opens behind Force but without his knowledge since there is only one other man in the Temple capable of silent entrances other than my father. Inhaling, I brace my shoulders for what I'm about to do. But first, I begin with a challenging question.

"What about their father? Doesn't he get a say?"

Force snaps to attention, a whirlwind of confusion in his eyes. "What? One of dozens of invisible men you've played Breakable whore to over the years?"

He acts like I had a choice. Like I was booking appointments. Like it was more than just survival. More than becoming who I needed to be, becoming who he wanted me to be.

"Your daughter is not a whore," Luc refutes, voice bordering on dangerous territory, the same tone he used when he fought my first client months ago. "And I am hardly invisible."

Force shakes his head, a few dark tendrils dancing on his brow at the same time he turns around. Matched in height, Force and Luc form a stalemate. Not only in countenance, but also in expression. Neither relents. Luc's eyes turn deadly. Nightmare blue eyes. The kind that can drown a man in cold blood. Father's are the opposite. Dragon eyes. The kind that reflect flames, that can set water on fire.

"Seems I've overestimated you this time, Director." My father breaks the silence. Axes it. "No, I should rephrase that. A director would know better than to allow his fantasy to become reality."

"Bliss is no fantasy." Luc shoves past Father hard to join my side, hand settling on my upper back.

Force rolls his eyes. Sways toward the two of us. "Allow me to prove you wrong."

In one swift move, he rips my nightgown, shredding silk as easily as snapping a thread. I know what he's showing Luc. The festoon of scars. Each one with a story to tell.

"Force!" Luc booms, going so far as to seize my father's wrist, but Force overpowers him and presses Luc's hand to my skin, to my spine.

"This one is my favorite. Looks different than the others," Force snarls. "The only one I never took a skin splicer to. Her very first scar."

When Luc shoves my father's hand away and collects me in his arms, Force straightens and rights himself, sidestepping us to continue explaining, "I needed blood, and she gave it. If you want that from her, then take it. Take her body if you want it. That's who we are, Luc. It's what it means to be a *man*. It's a man's nature."

Something twinges sharp in my stomach, reverberating throughout my body, especially my lower back. My knees buckle a little, but Luc is strong enough for all three of us.

"Mara is like all the others."

Force wanders toward the mirror on the opposite wall, which scans him automatically, making me wonder if it picks up on his arrogance. He continues, unhindered by the projection display offering him multiple different outfits from business to casual. "Even if she's had her fun adopting a different role, she will always return to her original state of being. Ready to submit to any desire. Meant for more palettes beyond yours." Force nods to him. "You want to play out a fantasy for a long time and be a repeat client, I don't care. But only a client, Aldaine. Mara will always be a Breakable."

"Bliss is no Breakable," Luc growls, countering Force, striding toward him only after I'm sitting in a chair.

Pain is something I'm used to. But this is new.

"She has just as much value as Serenity."

So does every girl.

When Luc reaches Force's side, my father dodges past him. Pushes back his shoulders as if they're tossing aside any annoying weights before answering, "Serenity has my blood in her. It is the only thing that separates her from the others. Only thing that gives her soul lightning. But not Bliss. She is meant for pleasing us. Worth nothing else. Get what you want from her and move on."

I imagine every one of Luc's kills from his past is in his clenched fist. But I just don't expect him to actually throw it. I wince when he cracks his knuckles against my father's face. As if I feel it when it lands, when Luc sends him stumbling to the floor. No, I'm feeling something much worse. And they're growing.

Force catches himself with his hands. There's a trickle of blood on his lip. He spits out more, red-tinged saliva. A tooth clatters to the floor like a popped piano key. Luc takes one step forward, squats, and grips Father's collar, bracing his fist again.

"Now you're acting like a man," my sadist father commends him.

"Apologize to your daughter," Luc orders.

I clutch the torn fabric of my nightgown. I must resemble some plump bird clinging to the random bits of twigs, string, and hair that make up her nest.

"Apologize to your own flesh and blood," Luc presses, looming closer. It's the first time I've seen my father cringe. It's subtle but there all the same.

Force tilts his head up to me before spitting more blood out to the side. "You are a man full of surprises, Luc Aldaine. Who could've believed Jacob would really fall in love with weak-eyed Leah after he'd already sampled the intoxicating Rachel?" Force winks. "If you understand the reference."

Luc narrows his eyes. "Only due to my ending the life of a priest and deciding to read the last thing he was holding." The former director gives a mirthless laugh. "Pity he didn't read more of it since I'm pretty certain the texts forbid using a cathedral as a front for a pedophile ring."

Force starts to laugh, throwing his head back before shaking it. "You're a real piece of work, Aldaine. Possibly even more than me."

Luc tenses. He looks like he'd enjoy ramming my father's laugh down his throat. But this time, it's Luc's turn to wait Force out. Luc won't relent until he gets what he wants...for me.

"Very well, Luc." Force sighs in surrender before turning to me as I clutch at my stomach. "Bliss..." He calls me by my real name for the first time in what must be years. "You have my most sincere and humble apology." He presses a hand to his chest to make a show of it.

I'm not fooled. Neither is Luc, but judging from his smile, it's simply a pleasure to hear the words. My father has just lost a few of his shark teeth which lacerate his tongue on their way up. It's enough for Luc, who releases his collar with enough force to fling Father back to the floor. Force calls for a medic bot. It'll likely take a day for the Immortal implant to repair his tooth. Luc wanders toward me as Force leaves, ordering multiple masseuses to his room. They double as professional ego strokers and self-pity encouragers, doctorates in professional babying. At heart, my father is a spoiled, selfish little boy.

Luc shakes his head, corner of his mouth twitching. "When you cart around that level of sadism, his Id is in constant need of nurturing."

"Luc..." I suddenly gasp, finally permitting myself to react to everything going on inside me. In the same moment, I feel a host of liquid slide down both my thighs.

"Bliss?" He places his hand on my waist and another on my shoulder, ready to raise me up.

Hunched over, I stare up at him and announce, "My water just broke."

Fifty-one
GrIef

SERENITY

By THE TIME WE ARRIVE, it's too late. A pool of blood pollutes the sheets. Luc's arms have become a cradle for Bliss while his body rocks her. Both on the floor together. No.

"No."

It's all Sky can say. He closes his eyes just after. Then punches the wall, leaving a fist-shaped hole there.

Something twists and turns in my belly. Chaotic loops and corkscrews rearranging my intensities when I see the two nurses carting away the stillborn babies in sterile plastic-like containers. My sister's sobs are so loud they could fracture the room, which is already on the verge of shattering into pieces. All these months, all that work to hide the secret, and they are just...gone.

I slide down the wall, grief rattling my insides, shaking them. A second later, Sky is holding me but not rocking me. His arms tremble with his own emotion. What I should do is go to my sister, hold her somehow. But Luc is a barrier between her and everything else. Couldn't so much as touch her right now. Realization dawns that they need to be alone. I need to give them this. I'm not supposed to be here. I'm just a Yang-shaped parasite who would suck on their grief.

As I break free from Sky and start to leave, I hear Bliss behind me.

"Serenity," she whimpers, her voice stretching, curving around my body like a double helix, reminding me that we are sisters, that we are twins. "I'm sorry. So sorry."

225

I hang my head. She shouldn't say that. It's not her fault. Maybe…maybe it was mine. For being the stronger twin, for taking what she was denied, for having the life she should have had. The life without the trauma—trauma that could have impacted her babies. The body doesn't get over that trauma. It's always there waiting, remembering even if the mind chooses to forget.

"Bliss…" Sky starts, but I grab his hand, tugging him away. Nothing we say will help right now. Absolutely nothing.

"Please tell Mom," is the last thing she says before we leave the room.

For the first time since entering the Temple, I feel cold. A numbness settles inside me. A soft snow but the kind that doesn't melt. I need…I need to *feel*. But first…I have to tell Mom.

"Meet me at Sharky's tank," I say to Sky. "I need to tell Mom first."

Since our wedding day, this will be the first time Sky and I have been apart besides the times I'm with Force. My father wouldn't like any space between Sky and me, but as far as I'm concerned, Force can go to the deepest pit of hell. As it is, I'm sure he's on his way to Bliss's Centre Room. Alerted by now as to the events. He won't want to be late like he was for my birth.

But when I knock on my mother's door, my father opens it, and it's the worst form of wrong that could ever be. Because his lips are pinched and his shoulders are stiff. Yet, he's shaking just a little with his chest thrust out. Hot black ink roiling in his eyes. A lion roaring in his blood. He only gets this way when…

No. Not in my mother's room.

Suddenly, Force smiles. A smile that reeks of a checkmate. He takes one step to the side to reveal my mother. Hunched over. Palms on the floor. Three sinister whip marks scrawled into her flesh. Fresh blood oozing from them to taste her skin. And the whip in Force's right hand.

He anticipates my action, so when I lunge for the whip, he flicks it, primes it against my chest. "Tsk, tsk, tsk, Serenity. The one you should be attacking is *her*." He sweeps the whip in the air, gesturing it toward Serafina. "When I came to her, she confessed everything to me about her knowledge of Mara's pregnancy." He pauses, licks his lips, and smiles. "And then begged me to punish

226

her."

I wish I could refute him. Throw it back in his face and say he's lying. But my mother nods, confirming his words. And with her voice cracking, she looks up at me. "Serenity..." She swallows the hoarseness, the pain in her voice. "You'll understand someday."

I run as fast as I can. So fast, the tears soar out of my eyes, dodging my cheeks on their escape. She's wrong. I'll never understand.

I don't understand anything anymore.

Fifty-two
Understanding

BLISS

SHE'LL UNDERSTAND SOON.
They both will.
In the meantime, he'll take care of her. And my body needs to heal.

Fifty-three

HeAling

SERENITY

A COUPLE OF HOURS LATER, LUC is in the middle of bringing Bliss back to her room. My curls lay as wet waves all down my chest and shoulders as I march straight up to them, stare down at my sister, and command, "Come with me now."

Bliss blinks once. Luc glances at her, lips parted.

Shifting his weight behind me, Sky shrugs, jutting his elbows out, hands still in his pockets. "I'd listen to her. She's got that look in her eye."

Luc sighs, dropping his arms to the side before surrendering Bliss to me. Slow but sure, I loop my arm around her back, securing my hand under her elbow. Throughout our entire trek down the hall, she peeks up at me, eyes skittering with questions, but her lips ask none. I don't offer her anything. When we turn the corner and reach the medical room, I use my barcode and enter with her, leading her to the cell generator. Considering we are identical twins, it doesn't take much to trick the machine.

I open it up, then motion for her to lie inside it.

And Bliss doesn't fight me.

I sit in a chair with my back to the machine after I close it. It hums to life. I swipe at the tears on my cheeks when I hear my sister whimper just a little because the healing process through the generator is painful. For an hour, it is painful. And I listen to everything…even if it's through my head in my hands. But the result is Bliss stepping out of the machine, able to move without

229

clutching her no-longer-swollen stomach. She can walk at a normal pace without pain. Without shuddering.

"Thank you." Bliss sits in the chair next to me, the hospital gown slipping down one shoulder.

"Don't say that," I snap, tugging at the ends of my hair from a sudden recognition. "I just made you erase whatever you had left of them." My thoughts are always too late to catch up with my actions.

Bliss smiles, pats my hand. "But now, we can escape that much quicker."

I look up. Perplexed. Bliss leans over, kisses my cheek, and tells me, "I love you, Serenity."

Groaning, I grate my nails into my scalp and stare at the ceiling as if it can help me navigate through the tetra that is Bliss.

She grabs my wrist, yanking it down. "Don't do that. You'll hurt yourself."

"What changed?" I ask, referencing her twins being gone. Is she in denial?

Bliss shrugs. "When Father found out. And when I pushed them out. I'm just...grateful. Grateful I got to carry them for all those months. And grateful to you." She nods toward me, nose nudging my cheek.

"Why?"

"Because without you, it never would have happened."

Fifty-four

QueRaN's PreSent

SERENITY

FTER BLISS AND I PART ways, I return to Sky and finally unload everything. And then, I ask him a question. Relive that same moment in the Aviary when I met him in my room. When he said it was time.

It's time again.

Sky searches my eyes just after he's relayed the plan. We have no time to waste. His smile is warm. It stretches across his face, injecting sunlight straight into my skin.

"And you can do it so the others will get out?" I confirm, thinking of all the girls Sky met while imprisoned. All the other Sunshines...all the other unicorns of the Temple.

Sky nods. Relief finds a host in me, multiplies, becomes a swarm. He tells me to change or at least to fasten on some pants below my long skirt. As soon as I'm finished, an alarm goes off. Blaring into my bedroom, echoing into the hall, and all through-out the Penthouse.

"Every level alarm is going off," Sky confirms, grin spread-ing. "Bomb threats, enough devices for them to evacuate, but they won't go off."

"Sanctuary waiting for us?" I ask as we travel down the stair-case. I say goodbye to the exotic fish in the spiral tank along with the miniature dolphins.

Once Sky opens the door and we enter the hallway where the alarm is even louder with the lights flashing, I glance at the eleva-tor, imagine riding it to Sharky's tank and planting a kiss on his head. For the past few weeks, I've taken more time to swim with him, preparing to say goodbye because I knew I couldn't bring him with me.

We round the corner of the hallway, almost smacking into a drone. Sky fiddles on his volu-screen and the drone moves on, sweeping around us to continue scanning the rest of the floor. Of course he's hacked the drones.

"How long before Force catches on?" I ask, keeping my hand curved around his arm as we move farther down the level to the west side.

"A few minutes, give or take. He's in a business meeting. Won't take him long to figure out what we're doing. But by the time he gets up there…"

"Up where?" I ask just as he deviates to the right, activating the automatic-security door that leads to what Sky tells me is a maintenance level…with a staircase. As soon as we start ascending it, I hear thunder from the other side of the hall right before the floor rocks beneath us.

Too loud.

I stumble, crashing into Sky's arms. "What's going on?" Confusion chokes me when I smell smoke, faint but wafting through the air even from behind the door. "But you said…the bombs."

Sky pulls up security footage on his screen, revealing one whole level in the Penthouse that has collapsed.

"Bliss!" I leap for the door, but Sky grabs my arms, hauling me back.

"Stop, she's fine," he warns before showing me footage of her and Luc a moment later. "But their exit is blocked." He motions to the rubble, pointing out the fifty-foot gap between them and the other side where the opposite maintenance hall closest to her room was. "Get to the roof now and I'll get them, make sure they get up there."

"The roof?" I warily eye the stairs.

"I've disabled the dome, Ser." Sky cups my shoulder, reassuring me with a smile. "You're finally gonna get your turn to fly."

While the plan is promising, I purse my lips, apprehensive about him leaving. "Sky…the last time this happened, the last time you left me alone…"

Sky winks. "No Mockingbirds this time, Ser. I'll be just a few minutes."

"And my mom?"

He gestures up. "Checked just a few minutes ago. She's waiting for us already. Now, scoot!"

Sky does first. Within three seconds, he's gone, the door closing behind him. At least it's a comfort to know my mom is on the roof. With that knowledge, I climb the two short flights and make it up to the roof.

But my mother is not here.

Instead, Queran is waiting for me, and I feel like such a fool. Pathetic selfishness fills me because I never told him, never considered him. And then, my foot crunches on something below me. I scan my surroundings, marveling.

"Queran!"

I gush at the hundreds of paper swans scattered all over the rooftop. They even coat the pool—dozens of tiny floating swans. Since Sky removed the protective dome, the shapes wisp this way and that to the bidding of the wind, the papers bumping against each other to create their own origami orchestra. Why would he do all this?

"Queran?" I repeat again, but this time in a question as he approaches me.

As always, his eyes are whimsical yet perceptive as they squeeze at the corners. A white-eye sky with pale blue iris clouds. And for once, the unordinary pale skin of his face is offset by his hair, coating the sides of his face. In the untarnished sunlight, the dark ginger strands have become gold. Dark gold shadows.

As Queran nears me, close enough for me to smell his sterile breath from beyond his parted lips, the corners of his mouth quirk upward as he retrieves the origami heart. The second shape he made for me on the first day we met.

Just once, he raises it to his mouth, makes a "shh" sound. "Sweet girl," he repeats his familiar phrase before kissing the heart just as he once had.

Suddenly, Queran unbuttons his coat and lets it drop to the ground below him, revealing his bare chest to me. Before, his muscles were always subtle, but they seem more developed now.

As if he's been using them more. Suspicion—foreboding—gnaws on my spine. I wish I could stop it, but it continues its ascent.

Next, Queran reaches into his pocket and retrieves another origami object. A paper woman with a long train of curling paper behind her. A wedding gown. A bride—me? One more object. A paper man. He presses them to his chest. Suddenly, I understand… and step back, thinking this will be more difficult than anyone who has come before. Perhaps even more difficult than Luc.

"Shh…sweet girl." Queran reaches out to me, his fingers so gentle when he lights them on my arm. I bend it before him, allowing him to open my palm and drop the paper man inside it. He's offering himself.

None of this makes sense.

I'm married.

And he's…Queran.

Two more shapes. The Yin and Yang.

"Bliss and me?" I question, brows furrowing in confusion.

Queran shakes his head. Points to the Yang shape, touches my chest once. Then, he gestures to the origami Yin and places it on his own chest. I don't understand…

Until he touches my waist. It's then I notice the bulge in his pants, which alarms me the most. It's not possible. I try to deny it, my eyes flashing back and forth between his lower regions and his eyes. Smiling, Queran folds his hand into mine.

I open my mouth, but before I can speak, Queran signals me with a finger to his lips. "Shh…follow."

Playing along for the moment, I sense I'm about to discover the gnawing sensation. Not so unlike needles dipped in lightning pricking the line of my vertebrae.

I trail him to the table near the pool. And that's when I see the giant paper swan hoisted to dangle in the air, undoubtedly through some magnetized force. But it's not the floating swan that causes my stomach to disappear into my toes. It's not the floating swan that steals all my breath and banishes it to some remote island. It's the paper bodies surrounding it. A mermaid, an angel, a girl holding a flower, a Venus flytrap, and all the others who have been found with the swan symbol carved into their chests. What I hope is only red ink stains the paper bodies, which spread around the hovering swan as if they are trophies. No, not trophies. *Presents.*

I try to swallow. Do my best, but my throat won't accept it. My voice is like a strung-up dry flower when I speak his name. "Queran." I clutch my stomach, willing the butterflies to stem the bile that wants to rise. The bomb was his doing. A diversion.

With one hand sinking onto my shoulder and the other onto my waist, Queran holds me, tries to draw me closer. "Sweet girl. Swan beauty. Most beautiful. Stay beautiful forever. With me."

The bile is too strong for my butterflies. Because I remember how Queran has seen every inch of me. How he's *touched* every inch of me. And I recognize the signs. Why he had to excuse himself more. Why he retreated to his room or the bathroom. Why he stopped the murders after learning of Bliss's pregnancy.

He doesn't seem offended when I vomit onto the ground, pouring retch onto the paper swans below me. Instead, Queran grabs onto my hair and holds it before rubbing his hand across the strands. When I straighten, both his hands join at my waist. If I try to run now, it would be more than easy for him to drag me back. Would he do that? Would he take what he wants from me? Only half my question is answered as he tugs me against himself, his groin thrumming against the back of my thigh, nose rubbing the side of my neck.

He motions to the pool, whispers in my ear. "Swim for me. Be my Swan."

"Queran." I try to pull away, sense him tensing behind me. "You're not...I mean, I'm not—"

With more strength than I could have predicted, my old preparer swings me around and stabs at me with his eyes. The whimsical blue clouds fade, replaced with a dark fury, quiet and calculating. No one would have ever suspected. Least of all me.

"Impossible girl." He raises up the origami bride, retrieves the one of himself, then puts them together. "Destiny."

His hands anchor on my hips right before he presses against me again, mouth nuzzling my throat. Oh, damn. I bite my tongue hard. Instinct causes me to pull away, but I can't run. Queran grips me with one hand while his fingers edge up to my blouse.

"Beautiful Swan. My Swan. I make you beautiful for eternity.

Just us."

What does he mean? Not releasing my hand, Queran gestures to a box underneath the table. He reaches under and withdraws what looks like a backpack. It takes me a second to realize it's a parachute.

"Skylar asked for my help…" Queran grins, raising it. It looks larger than a normal one. A double? "Package sent to me. Force doesn't monitor me." With my hand in his, he brings it to his chest and indicates, "Invisible."

"You weren't invisible to me," I refute, shaking my head. To everyone, he was invisible. Often, the preparers are, especially in Queran's case. For the first time, I consider how lonely life as a Penthouse preparer must be. Even Bliss is not the true Yin. Even she is known, even she is seen. Never Queran.

His lips part as he gazes at me, smile soft as swan down. "Sweet girl," he coos right before tossing the parachute over the side of the Temple.

"No!" I lunge for it, but Queran seizes me, protects me from falling because I've lost my balance.

"We will fly together, Swan," he whispers through my curls.

I start to sob because I know what it means for that parachute to be gone. But Queran isn't finished. He retrieves two others. A double and a single. And he reaches into his pocket for something else. A volu device, which he fastens to a cuff on his arm before bringing up the schematics for the Temple. And various floors. He taps on different ones in sequence, and I feel the ground shudder beneath my feet.

"Queran, what did you do?" I scream just as he picks up the double parachute and begins to fasten the harness around me, buckling it around my waist, looping it over my shoulders.

"Air before us. Fire behind us." He says nothing else.

Fire. He's burning the Temple down.

"Sky…"

I cry out his name before sprinting into a run as fast as my feet can carry me. To the closest door, but I hear Queran behind me, underestimate his speed because just as my fingers grab the handle, he yanks me back, hands caging my cheeks, lips pressing hard against mine. I shudder. Try to pull away, but his hands trample along my back, rooting on my waist and securing me close to him. He tastes like raindrops on glass, but the salt from my tears replaces the rain moments later.

Suddenly, the door opens behind Queran. My eyes turn saucer-wide at the sight of my father lunging. He grips the preparer by the nape of the neck, yanking him off me and slamming him to the ground. In the time it takes Force to press his boot against Queran's neck, my mother emerges from the doorway.

"Serenity." Force's voice is grim with a bite. Dark as shadow and claws. It's taken only a few seconds for him to observe all the paper swans and to process what's going on here. "I've already shown you what happens to murderers and traitors in my Temple. Now, I'm about to show you what happens when they screw with my family." Droplets of sweat careen off his nose, drop onto Queran's head.

In that moment, all I can see is Queran as a small boy. His hands creating little dolls out of twigs and fabric scraps, painting them with crushed berries. All I can think about is a little boy who was abandoned, who was bullied, who was Temple-plucked, and whose hands spent their whole existence creating beauty while he never felt beautiful himself. Until me. In the moment before my father's boot presses down to crush Queran's windpipe, my heart reaches to nudge Queran's.

I whisper two last words.

"See you…"

And then, Queran chokes on Force's boot, head lolling, eyes lifeless—a ghost-less corpse.

No sooner does he die than Sky finally appears with Luc and Bliss in tow. I don't know how he managed to get to the other side of the Temple and make it up the same staircase as my father and mother, but I don't care. I lunge for his arms, crying lightning tears. Not only from Queran but from the loss of the parachute. From the smoke and flames I notice creeping up the staircase. The aftermath of Queran's bomb.

Bliss slowly kneels beside Queran's still form, closes his eyes to leave him in peace. A paper swan brushes her bare ankle, and she scoops it up as if it's real.

"What's going on, Sky?" I sob into his shirt, watching my sister out of the corner of my eye.

"The Temple is burning, Ser. All the floors have been evacuated." He keeps his sentences short, offering nothing else.

"Queran threw one double parachute over the wall. Sky…" My voice breaks.

Force interrupts. "I've already got a helicopter en route." His eyes penetrate Sky's with a promise. "We will discuss your little escape attempt later."

Sky shakes his head. "There won't be a later. Chopper won't make it in time."

There must be some way to get out. But both windows in the Penthouse doors clouded over in smoke leave me doubting. My father's gaze flicks to the parachute harnessed around me. I know what he's thinking. He'll lock himself to me, force my mother into the other, and leave Sky, Luc, and Bliss behind. Force's smile is a powerful one. The one he wears when he's about to enact a superior plan, when he's ready to go to war. His smile is the king of all traffickers, abusers, virginity thieves, rapists, and murderers; he owns every last one.

As soon as he touches me, I snap. I fly for the weapon at his waist, jerking it away before he can use it. I use it instead. Sky's voice sounds more like dark cotton, muffled, as I whip my father once, twice, three times before I stop. I throw the whip away, hurling it over the side of the Temple so it becomes a black snake falling hundreds of feet to its death.

I won't become him.

Amidst the blood streaks on his back, Force grits his teeth and gets to his knees, but that's as far as it goes. Puzzled, I watch as he falls to the solid concrete, hand clutching his heaving chest. My mother approaches him, the ends of her dress sweeping across his cheek. Grinning great and golden as a firework lighting up the night, she kneels before him to say, "Shortness of breath, sweat soaking your skin, eyes heavy from fatigue…those are the signs of the final stage of the poison shutting down your heart."

My arms drop from Sky's shoulders. Bliss exhales, her warm breath like a white dove in the chilly air. Luc rubs her arms, soothing her. All this time, we were all wrong. Bliss isn't Yin. Neither was Queran.

My mother had the secret all along.

Force chokes, coughing up blood. "You will die," he seethes, gasping as a result.

My mother laughs, shaking her head, her hair diving onto his head. "You think this is a fast-acting poison? You seriously think I let you fuck me all those months because I wanted you to? The vampire betrayed you, Force." She leans over, mocking him. "Every time you kissed my skin, every time you licked me, every time you bit down...you were tasting poison. The type of slow poison that erodes implants. That finally shuts down hearts. With the right adrenaline rush."

Me. I was my father's final adrenaline rush. The irony. The Vampire dying at the hands of the Unicorn. From her poison. Too powerful for him. How could I have doubted her all this time?

As Force's head jerks from the poison injecting fire into his heart, my mother grips onto his jaw so she is staring right into his eyes. She raises her voice. "You said you would show Serenity what happens to those who mess with your family." He gurgles, blood and foam flowing from his mouth. We all see her crowd closer, hear her whisper, "I just did."

Force goes still.

And the Temple shudders even harder beneath us.

Lightning-fused panic shoots up my spine. I look to my mother to Sky to Luc and finally to Bliss...

And I can't stop her. I can't stop her from running headlong for the door behind us. Weighed down by the double parachute, my body misses hers, my hands hitting the door just as she closes it, locks it behind her.

"Bliss, *no*," I scream through the window. I start pounding on it, but even if I could break it, even if Sky could break it, it's small. Only gives me the image of her face. The image of her eyes. The gray in them steeped in melancholy and heartache.

I try the handle again and again, but Bliss summons me with her scream. "Serenity!"

I stop. Gasping. Crying. Pleading. Through it all, I gaze up at my twin.

"You have to go," she tells me. Her voice is firm, too firm. It's diamond hard. She's trying too much. Her eyes betray her. "Before it's too late."

One moment later, Luc cups my shoulder, squeezes it once, granting me a reassuring smile. I know that expression in his eyes. They've turned into steely blue ships. He's staying.

I grab at my hair, tears uncontrollable as more smoke billows from the staircase behind Bliss. She coughs into her arm. Before the fire can even reach her, the smoke will become her tomb.

"There has to be some other way." I shake my head violently. Slam my hand against the door a few more times. But the only other doorway into the Temple is already engulfed in flames. Any moment now, the entire Penthouse will come down. Urgency strikes. We have to get out of here.

Sky touches my arms, starts to clip himself into the parachute. Lips compressed. Jaw firm. Focused movements. His eyes speak of nothing but defeat.

Mom doesn't touch her parachute.

I try the door handle again, the dull clangs like a Morse code SOS blending with the muffled sounds of my sister coughing.

"Ser-enity." Her cough is an axe chopping my name in half. She covers her mouth, but yells through the fabric of her dress. "Thank you." She closes her eyes. "Thank you for everything." She plants her hand—just one—against the glass. Wind lashes my tears as I mimic her action, my fingers lining up so perfectly with hers, our identical fingerprints kissing. One would think the window is a mirror.

"I love you." She presses her forehead against the glass. "I can only say that because of you." And then, she chuckles. "I don't think—" She coughs again but manages to sputter out, "This is what you had in mind when you said love is dynamite."

I drop my head, shaking just a little when the inward laugh bubbles to the surface. How can I laugh right now? Sky urges me toward the wall.

"Serafina!" he barks at my mother.

Unlike me, she doesn't cry. Just stares at Bliss as long as she can. No words exchanged. In that moment, I recognize my mother is back inside the Centre on that fateful day. She is watching her daughter, a tiny slip of a thing, delivered and then rushed out of the room. Helpless to do anything but gaze at Bliss for as long as she can, committing her image to memory.

Finally, Bliss nods, and my mother clips herself into the parachute.

The ground shakes once more. Grows hot beneath our feet. Cracks.

Something inside me breaks when Sky hoists us onto the ledge.

All my butterflies shatter, wings fracturing, bodies rupturing, antennae splintering. As soon as Sky's feet leave the ledge, I'm in pieces, sailing into the wind. Turn my head just in time to see Bliss open the door—to see Luc safeguard her. It's the best word for how his arms surround her, hem her in, choosing to stay with her.

He chose to stay.

Fifty-five

My HoMe

BLISS

I'd always known I'd never leave. The Temple is more than my home. For a brief time, I thought I could, thought I could make it out there in the world. But as I watch Serenity flying away with our mother following her wind trails, gazing down at the Temple borders where they'll land, I know I could never follow.

I just never expected anyone else to be standing by my side.

Luc kisses me long and hard on the mouth as the fire builds, heating our shoes so they sizzle as the heat burns away at the soles. I taste every last precious second. In this moment, there is no smoke. No fire. Except for the flames we have created. A fire that will live on through Serenity and Skylar.

I have one last thought before the Temple goes down…

My father was right about one thing.

And I couldn't be happier!

Fifty-six

EscApe

SERENITY

*T*HE PENTHOUSE COLLAPSED FIRST, TAKING several other levels below it.

Those with private helicopters were the luckiest. Or those who could evacuate to the lower levels or to the Centre.

We land on the Temple outskirts.

Multiple tracks for public transportation whiz this way and that on both sides of us. They've already filled, carting away paying customers as fast as they can. Hundreds of private cars flee the Temple premises on cable tracks high above our heads. It's chaotic. Managers have departed since they have access to amenities like the private cars and tracks. They've left the girls. Many huddle in groups, trying to stay warm in the winter climate with nothing but pittances of clothing on. Others head for the public trains, but they won't be able to go very far. Not on Temple salary. The Glass District will pick them up.

Dozens of girls follow our every move, gathering closer to the couple who parachuted from the sky. A very familiar couple they immediately discover.

The Temple continues to burn in the background, but we are a reasonable distance away. Still, all I smell is smoke. All I remember is flames.

I'm in awe when Sky unclips our harness, discards the parachute, and climbs onto a nearby platform with a Temple statue of Force. The irony of it all.

He raises his arms, commanding attention. "Okay, listen up,

243

ladies!"

He calls out to the girls, voice booming, and dozens begin to crowd even closer. I pick them out one by one, recognizing many from the time my father imprisoned him. Others are familiar from Temple magazines.

"I recognize most of you. We had a few laughs together. I told you some stories. By now, you figured out they're true..." He looks to me, and I take it as a signal to wave to them. A few shake their heads in disbelief, but most just part their lips with ears primed. "But now it's time to get real. Glass District recruiters will be here soon. They're going to make you all sorts of promises. Tell you they'll pay you well, that regulations are in place, that you won't be hurt. I can't make the choice for you. But I work for the Sanctuary."

As soon as the word leaves his lips, I hear all sorts of evidence of Temple brainwashing. Giggles, eye rolls, heads shaking, defiant hands on hips or crossed over their chests.

"Listen!" Sky places a hand on his chest with one hand extended toward them. His eyes roam across the crowd of girls. A second later, I realize he's meeting each one of their eyes. "I know it seems hard to believe. I know the stories you've been raised with, the ones you've heard all your lives. And I can promise you they're all wrong." He pauses as if to double check they are listening. "No, the Sanctuary isn't some paradise..." Sky starts with the icy truth, and I hope and pray it won't backfire. "And I can't promise you it's all sunshine and rainbows. You're going to have to work every day. It's gonna be hard. Because what you've been through, what you've all gone through, is wrong and horrific and healing doesn't happen overnight." Sky takes a deep breath, hands dropping to his sides as he continues, "But I can promise you that you will never have to do the kinds of things you've done in the Temple ever again. I can promise that you'll be safe. You'll have food in your bellies you'll have worked for in good ways. I can promise you can take back your bodies and your power and own them for what they were made for. Not just for how some man can use them."

When he pauses, I survey the girls in the audience. Witness how some drop to their knees. I know those are the ones who are already saying yes. Others I must study closer, must see the tiny glints reflecting the sunlight on their cheeks. And others still have flint-coated eyes, which means it will take longer.

"There are thousands of us," Sky goes on to reassure them. "We can't be stopped. We have a transporter coming who can get you to safety. If you have family members, little sisters or brothers, we have lawyers who can help with that.

"I can't imagine what you've gone through, but I know others who can. Others who've been through what you have... They're living a better life, and they want that life for you. Just like I do."

Sky touches his chest one more time before gesturing to me. "You don't have to believe me. But believe Serenity. Believe..." He breathes deeply, and I realize what he's about to say before he even blows the words out. "Believe the Swan."

I wish I were better at this. Like Sky. It's not time for my lightning. It's not time for any of my fantasy stories. I think of my mother. I think of what she would say...and how. And then, I open my mouth.

"Every word he says is true," I tell the girls, my arms wishing they could wrap around the kneeling ones. I see Gull in every one of them. "I trust Sky with my life. You can, too."

No sooner do I say the words than the transporter arrives. Big enough for hundreds of girls. It runs on the Temple train line. A first-class transporter. The kind that can bypass all the major checkpoints. And if it's stopped, I'm sure there are backup plans for that.

"It's your choice," Sky tells them one last time before stepping down from the platform.

"Are you coming?" one girl cries out from the crowd. I recognize her. Halo.

Sky smiles. "Yes. We are coming."

Most of them go with us. Only a handful of skeptical ones stay. I bite down, chewing on my lower lip, remembering the time I threw a fit when Nightingale stayed in the Garden. This is out of my control just like it was then. Just like Sky said, we can't make the choice for them. I can only pray that someday they will see how much they're worth, how they're meant for something... better.

I just wish I could feel the same. But even with my mother

sliding into the seat next to me, all I can see is Bliss's face. Her eyes in my mother's. Her expressions reflected there. I wish I could focus on Sky, but he's in task-force mode. As soon as the transporter doors close, he pulls out his volu screen to create a record of the girls. He knows most of their names, but he asks more questions—if they have any family we need to get in touch with. A few have little siblings, plead with Sky to get them out of the orphanage or even the Glass District. Sky creates profiles, then starts sending information to his other contacts spread throughout the city.

"They're good people. They'll do their absolute best." It's all he promises.

I hear Bliss's voice in my head. Swipe away a tear. Mom sees because she squeezes my hand. It doesn't help. I need Sky. But they need him more.

So, I lean my head against the window, stare up at the moon. At its dark side that no longer reminds me of Bliss. Because she was the silver, the glow, the light reflecting the sun.

And I'm the reason she's dead.

HOURS LATER, I FINALLY STIR, my body a little achy from the position I've held. The Immortal implant will take care of that soon enough. The first thing I notice is the absence of all the girls. The only ones in the transporter are my mother, Sky, and me. Except it's a smaller transporter now. It still bears the Temple insignia, which allows us to go most places unhindered.

Next to me sits Sky, one arm wrapped around my body.

"What's going on?" I stretch, yawning the words.

The sky is that gray color right before dawn. It resembles a graphite rubbing. Fir trees hem us in on both sides.

"You slept throughout the night. And through the processing," Sky explains, shaking out his arm.

"I missed the Sanctuary?" I rake my fingernails through my hair, rubbing them into my scalp a bit before shaking out my curls.

"Mmhmm. Girls wanted to say goodbye to you, but you needed your rest. I promised we'd see them again soon."

I rub the sleep out of my eyes, yawn again, and then look up at him to ask, "Why? Where are we going?"

"Cause we need our own healing first. And...you'll see soon."

The sunrise is just painting the sky in fiery flamingo feathers when we reach the lake house. Little about it has changed. It's the time of day when the lake is the stillest. When I follow Sky out of the Temple cruiser, I hear the croaking of bullfrogs, hear hundreds of bird warbles and twitters from the trees around the water. I wince from the reminder of the Aviary, images of Luc and Bliss flashing before my eyes once more.

Sky places a hand on my lower back, then leads me inside the lake house with my mother following behind us.

Fifty-seven

HeaLing

SERENITY

EVERY NIGHT, SKY TAKES ME out, rows us to the middle of the lake and dumps me in deep water. But it doesn't nurse my skin the way it used to. The quietude beneath the surface doesn't snuff out all the Temple memories. My butterflies are still frozen. The water doesn't thaw them. Not even on the nights where Sky helps me with my clothes so I can swim naked.

I can't feel my butterflies. Or my lightning.

"Mom..." I say to her one night after a month spent in the lake house. "How did you jumpstart your body after everything? How did you turn yourself back on after everything he did to you?"

My mother's face looks radiant in the firelight. Not a trace of the Unicorn on her features when she answers, "I *chose* to love, Serenity. It's as simple as that."

I glance over at Sky, who stokes the fire for us. We're talking low enough he can't hear, but he seems to register we're discussing him. For the first time since we arrived, I'm finally talking about him.

"Mom," I murmur with her shoulder cradling my head. "I can't *feel* anything. It's all gone. Nothing left but that monster in my blood called Yang. I don't want it to come out." The explosion has kept it in a neat little cage somewhere inside me. Not in my blood anymore. But if I let my butterflies out, I'm afraid they'll bring the monster with them.

"Serenity..." My mother lifts my chin, steadies me with her gaze. "You can waste time for years like I did. You can let yourself

248

drown in all the memories. Or you can just *love* him. You can *choose* to love."

"How can I—"

"You might not feel anything. But you'll never know unless you try. I've lost one daughter, Serenity. I don't want to lose another. Kerrick is gone. I can't get him back. My only regret is not telling him I loved him one more time before your father took him." Mom nods to Sky. "He's been showing his love all this time. Don't you think it's time you let him? Healing doesn't mean letting go. It means holding on but letting yourself move on, too."

I look at Sky again. This time, he meets my eyes. Smiles. For a moment, I think a butterfly's wing twitches when he does.

"He's a good man," Mom confirms, pressing her lips together.

"I'm not the same girl he once knew."

"It doesn't matter to him. He loves you just the same. You know he does."

I stare at my hands. Realize they don't tremble like they used to. "I-I want it to *mean* something."

"*You* mean something. Together."

"Mom…I need your help. Please help me."

"ARE YOU READY?" SHE ASKS as we face each other. Our knees brush as we lean toward one another.

I purse my lips and nod.

"You look beautiful," Sky remarks, gesturing to the old white dress of my mother's we managed to find tucked away in a chest.

"Shh…no talking yet," my mother hushes him. She begins. "Love doesn't always feel kind. Sometimes, love is magic and flying on wings. But most of the time, it's just hard work. Going to bed every night and waking up every morning with one person for the rest of your life is the hardest thing you will ever face in this lifetime. To do that, you need more than just love. You need love seasoned by strength, seasoned by courage, seasoned by patience, seasoned by acceptance. Give Skylar the ropes, Serenity."

I place them in his capable hand, my fingers quaking. Just a tremor in their tips. I inhale, willing more breath into my being as he wraps the ropes around our wrists, uniting our hands together as my mother continues.

"You need strength to open your heart and soul to another human being because trust is a frightening thing. You need courage to overcome challenges together because they will come. You need patience to renew your love on days where you don't feel like it. And finally, you need acceptance because we are all born flawed and broken. So, be broken together.

"Do you promise to give all your broken pieces to each other?"

I thread my fingers into Sky's. Without closing my eyes once, I commit to him. "I promise."

"I promise." His voice is steady and even because Sky never looks back. And he always helps to turn my face away.

"Do you promise to give and receive?"

"I promise."

"I promise, too."

"Do you promise to move toward one another and not away?"

"I promise."

"I promise, too."

"Do you promise to bear life together, believe life together, have hope in a life together, and endure everything it throws at you together?"

I gaze at Sky, breathing out the words, "I promise to be your water and lightning."

He lowers his jaw, eyes meeting mine at equal level. "I promise to be your rocks and thunder."

I promise.

ONE HOUR LATER

This time, when Sky removes the dress from my skin, he follows with his own shirt and slides into the water before me. Arms reach out, welcoming me into the water's embrace with him. Tonight, I don't tread. I let him do it for me as I wrap my legs around his fortified waist that can more than bear my weight, just like his arms can. When he kisses me, I don't fight it. His mouth opens into mine. Not penetrating, not probing, not seeking…but sending. Slowly, I link my arms around his neck, tugging at the ends of his soaked waves as I accept what he's giving me.

"Sky…" I pause for a moment. Kiss his neck.

I can still feel the powerhouse of his legs pumping the water. By the strain in his forehead, I know it's becoming difficult. So, I pull away to tread water myself, but the ropes bound around our wrists hold us fast. We won't untie them until morning.

Sky reaches over to cup my cheek. His touch nurses me, skin overpowering the water to heal. "I will never love any girl in the world more than I love you, Serenity."

"I will never want to be loved more by any other man than you, Sky."

He smiles once before helping me back into the canoe. We take our time. Out here in the darkness is where we begin, just kissing and touching. Sensing each other. Sparks erupt in my stomach, shedding over my butterflies. Some land on their frozen shells. Strip them like peeling bark back even as Sky peels me back.

On the shore now with the sound of my breath catching in the background, he hauls the canoe to the ground before joining me once again and removing any leftover scraps of clothing we wear. Freed from their icy cages, my butterflies wake up now. When his mouth moves across my skin like a warm ribbon and leaves no trace of skin un-kissed, they rise. My mother was right. It just takes some time.

And there is no monster in my blood.

There are no demons parading themselves in my vision.

There is no remembrance of the whip.

There is no Force.

There are no other man's hands, no other man's lips, on my body but Sky's.

There is no Temple.

There is no world but the one Sky and I create tonight.

Harder than ever before, I kiss him back. Our bond solidifies. The melted gold hardening. Together, we fuse all the cracks and all the hairline fractures of our coin. Our faces will never look the same, but it's the first time I register they don't have to. Our paper petals fold over one another again and again, stems merging to become one. And we will grow together, live together, and die together. When we were born, we were created to love each other.

THREE HOURS LATER

"How are you feeling?" Sky asks, rubbing my bare shoulder, the glow of the fire casting shadows on his skin.

Closing my eyes, I sigh radiantly. If I could see myself, I imagine my smile *wouldn't* look magical. Not some floating lantern of a feeling. Not some fairy dust. Because this will never fly away. It's not lightning in a bottle either. It's just this unbelievable open door. It's opening myself to every moment. Steadying, supporting, and stabilizing until I'm stationary…unshaken. Rooted to Sky.

"I'll take that as a good thing," he comments after I snuggle into him, content.

It's nowhere near morning yet. Goose bumps roll across my skin. Sky groans a little because he must look away from me to stretch both our arms to add another log to the ebbing fire. He stokes it until it rears up again before returning to me—sitting before each other with nothing but firelight on our skin, reddening our cheeks and warming our blood. Shadows stir around us, but the fire threads us in its glow. We are one naked orb.

"What made you think of the ropes?" He fingers one of the braided fibers.

I touch my fingers across his. "I read about it. It's the oldest symbol. It just seemed right."

"And the idea of keeping them tied all night?"

"That was mine." I grin.

"Works for me."

Sky is careful when he picks me up by the waist and eases me into his arms, no longer content with the thinnest gap between us. I don't curl up there. Despite my slight wince, I spread my legs and wrap them around his waist instead, flattening myself against his chest, urging him closer.

"Serenity, we don't have to…again…if you don't want to. We can sleep if—"

Kissing him shows just how much I don't want to sleep.

FIVE HOURS LATER

Nothing left but glowing cinders, but we've created our own warmth. Beneath the wool blanket, our heat knits us together, stitches up the broken pieces of our hearts. Sky kisses my temple, supple warm lips lingering there as I sidle up against him.

"Penny for your thoughts, Ser?"

"Just thinking about you."

"Something when we were little?"

I shake my head. "No." Peer up into his face. "Just you. You're so beautiful, Skylar Luc Storm."

"And you, Serenity Bliss Storm."

It seemed right. Fitting to change our middle names because we'd always carry them with us. Creating a last name was something new, untried. Mom would always have Lace, but Sky and I needed something else to signify our new bond. Speaking our new last name feels like I'm holding an unbreakable snowflake. And I can put it in a frozen bottle to take out whenever I want to look at the crystal form we've brought to life.

Sky's chest is warm beneath my cheek. I memorize his heartbeat, tapping my finger to its rhythm, murmuring 'beat, beat, beat, beat' until I rouse his grin. That grin swirls the butterflies in my belly. With that one smile, he makes one giant butterfly tornado I feel all the way down to my toes. In another moment, I'm laughing beneath him just before his mouth swallows the laugh, his tongue tasting it.

SIX HOURS LATER

Finally made it to the couch. The blanket cocoons us now. In the background, I can hear the rain. Is it irony or providence there is a storm tonight? As soon as I flinch at the sound of a thunder crack, Sky tips his head to mine.

"You want to see it, don't you?" he asks.

I don't bother to conceal my sheepish grin. Sky rolls his eyes but follows that with a shake of his head before he unravels the blanket from our bodies. We've been anchored here long enough he has to steady me when I stand. Feeling a flutter engulf me when his hands touch my waist, I scold my butterflies because if I don't, we won't make it out of the house.

We don't bother dressing. "Just bring the blanket," I tell him.

Sky likes the sound of that.

I've always imagined heaven smells like rain. It's pouring. Puddles decorate the land in front of us. Wind rips across the lake—glorious hands pushing the water into waves. A flawless tendril of lightning dazzles the horizon before the thunder catches up, bellowing its protest that the lightning is always faster. But the thunder doesn't make me flinch. Sky does when he fingers a space on my bare back, centering his thumb on the lowest part of my spine.

"You'll catch cold if you keep standing here like this."

He's right. Already, raindrops careen onto my naked skin because I'm standing almost on the edge of the front porch, though my feet haven't brushed the first step. I only like the cold because it makes me appreciate the warmth of his body when he slides against me to wrap us both in the blanket.

Sometimes, healing hurts. New wounds and strains and infections, they'll still creep in, but maybe…just maybe…we'll be stronger this time. We'll never forget our old scars. Their imprints shape us, but they don't haunt us anymore. Sky and I haunt each other instead. In each other's blood and flesh, our hearts are roped together, forever set to stumble, climb, heal, laugh, and love.

Together, we stand. Patched. Mended. Rehabilitated. Restored.

We both comment on the storm roaring all around us. At the way the lightning and thunder play off each other, reclaiming us with our private and personal joke because we've done that our whole lives.

And we'll spend the rest of our lives doing that.

EIGHT HOURS LATER

Dawn summons me. Thanks to the rain last night, the land all around us glistens in the wake of sunlight riding across it. The scent of Sky's sweat hovers all around me. So potent I think I can scoop it up. Instead, I scoop up one of his hands and kiss his palm. Even if we've only slept an hour, he's like some creature in hibernation. When I kiss his mouth, folding his lips back, he still doesn't wake. But I know what will. My mouth doesn't leave his when I touch him.

Then, he kisses me back, faint growl in my mouth before we throw off the blanket and let the sunlight join our heat.

"Would you like bacon?" Sky asks.

The blanket falls a little, and I giggle before securing the thing around me again while answering, "Absolutely."

I can't help it. It might as well be a circus tent on my petite frame. It fits Sky better, but he doesn't bother with it. He has his robe right now as he slaps an entire pat of bacon on the pan.

We'll eat like kings today.

The bacon crackles so much I can almost imagine it leaping up and dancing a little jig. Thanks to the sound, I'm able to tiptoe quietly up behind Sky until I drop the quilt to the floor. Ugh... still can't surprise him because I notice his head flick up a second before I touch his waist. He doesn't even flinch.

"That's so annoying," I complain as I fiddle with his boxer shorts.

He pushes the bacon around a little before setting down the tongs. Turning around, he hoists me up with his big hands, setting me on the counter behind him. "I could smell you, Ser. Now, stay..." he orders like a master scolding a pupil. "You stole my energy the whole night, and I'm starving. Damn..." Sky curses, staring at me as I beam at him right before he puts his hands on my thighs, leans up, and kisses me.

"Sky," I murmur against his mouth when I hear the hiss of the bacon in the background.

"Ugh..." He groans and returns to the stove. "Aren't you hungry at all?"

I'm hungry for bacon and pancakes and eggs and hash and skillet potatoes and all the things Sky likes to make at breakfast because they all remind me of him. I tell him so.

"No chocolate fondue?"

I whirl my head back and forth, eyes crystallizing just on the surface. Sensing the ice-shard memories, Sky apologizes before flipping the bacon over again.

"Sky..." I slide from the counter until I'm standing right next to him, but I don't get too close to the stove because sizzling hot bacon fat flung against naked skin isn't the best feeling. "That night in the Temple…you said you were waiting for me, saving yourself for me."

"And…?"

"And all those nights we shared a bed, that one night I could tell how much you wanted—"

"It would've cheapened it," Sky states without reservation, his brow line wrinkling. "It was supposed to be here. In our place. On our own terms."

I ponder the words that feel like pages in my hand. Pages from Sky's journal. Just a few entry paragraphs in the present because I've already memorized the book that came before. Now, I'm stamping the ones of the future.

"You've gotta stop standing there looking gorgeous. Or I'll be burning this bacon in no time."

I toss my head back, laughing at the notion. "Well, if you'd stop burning up my insides."

"No chance of that happening." He leans over and kisses me again, lips pushing mine apart before he finishes, "It's why they call it a honeymoon."

"By the end of it, all the honey will be burnt and the moon will be gold."

Sky winks and then sweeps a hand around my waist, yanking me closer to him. "Count on it."

WITH MY BELLY FULL, I finally agree to put on some clothes. Not much. Don't even bother with undergarments—just stick to a simple peasant skirt and a blouse. I'm comfortable in my own skin because it's just Sky and me. But Sky wants to take a walk. And stretching my legs seems like a good idea. I don't bother with shoes. Not with how the rain from last night still moistens the earth.

I take Sky's hand after joining him at the bottom of the steps. Despite the coolness of the morning, his hand warms mine, seeps into my skin to join with the other flares there. He knows one kiss would detonate them, but he keeps himself at a reasonable gap.

"You're impossible, you know that?" he says after he catches me staring at him several times. "Don't you have anything else on your mind?"

I shrug. "A girl's got needs."

"Does it hurt, Ser?"

I bite my lip, not wanting to answer because it does. Feels like a cannon blazed through a trail of cheesecloth, but… "It's getting better. Easier. And better."

"Practice makes—"

"Better?" I interrupt him.

"I suppose. Look." He turns to face me and folds his palms into mine, tethering our fingers together and pushing on my hands just a little, "I know we agreed not to talk about anything until after the weekend, but you know it's harder to turn my mind off. There's still work to do. And your mother to think about when she comes back. Stock market may have slumped after Queran's Temple terror attack, but it doesn't mean we're in the poorhouse. Just the opposite."

"What did you find out?" I lean toward him as we embark onto the path that winds through a grove of trees on the property and links to a stone bridge.

"Just like he said. Left all his assets and holdings to you. The Syndicate, board of directors…they're hunting for you. Right now, they're rebuilding as much as they can of the Temple. More Museums are popping up to meet the demand."

There will always be a demand. The cynic inside me believes it. The magic girl believes something could be different. But teaching men to love instead of lust—to honor instead of harm—seems like an impossibility.

I share my thoughts with Sky, who strings one firm hand around my waist, tugs me toward him, and cups the side of my neck. "How those men miss out on the chance to love just one woman just boggles my mind. Serenity…you will *always* be more than enough for me."

On our way back, we pause when a Temple car cruises onto the long drive sweeping up to the house. At first, Sky tenses, but we both seem to register there's no danger. Not from one lone Temple car. As it slows, I recognize the driver—Dr. Moby. Though he doesn't turn off the car, allowing it to idle, Moby does close the door and approach us.

"Your mother was able to hold me off for a brief time, but I'm afraid I can do no more at this point."

All I can do is screw my brows down, confused before Moby motions to the digital cuff around his wrist, which he taps, summoning a sprite light. A spright light of Bliss and Luc. My heart stutters as I take in the sight of them. In her bedroom. I can see the familiar vanity in the background.

"Serenity." Bliss sucks in a deep breath, closes her eyes once as Luc squeezes her shoulder. "If you're watching this, it means we are both dead. Luc thinks this is pointless, but I wanted to be prepared. I wanted *you* to be prepared." She stares directly into the camera. "I knew you were always more likely to escape than me. If nothing else, this last will and testament will provide some answers. Now, you will understand why Mother allowed Force to whip her when I went into labor. It bought us the time we needed."

I hold my breath, suspecting, wishing, yet dreading, because I know what it means...for Sky, for me, for us.

"You saw what you needed to see. You had to believe it so *he* would believe," Bliss explains.

Luc leans over to speak this time. "In the unlikely event of our death because I plan to get us the hell out of this place and live for the foreseeable future, we want you to do the right thing, Skylar. You get them all to the Sanctuary. You have a life there."

Bliss smiles at Luc and then at the camera. "Their names are Kerry and Verity." All my butterflies' wings crack, dropping to the floor of my stomach when she reveals the information. "We are turning their middle names over to you. Serenity, I know what you must be thinking. If this is happening, then this is one area where Force was right. I will never be a mother, but you will."

How could she say that?

"That day, I knew I would try. But if you're watching this, then it means it has to be this way." The corners of her mouth lower right before her chin does, taking the rest of her face. Head bowed, Bliss continues. "There are some things you cannot change." Then, Bliss lifts her hand. Cupped inside it is her tetra-star...but with a tiny heart in the middle. "But thank you for helping me change.

Now, it's your turn. Time to fly to the Sanctuary, Serenity Swan."

I want to watch it again. And again. Anything to delay what's about to happen, but it's too late because Dr. Moby managed to steal away to the cruiser in the time Bliss was finishing. Now, he returns with two small bundles, one in each arm.

I grit my teeth, setting my jaw as Sky accepts them both. Except his eyes don't leave mine when he does.

"Don't do that, Ser," he lectures even as I dig my toe into the dirt. "Bliss and Luc left us a gift. Don't close your heart to them."

Now I know why Bliss acted the way she had when I took her to the CellGen after I believed she lost the twins. Why she hadn't been angry I healed her, thereby stripping her body of their memory. In the end, I'd helped because there hadn't been a loss. No permanent loss. At least not that she'd known about at the time. It also means she wanted to escape. She wanted to leave with us. Even though I'd known she'd forgiven me, even if I'd known we were finally sisters, I still hadn't known she'd wanted to escape... until now. In a way, I guess she did escape. In more than one way...

"Give me the girl," I demand of Sky, placing my hands on the pink bundle.

Peeling back a bit of the fabric from her cheek, I stare at Verity and search for Bliss, but all I seem to find is Luc. Her father's cheekbones, his mouth, his face shape...until she coos, gurgles, and opens her eyes. They are the color of dark moonstones. Of calm rain on a lake in the early morning. Of a lonely mountain clothed in fog and snow.

I find Bliss in them.

Then, I kiss Verity's cheek and return to the house to start this thing called *change*.

The Temple Twins

Discussion Questions

1. Discuss the first conversation Sky has with Force. How are their perspectives different? What does Sky mean when he reflects: as if any girl is truly tainted? How do different messages subscribe value to a girl based off her sexual history? Contrast secular vs. religious. Are the messages different for men? How so?

2. Discuss Luc and his reflections on how he was raised and the messages from his father regarding submission. How does Luc begin to change? What leads to those changes? How can we influence men, young and old, who may have this mindset to change?

3. Consider Serafina and how she tells her that her worth is intrinsic and shouldn't be based on others. Have you ever subscribed your own worth based off others' opinions or standards? How can we change this message in our society today?

4. Sky has many encounters with Temple girls. Where are they coming from? Consider the parallel to our society today for those in the sex industry. Research the backgrounds of those who end up in prostitution.

5. Compare and contrast Luc and Sky. Does Sky's compassion and respect make him any less masculine? Or does his resistance make him stronger? Reflect on how he chooses to see the little girl inside all the Temple girls.

6. Discuss the night Bliss and Luc first sleep together and her experience with other men. How they treat her verses how

Luc treats her. Research survivors of prostitution about their experiences with buyers. What is common?

7. Discuss Sky challenging Luc to love Bliss without conditions and to not treat her as a conquest. What would our society look like if more were taught this from a young age?

8. How does Serenity change in The Temple? What happens to her perception of Bliss? Does she still want to rescue her in the end? Consider how we might have the wrong perceptions of someone in this situation? How can we better love those who are hurting and suffering?

Acknowledgements

OR MY HUSBAND WHO IS truly the behind the scenes stage manager for my books. Thank you for all the little details from working on my website to encouraging me regarding my writing to listening to me brainstorm ideas. You are more than just one of the good ones. You're my Superman.

Again, I'm giving a shout-out to NANO since this is a two-part book. The deadline and pressure gave rise to a 130K word book.

Francine Rivers and even Disney ended up playing inspiration to Bliss's voice. Even though I preferred her seriously underrated little sister, Elsa offered tidbits for Bliss.

Rachel Moran: your Paid For memoir is the best resource I've ever come across for trying to understand those "in the life". Thank you for sharing your voice to the world. Everyone should be grateful for your words. And the testimony of any #metoo.

To the CTP Team: you've gone through some major trials and you're still fighting
and still working. A big thank you to my editor for getting this edited so fast. Your red pen is never daunting!

To all the anti-trafficking organizations out there in the trenches doing intervention, rescue work, awareness, prevention etc. Especially to Exodus Cry for my training which helped shape the discussion questions for this book.

Thank you to all the #metoo's of this world—trafficking survivors/victims and others—for being brave enough to speak up.

To those who are still in the darkness or still struggling with old wounds, you are valuable and priceless. And I pray there will be someone who will enter your life who will show you love like dynamite.

To my street team, old and new members alike. You are so valuable! Please keep reading because I depend so much on you! I keep your reviews in a special place in my heart.

Thank you to my mom for taking me to see Amazing Grace in the theater when it was released. It wasn't the seed, but it was God tilling the soil.

To my Savior for strengthening me on this journey. For changing my lens on December 30th, 2017 and giving me the drive to stick with it. I'm so glad I didn't stop writing.

Resources

RACHEL MORAN: PAID FOR: MY JOURNEY THROUGH PROSTITUTION: https://www.amazon.com/dp/B00C7735X8

EXODUS CRY'S DOCUMENTARIES: NEFARIOUS: MERCHANT OF SOULS AND LIBERATED: THE NEW SEXUAL REVOLUTION (AVAILABLE ON NETFLIX): https://exoduscry.com/tag/documentary/

A CALL TO MEN: http://www.acalltomen.org/about-us/our-leadership

NITA BELLES: IN OUR BACKYARD: http://inourbackyard.org/media-publications/

NATIONAL CENTER ON SEXUAL EXPLOITATION: https://endsexualexploitation.org/videos/

REBECCA BENDER: https://rebeccabender.org/

WOMEN AT RISK, INTERNATIONAL: https://warinternational.org/

SHARED HOPE INTERNATIONAL: https://sharedhope.org/

FOR MINNESOTA:

BEAUTIFUL AND LOVED:
https://beautifulandloved.com/

REBECCA KOTZ:
http://www.rebeccakotz.com/

BREAKING FREE:
http://www.breakingfree.net/

TEREBINTH REFUGE:
https://www.terebinthrefuge.org/

DON'T BUY IT PROJECT:
https://www.dontbuyitproject.org/

WOMEN'S FOUNDATION OF MINNESOTA:
https://www.wfmn.org/mn-girls-are-not-for-sale/

About the
Author

EMILY SHORE IS A MN author with a B.A. in Creative Writing from Metro State University and was a grand prize winner of #PitchtoPublication, which led her to working with professionals in the publishing industry. Her anti-trafficking books Ruby in the Rough and Ruby in the Ruins are her first indie-published books with proceeds benefiting trafficking rescue organizations. She is signed with Clean Teen Publishing for her anti-trafficking dystopian The Aviary. For every book sold, a personal donation will return to Women At Risk, International.

Throughout the years, she has connected with rescue organizations and survivors of sex-trafficking and injects the truths she's learned into her books for youth. She loves motivational speaking on the issue of sex-trafficking and always hopes for more speaking events in schools, churches, and libraries. Please contact her on her website if you are interested in hearing her speak. In her spare time, she loves attending any abolition events, baking, acrylic painting, interior decorating, and spending time with all the little girls in her life.

Emily lives in Saint Paul with her husband and two daughters. Their goal is to adopt a little girl from India.